HIDDEN IN DARKNESS

Alice Winters

Hidden in Darkness Copyright © 2018 by Alice Winters. All Rights Reserved.

All rights reserved. No part of this book may be reproduced in any form or by any electronic or mechanical means including information storage and retrieval systems, without permission in writing from the author. The only exception is by a reviewer, who may quote short excerpts in a review.

Cover designed by Cate Ashwood Designs

This book is a work of fiction. Names, characters, places, and incidents either are products of the author's imagination or are used fictitiously. Any resemblance to actual persons, living or dead, events, or locales is entirely coincidental.

Alice Winters
Visit my website at www.alicewinterauthor.com

Printed in the United States of America

First Printing: Feb 2018
ISBN: **9781731014870**

PROLOGUE

~**Lane**~

I know I have to run.

I know I have to get away.

But I can't. I can barely move.

My hand hits my leg, and I'm shocked by how close it is. I jerk my hand back as everything compresses around me until I feel like I can't breathe, but I can't let the darkness take me. Not yet.

I know that I have to move.

There's noise outside the room. I can hear it, but it's getting farther and farther away from me. Desperately, I grip onto the noise since it's the only thing that feels real at this moment.

Calm down, Lane. This is what you're trained to do.

Is it? Am I trained for situations like this? Situations where I have been thrown into the darkness, where the walls collapse down tight on top of me until I can't breathe? It's almost bad enough that I can forget the throbbing that is consuming every inch of my body.

My hand is shaking as I strain my fingers in an attempt to reach down and touch my leg. My pants are wet, but I could have figured that out without even touching them. My wrist aches against the restraint, so I give in, letting myself rest at a more comfortable angle.

I need help. I need medical attention.

I need to get out.

I need to live.

The duct tape around my wrist is wet, slick with blood. I pull on it as the bruises scream, but I can't stop because I don't know when he'll come back.

Five hours?

Five minutes?

Five seconds?

I need to get out.

Straining, I twist and pull my left arm as the tape bunches. The struggling is causing the blood to run against the tape until it begins to slide. My aching hand screams as I twist and pull until I feel it start to give. I pull it free and slump down in the chair.

Now just one more hand.

I feel like I'm going to pass out, and for a moment, I have to focus on staying alert.

My fingers are shaking as I reach over until my hand bumps into the arm of the chair. This one is tight against the chair instead of loose like the other. The tape on this wrist is dry, so I run my fingers over it until I feel a slight catch. I can't tell if it's a ripple in the tape or the end of it, but I begin to dig at it with my fingernails. Each bump of my left hand against my right makes it ache. My hand feels like it's broken, but I don't think it is. All I know is that each tug of the tape makes me want to scream, so I grit my teeth and pull. I even my breath, breathing in for three seconds, breathing out for three seconds.

I can't pass out.

My hand goes around and around, tugging and pulling at the tape, but I can't tell how much is left. I can't tell if I'm close to the end or still at the beginning.

I can't tell anything in this dark world.

The tape pulls free, and I can't help the smile that touches my face.

I'm free!

For now.

Instead of tossing the tape to the ground, I set it against my bleeding leg and begin to wrap it around the wound. I pull it tight and have to grit my teeth as I keep it pressed against the wound. I wind it again and again as heat begins to consume my body, telling me that I'm close to passing out.

I can't…not yet.

I tuck the end of the tape in, praying it'll stay. Slumping against the chair, I feel nauseous as sweat soaks my shirt. I have to waste a precious moment regaining my composure until I feel prepared to make my escape. If I make a single mistake, this will be over. I won't get a second chance.

It doesn't matter how much pain I'm in, I know that if I don't make it out of here now, I will die.

Using my one good arm and the arm of the chair, I push myself to my feet, favoring my left leg. I know where the door is; it's in front of me. But I can't remember how far away.

Four feet?

Six feet?

It feels like a mile as I take my first step. My weight comes down on my leg, and I nearly fall to the ground, but I manage to steady myself. When I hit the door, I am elated. I have made it this far. I can make it. I can do this.

I set my hand against the cool metal door and slide it to the edge until I feel where the door meets the doorframe. Then I run my hand down until I hit the doorknob. Desperately, I grab onto it and pull.

It gives easily in my hand, making me want to grin at their mistake, but I can't get the grimace off my face.

They're not afraid of me escaping.

How far can a blind man go?

I'll show them how fucking far I can go.

I step out into the hallway as I try to remember the path I was taken in through. Back when my world wasn't consumed by darkness.

There were stairs. I remember the stairs that I was dragged down; now I just have to find them. With my good hand against the wall, I begin to walk. Each step as painful as the last. It feels like the world is closing in on me as the darkness consumes me.

There could be a man directly in front of me, and I would never see him until I am on him. They could be laughing at me as I drag my body through the hall, praying for stairs I am not sure I will ever find.

My hand touches a door and I debate opening it, but even if there is a gun sitting right inside, I can't do anything with it. I am useless now.

No, I am not useless. I can get out of here.

My hand slides forward, dropping as the wall falls away. I don't realize how much weight I had been pressing against it until I am falling forward. Desperately, I reach out, hoping to catch myself, but the moment my right hand hits, my wrist gives, and I slam down onto the stairs.

I dig the nails of my left hand into the step as I lie against them.

Well…I found the stairs.

I grab onto the next step and pull myself up, first placing one knee, and then the next as I crawl up them. I know I need to get to my feet, but I'm not sure I can. Carefully, I slide each hand forward, feeling my path as I edge up each step.

When my hand doesn't reach another step, I stretch it out, feeling the path before me until I hit a wall. I slide my hand along it until I find a doorknob and turn it. I pull the door toward me, but it won't give, so I push it away.

For all I know, I'm stepping right into the pit of vipers. I can't check, I can just listen. As I step through the door, I feel the cool air on the left side of my face. Slowly I turn my head as if I could see something and move toward it.

Could this be a door leading out? Could it be this simple?

None of this has been simple so far.

My hand hits a door, and suddenly I can feel the cool metal. I move my hand until I find another handle and pull it open. The smell of fresh rain fills my nose as I grasp onto the sound of birds in the distance.

I have made it outside, but it doesn't mean I'm free.

The wind blows, disrupting my hair and angering the wounds on my face. I want to lie down. Just rest for a moment, but I know that if I do, I won't get back up, and I can't give up. I've made it too far now, but doubt sets in regardless. I have no idea where I'm at; I can't grab a car and drive away. I am lost in this world of darkness and can barely breathe. My chest feels like it's compressing as I take my first step. I can hear gravel beneath my feet as I reach out, wishing to find a wall to support me.

There's nothing left, making me feel like every step I take could lead to my death. Like I would fall into a pit and drop straight to hell.

Then I hear it.

A dog barking.

The sound is distant but steady.

A rhythm, almost.

Constant.

It could be leading me to my death, but it could also be leading me to my freedom.

So, I begin to walk. Slowly placing each foot in front of the other. It feels like a dream, almost like I am walking on nothing and everything. Carefully, I keep moving forward, forcing one step after the other.

The barking grows louder.

It feels like I've walked for hours.

Or days.

Or a lifetime.

I will reach that dog. I will reach it, and I pray that when I do, it will lead to my freedom from this hell.

CHAPTER ONE

~Felix~

I check my phone for the fourth time to make sure it's the right address, as if I have forgotten how to read and might be at the wrong place. But I hate going to places I have never been to before, so I check it one more time, just in case. When I'm certain that I'm at the right location, I get out of my car and walk up the sidewalk, toward the gray, one-story house. It has a small porch with some weathered wicker chairs set out on it. I walk up the steps and across the porch to the dark blue door. I knock on it, before stepping back and waiting. It isn't long before the door swings open, and a man in his forties looks out at me.

He smiles at me as he swings the door open wider. "You must be Mr. Wake," the man says as he holds his hand out. His brown hair is cut short and gray hair is starting to mix in. He has dark blue eyes that are hidden behind black-framed glasses.

"Yes, I am," I say as I take his hand and shake it. "Just call me Felix though."

"I'm James Dixon. I was the one that talked to you last night on the phone."

"It's nice to meet you," I say as I look up at him. Sadly, I seem to have to look up at half the population. Not half the adult population, but half the population as a whole.

"Please, come in," he says as he holds the door open for me. "I'm glad to finally meet with you in person. I've been very busy, so I was unable to do the interviews, but Dani thought you were the best choice, so here we are."

"Yes, thanks for giving me this opportunity," I say with a smile.

"Right this way," he says. "You can meet Lane, and then I'll show you around the house."

"Okay," I say, looking around curiously as he leads me through the kitchen and into the living room. The house is very nice but noticeably bare. It looks like someone had just moved in and had forgotten to decorate any of the rooms. There are no pictures on the walls or anything that looks personalized. Everything looks like it was bought from a home décor store and just stuck on the wall or on a shelf without any meaning to it. It reminds me more of a house ready for market than one actually being lived in.

The television is on in the living room, and in the middle of the room is a man in a wheelchair. His back is facing us, but he turns his head a little in our direction, telling me he's heard us.

"This is Lane," James says, and the man turns his head a bit more in our direction.

"James, if that is someone to babysit me, I swear to God I'm going to be so pissed," he growls.

Clearly, I've made an excellent first impression, and I haven't even opened my mouth yet. Generally, I get a few words out before people decide to hate me.

"It's not," James says calmly. "Go ahead, introduce yourself."

I walk around to the front of the wheelchair the man is sitting in. His head turns as he tries to follow the sound of my footsteps with his ears. I can see a stretch of a healing red cut running along his left cheekbone, hidden slightly by the dark sunglasses he's wearing. Even though he is in his own home, the fact that he is blind must bother him enough that he feels like he needs to hide it. He has a blanket lying over his lap, but I know from the interview that he had hurt his left leg. All this from a drunk driver hitting his car. He'll be blind forever because of another man's negligence. I guess I would be a bit of a grouch too if someone had ripped my vision away from me.

"Hi, Mr. Price, my name is Felix Wake," I say.

"And, Mr. Wake, what are you doing in my home?" he asks as venom drips off his words.

I look over at James and raise an eyebrow as I realize I'm not welcome.

"Felix is going to be assisting you until you get better," James says.

"I don't need help, because I am not helpless." He's scowling at us and I know that if I could see his eyes they'd be glaring at me. He looks to be in his mid or late thirties with rich brown hair that looks a bit unkempt. The right side is sticking straight up, and the left lies naturally. His facial hair looks scruffy, like it hasn't been trimmed in a while. His cheeks look hollow like he is beyond exhaustion, but it is clear that this man used to be quite active by the way his T-shirt clings around his muscular arms and stomach. So honestly, it's not my fault that I can't help my straying eyes.

"Felix will be staying in the guest bedroom and will take care of the cleaning, cooking, and care for you," James explains, and I hope he hasn't noticed my betraying eyes.

Lane laughs, but it's not a happy laugh. "It's my house; I can decide what to do with it and how to take care of myself," he says. It's like every time he opens his mouth he looks just a bit uglier. Who am I kidding? The man is gorgeous.

"Well, Lane, he's moving in tomorrow," James says. "So, you better get used to it."

Lane seems to decide that he's done with the conversation and starts to ignore us. Instead, he aims all his concentration toward the TV, making James sigh. "Right this way, Felix."

I follow as he leads me over to the hallway. Even these walls are empty of pictures and color. Just white walls, white trim. It feels sterile, like a hospital or a school.

"First door on the left is the bathroom," he says. I glance through the open doorway as he continues walking. "Next door is Lane's room. Then yours is right here."

Lane's bedroom door is closed, but James pushes open the door to the guest bedroom. I peek in, but from here all I can see is the full-sized bed. I run my hand through my ear-length, blond hair and pray that I had made the right decision coming here. I worry at a tip of my hair before dropping my hand down.

I glance over at James, who is staring at his phone. "Is it alright with me being here?" I ask a bit skeptically. Clearly, the occupant of the house didn't want me within ten miles of him, and we hadn't even shared words yet beyond an introduction.

"Of course. Don't listen to Lane. I make the decisions, not him. He thinks he can do everything, but I don't want him alone all day. He can be reckless at times, and I know if he's alone he'll end up doing something stupid and hurting himself. Really, he's not a bad guy. He's is just…not taking this well. He's angry and upset, so he seems to be lashing out at anyone that looks his way. He is used to being independent and self-sufficient, not relying on others. You alright with this?"

"Yes, of course," I say as I glance into my room. It looks as bare and lifeless as the rest of the house.

"Here," James says, pulling my attention back to him. I notice that he's holding out a credit card, so I reach for it. "Buy groceries for Lane and yourself with this. It can also be used for whatever necessities are needed. Dani said she'd already gone over all the details with you. Are there any questions?"

"Not that I'm aware of," I say as I clutch the credit card in my hand, slightly unsure of what to do with it.

"I'll see you tomorrow then," he says. He shakes my hand again, but for some reason, I feel like "if you decide to come back" had been hanging onto the end of his words.

He turns around and continues back through the hallway, so I follow him into the living room.

"He's not gone yet?" Lane grumbles.

"Not yet," James says.

"Did you tell him the last babysitter didn't make it a day?" he asks like he's proud of himself. I'm kind of proud of him because I can't imagine that would be easy to do.

"Nope, but now he's well aware," James says with a grimace.

I can't help but grin. To me, that sounds like a challenge, and one thing I do enjoy is a challenge. "I'll be back tomorrow to start," I say, trying to sound very happy about it. "Can't wait to see you again, Lane!"

"Don't bother coming back," he growls, and I almost laugh as I head out the door.

***

I knock on the door, but James must have seen me pull up because he pulls the door open before my hand even hits a second time.

"Good to see you back," he says eagerly. "Sorry to run, but I need to be home by six. You have any questions?"

The bag is weighing down my arm, and right now I just want to find a place to put it. "Not that I can think of," I say.

"Here's my number. If you need anything, don't hesitate to call," he says as he passes me a piece of paper with a list of contacts. His number is handwritten at the top, and I notice the rest of the numbers are for doctors. Not a single contact looks like a family member's.

"Thank you," I say.

He smiles and passes by me, leaving me in the house alone with the man who hates my guts. That's alright, I've lived with people that hated me before. How could this one be any worse? I carry my suitcase down the hall, between the white, looming walls, and set it just inside my bedroom door. Then I walk into the living room where Lane is sitting before the TV that's playing a movie. He doesn't even look in my direction as I walk in, instead, he stays facing the TV with his blanket around his lap and sunglasses firmly in place.

"Lane, it's Felix," I say. "How are you doing today?"

He doesn't move, just completely ignores me as he taps the edge of his wheelchair with his finger.

"Do you need anything?" I ask.

Silence. The TV is playing *The Hangover,* which he doesn't seem to be enjoying. It's the part where the man jumps out of the trunk, but he's acting like it's a movie about the Holocaust.

I walk over to him. "Is your water full?" I ask as I pick the bottle up. It's full, but the water is warm. "I'll get you something cold. Just water or something else?"

"Maybe I want my water warm," he says.

I debate saying something, but I don't. It probably wouldn't look good to bad-mouth a blind man, so I put the lid back on and set it down. "Alright, one warm water coming right up," I say. I pause, waiting to see if he'll say anything, before sighing. "I'm going to go unpack. If you need something, don't hesitate to ask."

I walk back to my bedroom where I toss my suitcase on my bed and open it. The room is bigger than the one I'd had at my last apartment, which really isn't saying much. This one has a nice full-sized bed, which is an upgrade from the twin I had still been sleeping on at the age of twenty-five. There is a dresser in the corner and a desk, but the room is simple. When I pull the dresser drawers open, the smell of fresh wood touches my nose. I put my underwear and socks in the first drawer, shirts in the second, pants in the third, and sweatshirts in the last drawer. There isn't much else in my suitcase. A few books, a few movies. Everything else I own is in my car since I had decided to completely move out of my apartment. I didn't need it if I am living here, so what's the use of paying rent on it? And it isn't like I would have trouble finding another dumpy apartment if this didn't work out.

I walk back into the living room. "Do you need something?"

"Please, just go away," he says sharply.

Alright. I walk into the kitchen and rummage through the cupboards, but there isn't much. Thankfully, there is enough to get by until tomorrow because I really don't feel like grocery shopping today. I'm sure I won't feel like grocery shopping tomorrow either, but it has to be a little easier using someone else's credit card. I walk back into the living room and sit down in a chair. There's not much left of the movie, so I wait until it's over.

"I need to go grocery shopping tomorrow, so I'm wondering if you could tell me what types of food you like?" I ask as soon as the credits roll.

He keeps his face forward, refusing to even turn his head a fraction in my direction.

"How about meats? You like chicken?" I ask.

He ignores me, so I just lean back and watch the TV.

"You want to sit in a chair? That wheelchair can't be comfortable."

Ha, like I would actually get an answer!

When supper time comes around, I cook rice and chicken since that is basically all that I can find in the house. I dish it up into a bowl, grab a fork, and carry it into the living room. After setting his tray up in front of him, I place the bowl on it.

"I made rice and chicken. There wasn't much else in the house, so this is what we'll have to make do with. I put your fork on the right," I say.

He doesn't even turn his head toward the food.

"I'll be back," I say before getting up and walking into the kitchen. I watch from the doorway as he slowly reaches for his fork. He has a brace on his right hand, but he tries to set it against the bowl, so he can feel it. I know that his hand isn't broken, but he seems to be having trouble using it. I know he doesn't want me to watch him fumble, which is why he refused to eat in front of me. I sigh and eat my food from the doorway of the kitchen, so I can watch in case he needs something.

When he's done I walk back in. "Was it okay?"

"No," he says.

Of course not.

"What would you have liked different?"

"All of it."

Of course.

"Well, I'm sorry, but that's how I cook. If you'd like something specific, I'll make it for dinner tomorrow."

I don't even expect an answer, so I pick up the bowls and wash them in the sink before drying them. After a few hours of TV, I get no response when I ask if he wants a snack or if he wants to take a shower.

"Alright, bedtime," I say.

"I'm not a child."

"Never said you were," I say. But since he can't do anything about it, I grab the back of his wheelchair and wheel him down the hallway and into the bathroom. "Toothbrush…where's your toothbrush?"

"Up your ass," he says.

"Nope, I think I would have noticed it there," I say.

I open the cupboards and finally find it in the end drawer. I put toothpaste on it and wet it. "Here you go," I say as I place it in his hand. He instinctively grabs it, and I'm thrilled when he finally brushes his teeth. When he's done, I put the toothbrush back where I found it.

"I need to pee, so leave," he says as he tries to show me out with a wave of his hand.

"You expect me to leave while you try to pee alone?"

"Yes."

"No."

"What, you want to fondle my dick or something?"

Maybe.

"Your leg is hurt, and your hand is hurt, so I think I'll help you onto the toilet. I can leave then if you insist, I just don't want you to fall," I say as I wheel him over to the toilet.

He's bigger than me, so I put the lock on the wheelchair and wrap an arm behind his back. With his help, I manage to get him up. He slides his pants down, so I guide him onto the toilet.

"Alright, I'm leaving but only if you promise to tell me when you're done. Don't do something stupid on your own."

He ignores me as I walk out and shut the door. It isn't long before I hear a loud *crash,* so I yank the door open to find Lane half on the ground with everything knocked off the countertop. Quickly, I rush over and grab him, so I can help pull him into the chair.

As I help him, I don't even bother saying anything because I can tell he's mad at himself and would probably snap at me if I did. Instead, I kick the stuff on the floor out of the way and wheel him through the doorway and into his bedroom. "I want to check your wounds and then you can go to bed."

I ruffle through the mess that James had left for me, but I get the gist of what's there. "I have to pull your sweatpants down, alright?" I say as I do just that, so I can get to his thigh. I look at the staples, which seem to be healing well. It won't be long before he'll be able to get them out and get out of the wheelchair. I clean the area and help him back into his sweats. He also has a cut on his arm and a small one on his other leg that I check. "There. Everything feels alright?"

He ignores me, so I help him up into his bed and pull the sheets over him.

"Can I check your eyes?" I ask since I haven't seen him with the sunglasses off yet.

"No, I've already taken care of them."

"Are you sure?" I ask.

"They're fine."

"Goodnight. If you need anything, wake me up. What time do you usually get up in the morning?"

Silence.

"Yeah, me too," I say before walking out of the room.

***

I wake at eight and help Lane into the living room without much incident and without any kind words from him.

"Do you want to sit in a chair or lay down?"

Silence.

Oh, I can only be nice for so long. "Lane, I am speaking to you," I say. "You're not *deaf*. Answer me."

"Just leave me alone. I want to be alone!" he says as he slams his hand down on the arm of the chair.

I honestly think he just wants to rot in that chair and let depression consume him. "Well, sorry, but your pity party of one just gained a new member," I say. "And guess what? I'm not leaving. I'm going to help you whether you like it or not because I get paid, which I like."

He turns his head toward me. "Did you seriously just say that?"

"I did, and in retrospect, it *might* have been a bit mean. *But* I feel like you also thought it was slightly funny," I say.

"So, you're a comedian now?"

"Oh no. I just say stuff that gets me in trouble, but no one's here to yell at me. If I keep getting paid I'm staying. It's your choice whether you want it to be a fun and pleasant experience or hell."

"My life is already hell."

I snort. "Trust me, buddy, I can make it worse. I could…put you in the corner…take away your blanket…feed you dog food," I say as I try not to laugh.

"Can't be any worse than what you fed me last night," he says, and I feel like I can see a slight upturn of his lips. Maybe he isn't all bad.

I laugh in surprise. "You are pure evil."

"Then maybe you should leave now."

"No, I'm not going to." I grab his water bottle and go into the kitchen where I run the water until it is almost hot. I fill up his cup and carry it into the living room where I hand it to him. "Here's your water."

He takes it from me and I watch with a grin as he takes a sip of it and spits it out. "What is this?" He shakes the cup and water sloshes out.

"Yesterday you said you liked your water warm."

"Oh, really funny," he says, but his words don't have the venom they held earlier. He throws it at me, and let me say, for a blind guy, he has a really good aim. It hits me square in the forehead and I stumble back as water showers me.

"Ow!" I snap as I grab my head. It feels like I should have a welt the size of an egg on my head.

"Did that hit you?" he asks as he tries to hide a grin.

"I'm going to have a brain tumor now."

"I don't see anything," he says as he looks quite content with himself. "Not even a red spot."

"Hmm. I'm going to buy you cat food for lunch," I say.

"From the limited amount of time I have spent with you I have decided that you're actually quite mean. I guess you're really not the little happy boy you were pretending to be yesterday," he says.

"Being around you for any amount of time can turn a saint into a sinner," I say.

"If you're insistent on joining this 'pity party,' go make me some oatmeal."

"I thought you didn't like my food," I say.

"Hopefully even you can't ruin oatmeal," he says.

"One could hope," I say as I turn from him and walk into the kitchen. I pour the little packet of oatmeal into a bowl as well as some milk and slip it into the microwave. Then I pull open all the wrong drawers before finding the spoons. Once the oatmeal is cooked, I carry it into the living room and set it down in front of Lane. "Spoon on the right."

He reaches for it and touches it gingerly. I think he is waiting for me to leave, but I don't. I honestly can't. I also can't wipe the grin off my face. He sticks his spoon into the oatmeal, grabbing a spoonful before raising it to his mouth.

"What is this? Soup?" he asks as he tips the spoon and everything runs off.

"I *may* have added a bit too much milk," I admit. I hadn't done it on purpose, but instead of trying to drain any of the milk, I had decided he could drink it with a straw if he is going to be mean.

"How did you get hired?" he asks in shock.

"Honestly, I'm not sure," I say. "I guess I'm good at talking women into things. Alright, I'm going shopping. You going to tell me what you want?"

"I want you to leave. I mean, if I have to suffer and be taken care of like I'm an invalid, I would at least like someone that cooks."

"Yeah, I don't think I can buy cooking skills at the store. So, think of something edible. How about meats. Are you picky?"

He tries to eat the oatmeal, but every spoonful is just milk. "Is there actually any oatmeal in here?" he asks.

"Just drink it," I suggest. "So, I'm just going to go buy you things and hope you're not allergic to any of it. You want to go with me?"

"Absolutely not."

"Okay. What would you like to do while I'm gone?"

He gets a look on his face like he has a bright idea. "Why don't you go get me a book? Oh, and set up a puzzle for me, too," he suggests.

"Alright," I say. I walk into the hallway and turn left into his bedroom. There's a bookshelf shoved against the wall filled with books. The man must have loved to read because it's overflowing out onto the floor. I pick the first book off the top of the pile, walk back into the living room, and set the book on his lap. "Here you are. I couldn't find a puzzle though, but I can pick you up one at the store. A thousand pieces wouldn't be too hard for you, would it?"

The expression on his face shows me his shock. "Oh ho…that's *mean*," he says, unable to hide his grin. He grabs the book and chucks it at me. Thankfully, this time he misses and the book skids across the floor.

"You asked for it!" I say as I pick the book up off the ground and set it on the coffee table. "Want the TV on?" I ask as I pick up the remote.

"As long as you don't do it," he says.

I turn it on anyway and flip through it until I find the Spanish movie channel, really hoping he doesn't know Spanish.

"How'd you know that this is my favorite channel?" he jokes.

"I'm good like that. I'll be back in an hour or so. I have my cell, so if you need anything I have my number dialed in it. All you have to do is ask Siri. You do remember my name, right?"

He picks up his phone, holds the button and lifts it toward his face. "Siri, call shit for brains."

"*I don't see Shit in your contacts. Should I look for locations by that name?*" Siri asks.

Nice.

I grab my car keys and walk out the door.

CHAPTER TWO

Juggling the bags in my arms, I walk up to the front door and pull the screen door open. I grab the door handle and twist.

It won't turn.

It's very clear that somehow the door has been locked. I must have bumped it on my way out, but I'm not quite sure how that could have happened. I set all the bags down by the door before walking to the back of the house. I grab the handle of the back door, but it won't budge either, and I *know* I'd unlocked it this morning.

"Not funny, Lane," I grumble to myself.

I run around to the front of the house and peer through the living room window. Lane is still in front of the TV, so I start to beat on the glass.

"Let me in!"

He turns his head in my direction and gives me this big-ass grin that just brightens up his handsome face. Then he lifts his good hand and flips me off.

"You are not funny!" I yell as I beat on the window. "I have groceries that'll get hot!"

He just grins at me with that stupidly gorgeous face of his. I start checking all the windows, but they're all firmly locked, so I go back to the living room window.

"I hope you get hungry and have to take a piss!" I yell.

He just waves and turns back to his TV, so I sit down on the front porch and pull out my phone. I can hear his phone ringing inside.

"Hello? How can I help you?" he asks, sounding far too nice.

"This isn't funny, Lane. I have groceries that are getting warm out here. They'll be spoiled."

"Who is this?" he asks like he's confused.

"Lane, it's *really* not funny."

"I'm sorry…I think…I think you have the wrong number. Goodbye."

He hangs up on me, so I sit down on the porch and break out the cookies and milk. I eat about three or maybe seven as I lounge back in the hot sun and wait. I assumed, wrongly of course, that after an hour or so he'd let me in. After I've run out of things to do on my phone, I decide to give in and call James. He seems to be the only one Lane listens to.

"This is James."

"James, this is Felix. I'm having a bit of an issue—"

He groans. "Oh great. What now?"

"Well…Lane's locked me out of the house."

"You don't have your keys?"

"The door was open when I left," I say. "I didn't think about grabbing them."

He sighs. "I understand. I'll call him and see if I can get him to open it."

"Thank you," I say.

"Of course, but remember this from now on."

"Oh, *trust me,* I will."

It's at least twenty minutes before I hear the door unlock. I yank it open as Lane runs his wheelchair into the wall on his way back into the living room.

"You're really funny," I say.

"I thought so," he says from where he's disappeared into the living room. "It's the most fun I've had in a while, if I'm being honest."

"I have to throw away half of the stuff I bought, so don't expect anything edible for supper."

"Oh, don't worry, I wouldn't anyway."

I drag the groceries into the kitchen and toss what's warm and put the rest away before walking into the living room.

"I was hoping if I locked you outside long enough the heat would get to you," he says.

"Sorry," I say. "I'm not a dog."

"Fooled me."

I make Lane some ravioli from a can for lunch and set it down in front of him.

He puts the spoon in his mouth and sits up straight. "This is absolutely delicious! You finally figured out how to cook!"

"Shut it," I say as he laughs to himself.

When I'm finished eating lunch, I clean the house. It's already clean, but there are a few things to pick up. When I walk toward the kitchen, I look into the living room to check on Lane and notice he has the book I'd left on the coffee table. He's slowly touching the pages before turning them. It kind of makes me feel slightly bad for the guy even though his personality is as rotten as the food he forced me to leave out in the hot sun.

I walk back into my bedroom and shift through my clothes to find my MP3 player. "Hey, you have a computer?" I yell.

"No."

"Well, you do. I saw it when I was cleaning."

"Then why'd you ask?"

"Can I use it?" I ask.

"No."

"Please?"

"No."

"What if I do anyway?"

"You can't. It is password protected."

"I know. I tried 'Big Ass Titties,' but it didn't work."

He tries not to submit to my joke, but I can see a hint of a grin. "Will you leave me alone if I give it to you?" he asks.

"Gladly."

"Fine. Get under the Guest page. The password is 3286."

"Thanks," I say before walking into the computer room. Sitting down in the chair, I open the laptop before logging in and plugging my MP3 player into it. Once settled, I begin to scroll through the site until I find an audiobook by one of the writers he has in his room. It's newer, so hopefully, he hasn't read it yet. Of course, I use his credit card to buy it. I walk back into the living room and mute the TV. He doesn't even twitch, so I wonder if he was even listening to it. I stick one headphone into his ear, and he grabs for it.

"What is that?"

"My headphones."

"Why—"

I grab his hand in mine and place the MP3 player into it. I take his thumb and run it down to the first button. "This is to get back to the different songs, so you really don't even need to worry about it. But here," I say while pushing it down, "is play. Right is fast forward, left is rewind. Alright?" I push his thumb over it again. "Play, pause, fast forward, rewind."

"What is this ancient technology?" he asks.

"I apologize that not all of us are rich," I say as I press play and it starts playing the book.

He doesn't bitch anymore so I leave him be. I make supper with what I have left from the ordeal and set it before him, but he's still listening to the book.

"How about you pause that, so we can have a wonderful dinner chat?"

"No, thank you."

I pull it away from him and shut it off. "So, Lane…tell me something about yourself."

"I was listening to that."

"Yeah, and I own it, so you should be sucking up to me. Tell me how great my food tastes."

"Tastes slightly better than that stuff those astronauts eat."

"You hurt me. So…What other authors do you like to read?"

"None."

"Do you like horror? I like horror. But right now, I've been reading this author that is hilarious—"

"If you like it, I'm sure I won't."

"I'm sure," I say. "But he's a great writer. Makes me laugh every time. I'll put his book on when you're done with this, alright?"

"Fine."

"Good! See, we're bonding."

He huffs. "Bonding…uh huh."

I laugh. "Do you want a shower tonight?"

"No."

"You're just never going to take a shower?"

"Yes."

"Come on, it won't hurt, I promise."

When we are finished eating, I clean up our plates. Then, before he can utter another refusal, I grab his wheelchair and direct it into the bathroom. I run the water until it's hot and turn to Lane. I have to steel myself first. Remind myself that I can't ogle the blind man even if he looks like a Greek god. He'd really have a good reason to fire me if I'm jabbing him with a hard-on as I try to help him back into his wheelchair. I grab his shirt and start to pull it off. It's like unwrapping a Christmas present as I eagerly peer at the muscles I am revealing.

He waves me away like I'm a stray animal. "I don't need you to undress me."

"You have one working hand. Are you that good with it?"

"Astoundingly good," he says.

"And your shirts are so tight, can you even peel them off your muscles?" I ask. I squeeze his rock-solid arm as I pretend I'm doing it to add to my joke.

He snorts and tries to push me away again.

I ignore him and help him out of his shirt while I half-heartedly try not to look at his muscles. I mean, the man had clearly worked out *and* he is also blind, so I can look and admire all I want with him none the wiser! This man is a work of art and a decent specimen if you can dissect all the rotten pieces aka: his personality.

I wrap my arm around his back, pressing my hand against his muscular arm as I try to hold him up while he slides his pants down, although I honestly feel like I'm doing more holding on than holding up. As I'm bending down to help pull his pants off his feet, he's refusing to hold onto me for support, so I cling onto him, not because I want to touch him or anything. I assure myself that it's because I don't want him to fall or injure himself. Then I'm left with the awful duty of not letting my eyes wander down his body. I mean, it is kind of wrong to stare at a man that doesn't want to be stared at, right? But he's built like a god, and seeing him naked before me makes nasty thoughts fill my head. Like him pressing me up against the tub wall and pounding into me.

"You feel like a scrawny little girl," he says.

And all the built-up desire is now gone.

"Sorry, I'm not built like Thor," I say.

"How tall are you? I feel like we're the same height when I'm sitting down."

"I am average height," I lie.

"For a fifth grader. How tall are you? Are you even five foot?"

"Of course!"

Barely.

"The thing is, no matter how many times I tell you that I'm fine to take care of myself, you won't listen. The only reason I let them stuff me into this wheelchair is that I can't use crutches right now."

"I am helping!" I say.

He reaches down and wraps his good arm around my waist while putting all his weight on his good leg, then proceeds to lift me about six inches off the ground. "I could bench press you right now." He sets me back on my feet before sitting on the edge of the tub.

"Knock it off! You're going to hurt yourself trying to prove how manly you are!" *And you're going to give me a chubby if you keep touching me like this*, I think to myself.

I'm going to hell, aren't I?

"Sure," he says, and I'm not sure if he's answering me or he's gained the ability to read minds and is agreeing that I have a one-way ticket to hell.

Either way, I help him into the bathtub and sit him down on the stool.

Felix, keep your eyes up.

"Can I take your sunglasses off?"

"No."

"You're going to take a shower with your sunglasses on?" I ask.

"Yep."

"No, you're not," I say as I snatch them off and set them on the counter. It's my first time seeing him without the sunglasses since he always has them on when I leave the bedroom at night and back on when I arrive in the morning. His head is turned away from me, probably so I can't see him, but I can tell that his eyes are cloudy. The skin around his eyes is damaged like it was burned. The burns are worse directly under his eyes, especially near the tear ducts. With the sunglasses on, I could barely see the edges of the burns, which is probably why he always wears them.

I pull the showerhead down as he reaches up for it.

"No. What if you spray your wounds?" I ask.

"I won't. I'm not brain-dead."

"You will be if you don't shut up," I say as I tip his chin back and run the water over his hair. He then proceeds to act like his life is over as I wash his hair. Once I have finished rinsing his hair, I put the showerhead in his hand. "There, now you can wash whatever you want. Just don't scrub your dick raw, I don't want to bandage that as well."

He turns the showerhead so quickly that I don't have time to stop it and sprays me in the face. "Oh sorry, it slipped."

I rub the water out of my eyes. "That was not funny," I say as I hunt around for a towel to wipe my face off with.

"I don't know, I thought it was funny."

Once I have wiped the water from my face, I sit on the sink counter and I wait, sort of glad, sort of sad that there is a shower curtain between us. Because if there wasn't, I'm not sure I could have kept an erection at bay. It has been *far* too long since I've had evening company. And never have I had company that looked like him before.

"Are you done playing with your ducky yet?" I ask as I turn to the shower curtain.

"What, do you want to help?"

Yes, please. "Funny," I say as I yank the curtain back. "I'm missing my favorite show for you."

"What's that? *Big Breasted Nuns*?"

"No, but I heard that was renewed for an extra season," I say sarcastically as I turn the water off and reach for his towel.

He smirks. "Of course you'd be into that kind of stuff."

"You'd be surprised what I'm into," I say as I dry him off none too gently.

"Are you drying me off with sandpaper?" he asks as he tries to grab for the towel.

"Nope, with love," I say.

"I feel bad for the person you fall in love with," he says, and I can't help but laugh.

I reach in and grab his arm as I help him from the stool onto the edge of the tub. Then he swings his legs over while batting me off like I'm a gnat. I ignore him as I grab his clothes and move toward him.

"Nah, I'd rather be naked."

Does this man insist on tempting me?

"I have been naked this entire time, so you might as well," I joke as I take his hand and pull him up so I can lower him into the wheelchair. After he brushes his teeth, I try to look anywhere but at him as I wheel him into his bedroom. I know he's just trying to gross me out or get me to leave or something, but he is causing the complete opposite effect. I wheel him up to his bed, but by the time I put the locks in place, he's clawing his way up onto his bed with his one good hand and leg.

"What kind of work did you do? Or were you so in love with yourself that you just worked out in front of a mirror while jacking off?" I ask as I throw the blanket over him, all the way up over his face.

"Why don't you put that mouth of yours to good use instead of just annoying me," he suggests as he pulls the blanket down.

WHAT? "Really? You do know I'm a male, right?" I ask.

"If you have a problem with it you know where the door is," he says with a smirk. Oh…he thinks he's going to get rid of me by playing the gay card? Two can play that game.

"Don't worry, I don't. Actually…I'll help you with that problem, for the right price," I joke.

He laughs as he turns his head in my direction. "Oh, so now my babysitter is going to prostitute himself?"

"Oh, you'd be surprised what I'd do for a little bit of money."

"Ten bucks," he jokes.

I stare at him like he's an idiot before realizing that he can't see my expression. "I'm sorry, but I'm not that cheap," I say.

He grins. "Sorry, that's all I'm offering. I'm afraid your sex will be as good as your cooking."

I can't help but laugh. "Oh! Not funny. I will tell you that sex with me is *hopefully* better than my cooking."

He laughs. "You're honestly not going to run? I *was* just joking in hopes of disgusting you, but…if you're offering."

"No, you asked. I must be a good babysitter and do as I'm told. Can't get fired now, can I?" I ask as I crawl up onto his bed. I'm half expecting him to tell me to fuck off.

But he has this smug little grin on his face like he knows I'm not going to do it, while I've got a grin on my face while waiting for him to tell me to stop. But he doesn't, so I straddle his waist and lean up to his face. After the shower I just witnessed, this sounds like the perfect end to my night. Otherwise, it would have just been me and my hand.

"Fine, tough guy," I whisper in his ear. "But if you lock me out of this house again, I swear I'll strap you to the toilet and leave you there."

"I look forward to it," he says. "Now come on. Stop putting it off and show me what that mouth of yours is really better used for." He reaches out, moving his hand around until he touches my head and tries to push it down.

"You better be careful, or I will bite," I warn as I slide down his body, careful to avoid his leg. I run my tongue over his nipple, taking it between my teeth and pulling on it.

"Ow," he says while trying to bat me away.

I laugh as I move down to his waist and lick the area his jeans would lay. I slide my hands up his thighs, but I'm careful to avoid his cock on all sides. I am too busy admiring the tightness of his muscular legs.

"Are you just going to be a tease?" he asks.

"You're only paying ten dollars so I'm giving you ten dollars' worth of my time."

"Fine, twelve."

"Funny," I say as I slide my hand up his good leg.

"Fifteen, and that's my final offer. I would have more to give you, but you wasted all my money when you threw out all that food."

I sigh, like I'm really annoyed. "Fine, I'll do it, but this is my donation to the handicapped," I say. "It'll be my good deed for the year."

He laughs until I run my tongue over the tip of his cock. That shuts him up real fast. I swirl my tongue around the tip before taking the head in my mouth, which makes him groan. The noise sends excitement down my body, like I can finally get him to acknowledge or want me the way I have wanted him since I met him. Teasingly, I slide my hand down to his testicles and tug them gently. I move my mouth down as my tongue runs over him. I can feel him growing hard in my mouth as I slide my other hand down to rub the base of his cock. Pulling my mouth away, I run my fingers up from his testicles over his cock, allowing my fingers to dance over it so softly. I feel him fight to keep from rubbing against me. I move my body up to his, allowing his erection to rub lightly against my body as I slide up until I am eye-to-eye with him. I lean over to his ear and bite his earlobe.

"Want to have sex?" I ask. If he says no, I'm not sure I'll even bother to finish him off. I'll go cry in my room. I wanted him now. I needed him inside of me.

"How much is that going to cost me?" he asks, turning his head a bit in my direction.

I grin, already knowing that I have won this game. "First one's free," I say, nipping his neck. I lick and suck at the red mark I've created, causing the color to deepen.

"Oh, I've never been a man to turn down something free," he says as he reaches for me. His hand feels its way up my arm until he finds my T-shirt. He tugs it up, so I help him get it off me. Then he runs his hand down my stomach until he catches my jeans. I feel his hands move over my pants in search of the button, so I reach down and help him. As he pushes them down, I lean back, so I can pull them off.

"You have any condoms or lubricant?" he asks.

"Yeah. You don't have any in here?"

"Maybe…somewhere."

"How can you not know where it is? Don't you ever get laid?"

"Not in my house."

"You a one-night-stander?" I ask as I grudgingly get up. He doesn't answer me, so I head back to my bedroom and dig through my bag until I find what I need. It took me a bit since it'd been a while since I had even needed any of this stuff. I wasn't much of a commitment person so any sex that I wanted, I had to hunt for. And most of the time I'm just too damn lazy to look.

I head back to the bedroom where Lane is waiting for me. I can tell he knows I'm there by the tip of his head, so his ear is closer to me. But for a moment I just admire the man as he sits up on the bed completely naked. His body is still slightly damp from the shower, the water glistening on his chest. His cock is hard and ready because of me. The sight is enough to make me want to rush ahead, get to the best part. Jumping onto the bed like I'm a child, I say, "Found them," as I smack his face with the pack.

"They expired?" he asks as I crawl up onto his lap.

"Probably," I say. "You can't see, so it doesn't matter."

"I'm not sure that's how it works," he says as he touches my stomach. His fingers feel around like he's trying to get his bearings, so I grab his hand with my right one and slide it down to my groin.

"There, I thought you might need some help."

"Not from you," he says, but his fingers wrap around the base of my cock, massaging and stroking me gently. I grab onto him, eager for the attention I'd gone too long without. He grips me harder, making my hips jerk forward, eager for the friction of his skin against mine. His fingers trail down my cock to the tip where his thumb slowly circles.

For a moment I'm lost in his touches, wishing to just allow my body to succumb to each stroke, to each movement. I'm not used to being the one in charge of what comes next. I rub some lubricant onto his hand, so he slides his hand down my back to my butt where he runs his finger over my entrance. My body shivers in anticipation as his finger teasingly circles around it. He slowly pushes a finger inside of me as I set the condom against his tip and roll it over his cock. He pushes another finger inside of me, stretching and stroking me as I rub lubricant down his thick cock. I lean forward and kiss his lips gently and though he kisses me back, I can tell he's hesitant. Each touch, each action is tentative as he tries to navigate a world where I can see everything that he cannot.

I moan as his hand finds my cock and strokes it gently. His other hand is busy sliding over my butt, fingers rubbing inside of me. His muscles are taut as he leans into me, lips finding my skin.

"Am I going to hurt your leg?" I ask even though I don't want to. I don't want to do anything that might stop this.

"No, it's fine," he says as he pulls his fingers out of me. My body instantly misses the pressure, but I know what he wants next, and the thought excites me as I settle myself above his waist.

I take his cock in my right hand and slowly lower myself down until just the tip is touching me, but I don't go any farther. Slowly, I press down against his cock until his tip is pushing against me. I feel just the tip slide in as I push down harder.

"Oh shit, I haven't had sex in a while," I say since it's really tight.

Slowly, I drive all the way down on him and hesitate, so I can grow used to him inside me. The pressure is intense, making me grab onto him as my cock aches for his touch. He leans forward until his lips brush my cheek and his hand sinks into my hair. I open my mouth just enough to feel the touch of his tongue as his hand moves to my cock, touching me, relaxing me. I slide up just a bit, loving the friction of him before pushing back down on him.

"I'm not hurting you, am I?" I ask.

"No, I think you may have cured me," he says softly.

I can't help but laugh. "Oh buddy, I ain't that good," I say. "If I was, I'd be worth more than ten dollars."

He grins and thrusts up inside of me, making my back arch as I grip onto him. I slide up, almost off him, before pushing back down as he goes deep inside of me. His cock hits that perfect spot inside me, causing ecstasy to rush through me. He moves his hips, pushing again against that spot and I moan as I grab onto him.

His hand rubs me just right and the feeling of him inside me pulls me over the edge. As he thrusts up into me, making me moan, I wish he could toss me down and fuck me harder. I grip tightly onto him as I feel his body tense as he moans.

Slowly, I slide up and off him. "Dammit, I broke a sweat. I hate working while fucking," I say. "That's why I usually just lie there and let someone else do the work."

He snorts. "Aw, I almost feel bad for you," he jokes.

I roll over onto my back as I stare up at the ceiling for a moment. I'm not quite sure what to do as we both lie in silent bliss.

"So…was it as bad as my cooking?" I ask, and Lane starts laughing harder than I've heard him laugh before.

"No, it definitely wasn't bad," he says with a grin.

"That's good," I say as I lean over him and reach for his shirt that's on the floor, before wiping him off with it. "I used your shirt, hope you don't mind. Do you need anything before I go to bed?"

"No. Just make sure you're around for tomorrow night."

"You're so funny," I say. "Good night."

"Have a good night, Felix."

I throw the blankets back over him, toss the condom in the trash and walk to the bathroom for a shower.

CHAPTER THREE

"I guess I have to go grocery shopping *again*," I say.

"Have fun!" Lane says like he doesn't realize what I'm hinting at.

"Hmm, guess what? You get to have fun with me," I say as I grab his wheelchair.

"No, I'm not," he says as he grabs the wheel with his good hand and holds it still. I yank at it in the plan of dragging him across the living room floor, but instead, he just sits there with a grin as I tug with all my might.

"Yes, you are," I say through gritted teeth. "You'll just lock me out again if I don't."

He tries elbowing me with the other arm as I lean out of his path. "No, I won't. You have a purpose now."

"To be your fuck toy?" I ask like I'm in shock.

"You said it, not me," he says.

"Come on," I snap.

I grab his hand and force it onto his lap, but he's too strong for me. I yank my belt off, wrap it around his unhurt hand and use a nice pulley method to drag his hand up onto his lap. Quickly, I roll him through the room and nearly unseat him when I hit the doorframe.

"What the hell!" he yells in alarm as he grabs for the armrests. "You nearly killed me!"

"Nah, you're fine," I say even though I had hit the doorframe so hard he probably has whiplash.

"I hope you never have children. It'll be survival of the fittest in your house."

This time I ease him through the door before heading toward the car waiting in the driveway.

"That's why I'm going to learn from all of the mistakes I make with you," I say. I yank the car door open and grab him around the waist. I can't get him to even budge from the wheelchair. "Don't you want to go out?"

"No," he says bluntly.

"Have you gone out since the accident?" I ask.

"I have no desire to."

He's like a stubborn child that you can't reason with.

I feel bad for him though. I know he doesn't want to go out because the house has now turned into a "safe" area for him. A place where he can pretend everything is how it used to be.

"It'll be good for you," I say as I try to hoist him up again, but he just casually sits there with a jiggle to his leg, *knowing* there is no way I can pick him up.

He lounges back in the chair as I stare at him. Then he pulls his arm free before sliding it down to the wheel. He gives it one solid jerk, and suddenly he's headed back to the house.

"Wait! I'll take away my MP3 player!" I yell at him.

He hesitates for just a moment, before continuing toward the direction of the house, although he isn't heading to the door but instead the bushes. "That's alright."

"You won't get any more sexual 'favors' from me," I snap.

He slows to a stop and sits there, so I run up. "Fine, I'll go with you."

"Of course you will," I say as I wheel him back to the car. He helps me get him into the passenger seat, and after he's seated, I close the door. My car is old and boxy, with a trunk big enough to hold five bodies, so the wheelchair easily fits in it. After I slam the trunk shut, wheelchair tucked inside, I get in the car and start it. The music jumps to life, making Lane jerk back in surprise.

"Jesus Christ!" he shouts.

"Where?" I ask as I turn the volume down. "Wait a minute…I thought you were blind. How'd you see him?"

"No, I'm now deaf. What were you listening to?"

"Something super cool and sexy, I'm sure," I say as I back the car down the driveway. "Like if you heard me singing, you'd probably just jizz in your pants."

"Hm…you're awfully confident."

He seems nervous, though, since he keeps tapping his foot impatiently and leans against the door as I drive. I glance over at him and wonder if it is wrong of me to pressure him into going since he is clearly uncomfortable about the whole thing.

"So…what kind of music do you like to listen to?" I ask.

"Not whatever this is. I don't know what's worse. The sound of this music or the sound of your car dying."

"I noticed a nice little sports car sitting in your driveway. Would you rather listen to it instead?" I ask.

"You're not even allowed to look at that car."

"I already did." I look over at him as I stop at a red light. "I'll just start driving it around, you won't even notice."

"And when the big black and white car with the shiny lights begins to follow you, make sure you don't crash it," he says.

I laugh. "No, that's alright. I love my car."

"How old is this thing?"

"Dunno, but the wheels are made from stone. I bet that's what you're hearing," I say, and he smiles.

I'm glad to see the look on his face because I want him to realize leaving the house isn't that bad. I can't blame him for feeling like this though. I can't imagine losing something as life-changing as your eyesight. Everything would be so different…so much harder. I would never get to see new people I meet; everything would just become words. Movies would just be audio. A life suddenly drenched in darkness.

"How far away is this place?" Lane asks.

"We're here," I say as I pull into the parking lot.

I park the car and get out before going over to his side so I can set up the wheelchair. With a lot of help from Lane, I get him out of the car and into the wheelchair. I wheel him inside and look at the carts, unsure of what I should do.

"Well?" Lane asks. Since we haven't moved in a bit, he probably thinks I've just pushed him into the store and made a run for the exit.

"'Well' is right. How am I supposed to wheel you and a grocery cart at the same time?"

"Such a conundrum," he says. "I think we need to go home."

"Nah, I love figuring things out." I grab a basket and shove it into his hands before wheeling him over to the milk. I grab a gallon and put it in the basket. It seems to fill up half the basket as I question if I could get Lane to push a cart while I push him.

"Why am I holding this?" Lane asks.

"Because I'd already bought all of this the other day, but somehow it's all spoiled now," I say as I toss some cheese into the basket.

The basket doesn't take long to fill as I toss lunchmeat and pickles inside. "Do you like healthy stuff?" I ask. "What about salad?"

"Are you making it?"

"Yes."

"Then no."

I set a bag of lettuce on his head, which he grabs, but not before I jab his cheek with a cucumber. "You're used to this now, aren't ya?" I ask as I poke him with it.

He snatches it from my hand and holds it up. "Nah, mine's nicer than this. Unless you're talking about yours, then you'll need to grab one of those pickling cucumbers."

I laugh and start just dropping items onto his lap. "Funny."

"What the hell are you doing?" he asks as I set some donuts on top.

"Basket is full."

"I can tell, it's cutting the blood flow to my wounded leg."

"Yeah, well, whose fault is that?"

"You're not a real good babysitter," Lane says. "Actually, you're really abusive. How much are you getting paid?"

"Nowhere near enough," I assure him as I head for the meats. My attention is drawn to a display shelf overflowing with bestsellers. "Ooh! I've been dying to get this book!"

I turn Lane quickly, causing the wheelchair to ram into a shelving unit. Lane is jerked forward, and a package of sliced cheese tumbles off.

"What are you doing?" he asks.

"Sorry! It's heavy with all this stuff in it."

A woman very rudely glares at me as she walks past. Like she thought I was doing a poor job of caring for the wounded.

"Ooh, that lady just glared at me," I say.

"I'd give anything to be able to do that to you as well," he says as he tries to right all the products he is trying to hold.

"Can't imagine why."

***

I yawn as I stretch out on the couch. "Lane?"

"Hm?"

"I'm bored."

"Great, want to play checkers?" he asks as he turns his head in my direction. He had been lounging on the couch, listening to the audiobook, before I interrupted him. Sunglasses firmly in place even though I've told him to leave them off.

"Really?" I ask eagerly. "I suck at checkers."

"You suck at everything else in life, why would I think that would be any different?" he asks, and I snort.

"Tell me a secret, Lane, were you abandoned as a child?" I ask curiously. "Is that where your hate originates from?"

"I have a game we can play. Go get me some duct tape," he suggests as he pulls an earbud out and twirls it around by its cord.

"For what?" I ask as if I'm really interested.

He smiles at me, but the look is suspicious. "It'll be really fun, just come here, and I'll show you."

"Alright, where's it at?" I ask eagerly like I can't think of a million things I would rather do.

He waves his hand at me like I'm a stray cat he would like to shoo off. "I don't know, find it yourself."

"Why don't you know where anything is in this house?"

"Because I moved here not that long ago."

"Oh. Alright, duct tape, right? Are we going for a little S and M bondage style?"

"Was the plan."

"Ooh, you had me at S." I jump up and walk into the kitchen. I pull open the fridge and grab two string cheese sticks before heading back into the living room. "Want a cheese stick?" I ask as I smack him in the face with it. He quickly snatches it from my hands before I can even pull back.

"Do it again, and I might ram my 'stick' up your ass."

"I might like it," I purr.

"Where's the duct tape?" he asks as he fumbles with the wrapper. I watch in amusement instead of wasting energy helping him.

"Changed my mind." I pull a piece of my cheese off and drop it in my mouth as I watch him struggle with the wrapper.

"Why didn't you take the wrapper off?" he asks.

"I'm trying to make you grow as a man," I say as I pull another piece of the cheese off and dangle it above my mouth before lowering it in.

"There's only one way to make me grow anymore," he says.

I snort. "For fifty bucks you can show me."

"Get over here and unwrap my cheese."

"Ooh, is that what we're calling it now?" I purr.

He holds the cheese stick out to me, so I grudgingly take it. "I don't know, but in my last job I got to fuck prettier boys than you."

"You don't even know what I look like," I say as if I'm offended.

"What do you look like?" he asks, sounding genuinely curious.

I pull the plastic apart, freeing the cheese. "Plain...boring. Blondish brown hair, brown eyes."

"How old are you?"

I hesitate for a moment, wondering if he'd be annoyed to know that I am at least twelve years younger than him. "How old do you think I am?"

"Mentally you're twelve, physically...twenties?"

"You're right, I am in my twenties," I say as I walk over to him and sit on his right leg, though I'm careful of his hurt one. I start to repeatedly smack him in the face with his cheese until he snatches it out of my hand quicker than I could have, and I'm not blind.

He starts eating the cheese like a savage. Not even pulling a single string but instead biting it like a feral animal. "So, compare yourself to someone so I can get an image of what you look like. Because right now I envision you as a whiny, little dwarf like off *Snow White*."

"Okay, so you know when you're walking through the mall and there's this person that's just...gorgeous. Like so gorgeous you just stare at them? But you're like man, I shouldn't stare so you end up doing like a double take? Yeah, you know what I mean. Like even if they're of the gender you're not attracted to, you just appreciate their beauty? I'm the person you run into because you're so busy staring at them."

"So...you look like a trash can? Is that what I'm hearing?"

I laugh. "Exactly like one."

He tosses the wrapper on the floor as he finishes the cheese stick. "Since you're sitting on my lap, does that mean it's story time or fuck time?"

"Depends on how thick your wallet is."

"Thicker than your dick," he retorts.

"Damn, guess I better get to fucking you, huh?" I ask as he grabs my shirt and yanks at it impatiently. It catches under my chin, so I grab for it. "Give me a minute! You're choking me!"

He shrugs like he doesn't much care if I'm still alive at the end of this and instead turns his attention to my pants, tackling the button. I stand up to pull them off and push them down my hips. I can step out of them as I watch him unbutton his own. "I can't wait until I can use my leg."

"Just a couple more days," I say. "But then you'll probably be stuck with a cane or a walker until you're stable enough."

"Oh, they're really funny if they think they can force me to use either of those."

***

After a painful week of Lane refusing to use the walker he was ordered to use, we're finally free of it. Not because he is supposed to be free of it, but because he broke it on "accident" when I wasn't around. Then he lied and told me the physical therapist said that he was good to go.

It made me look like a *really* horrible babysitter when the therapist asked me how I could be letting him walk around without a walker.

"So?" I ask as I pull the car door open. "You're a free man. No wheelchair. No walker. Just your little jabby blind person stick."

"Thank God," Lane says as he gets out of the car and begins to walk toward the house while refusing to use the aid of his white cane. Since he refuses to even take it, I grab it and smack it around a bit just to test it out.

"Now, chop chop. Off to bed we go," he says.

"I'm not a blowup doll you can stash under your bed while you're waiting for your mom to leave," I say.

"You're right. If you were, I'd have at least made you human-sized."

"Funny," I say as I hold the cane like I was preparing to hit him across the back of the legs.

"Get up here and open the door," he says even though he's nowhere near it. So, as I walk past him, I loop my arm through his and pull him after me. "I don't need help. I am perfectly capable without help." As soon as I let go he runs into a fake tree.

I force the cane into his hand in hopes he'll take it. "Wave it around a bit, feel your way through the house."

He smacks the wall so vigorously that I'm surprised the cane doesn't break.

"Do you even know this house at all? Because I'm assuming you don't," I say. "Do you want me to give you a tour?"

"Yes, into my bedroom."

I grab his arm and head straight for his bedroom. He tosses the cane along the way, and once in the bedroom, he grabs onto me.

"Whoa, it's noon, I'm hungry. Not feeling it."

He begins to unbutton my shirt with eager fingers. "I am, and I'm your employer. If I say act like a dog, you bark."

"Woof," I say, and he grins.

"Idiot," he says as he yanks my shirt off and quickly pushes my pants down without bothering to unbutton them. I help him out of his shirt as he pushes his own pants down and grabs me. "Where's the bed?"

"I don't know, there's no way I'd ever find it since I'm an idiot."

He pushes me back and luckily, I fall onto the bed. "You don't sound dead, so I think I found it," he says as he walks forward until he hits it with his knees. Then he crawls up onto the bed, straddling me. I slide up until I'm completely on the bed and he follows me.

"This is your day of glory. You better not screw it up."

"I like it when you talk dirty to me," he says, and I laugh.

Instead of reaching for him, I just watch him. When I first met him, I had been worried if we would get along. It wasn't like I couldn't handle living with someone I didn't get along with; my entire childhood was like that, but he is nothing like my first impression of him. I watch his hands slide up my waist, toward my chest. His fingers make it feel like electricity is running under my skin and I shiver. My hands are aching to touch him, so I slide them up his hard chest, allowing them to snake around to his back as I draw him closer to me. I lean forward, pressing my lips against his as he gives in to me.

He captures my entire body with just the movement of his lips, and I'm entranced by them. When he pulls back, we are both breathing heavily, but he doesn't stop kissing me. His lips move down my throat as my hands explore his back, down to his butt. I squeeze the round muscle of his ass before dipping my finger between his cheeks.

"What are you doing down there?" he asks.

"Just exploring," I say innocently.

"Explore elsewhere," he says, and I laugh.

He shifts his body, and I feel the hot length of his cock brush against mine. I thrust my hips up and moan at the friction, but it's not enough. I need more, and he must sense it as his hand slides down and wraps around my cock, stroking me quickly. I press up against his touch as my fingers trail a path down to his cock. He groans as I wrap my fingers around him, teasing the tip with my thumb before pressing his cock against my own.

He reaches out with his free hand and feels around until he finds the lubricant. Slick fingers push against me as I open my legs wider to accept him. He moves inside of me like he already knows me. We may not truly know each other, but in the silence of his room, it is clear that we understand each other. We can feel each other and a part of it worries me. I have never been good at dealing with another human on an emotional level as I've never understood relationships or commitments. I never believed in them. But this? This I can handle. I can feel his touch, I can sense his lust, and I know it is finally something directed only at me.

He slides his fingers out of me, but before I can murmur a complaint, I can feel his cock pressed against my entrance. I wrap my legs around him as he thrusts into me, making me gasp. My body trembles beneath his touch as his lips gently find my own. Then he moves, sliding out then in gently at first. He shifts slightly before thrusting in, hitting that spot inside of me, making heat rush through my body as I moan and grab onto him desperately. He holds himself up as his other hand slides between my legs and takes my member between his fingers. He thrusts in harder this time, and I feel him there, tight within me. I grab onto him as the feeling spreads over my body until I can't handle it anymore. There is no way I can hold out any longer with the way he is driving me crazy. I can feel my body tighten around him as his head tips back and he thrusts hard into me. His hand pumps me as I come, his grip tight on my sensitive skin. Panting, he pulls out of me, but instead of getting off me, he sits on my waist.

"Your ass is heavy," I breathe as I watch him. His brown hair is sweaty and stuck to his head. I want to make a comment about him breathing so hard because he's old, but I am probably just as breathless, and I hadn't even done any of the work. "How old are you?"

"Thirty-seven."

"Shit, you're old. Is that why you have such saggy nuts?" I joke.

"You must be pretty ugly if you're willing to sleep with me then," he says as he sets his hands down on my stomach. He moves them up my stomach and over my nipples before reaching my collarbone. One hand stops on my chest and the other ventures up over my chin.

I watch him closely as he leans over me with such concentration. He seems hesitant like he doesn't really want me to notice what he's doing but doesn't stop. His right hand slides up my throat as his index finger makes an arch over my lips, then back down my cheek. He moves his other hand up past my eyes before sinking it into my light hair. The entire time I watch his unseeing eyes as I wonder what it would feel like to suddenly have my vision ripped away from me. All the things I would miss. Or how it would feel to have no idea what he looked like.

"Your hair is curly and long."

I really don't think to my ears is that long, but I guess he seems to prefer his hair cut short. "It's not curly, it's a little wavy. It gets messy like this when I go to bed with it wet. What are you doing?"

"I'm trying to feel if you're ugly," he says.

I laugh, and he runs his hand back down over my lips. I open my mouth and lick his finger.

"Disgusting," he says as he wipes the slobber off on my cheek.

"Ew," I say.

"What color is your skin?"

"I'm paler than you," I say.

"Is that pity I hear in your voice?" he asks. I watch as he reaches out and grabs a pillow before pressing it over my head. "I'll smother you."

I laugh as I push it off, but I can tell I've made him a little embarrassed. He doesn't like anyone acknowledging the fact that he can't do everything the same way as he had before. "Sit up for a moment."

He does, and I roll over onto my stomach. "Now, I bet you should feel my back over. I have always heard that the way to truly see someone is through their back."

"I'm not giving you a back massage," he says as he jabs me between the shoulder blades with his finger.

"That's not what I said," I say. "I've heard you learn a lot about a man from their back."

"You're not a man," he says as he slides his hand up my back and grabs a handful of my hair. "Why's your hair so silky? It's like petting a dog."

"It's how I seduce men and women," I say. "Fuck, I'm so good, you don't even need to see me, and you're already seduced."

He snorts. I notice he doesn't return to touching me, and I want to tell him that he can. He's acting like he's been caught doing something wrong or embarrassing.

"Are you hungry?" I ask, hoping to shift his mind to something else.

"Yeah…sure," he says as he gets off me.

"What do you want?" I ask as I sit up.

"Felix?"

"Hmm?"

"Whatever you make tastes like cat litter, so it honestly doesn't matter to me."

"Well...there *are* different types of cat litter," I say as I grab my clothes. I go into the bathroom and get cleaned up before pulling them on, then I head into the kitchen where I make him a lunch meat sandwich. I mean, I can't ruin that, right?

When he hasn't emerged by the time I'm done, I head back toward his room. I quickly stop before he hears me because he's sitting on the edge of his bed with his face in his hands. I can't tell if he's crying or not, but I feel awful for him. I can't imagine what he's going through right now. How hard everything has to be for him. I didn't know him before the accident, but it's clear that he isn't thriving in this new life.

What I do know is that he'll get pissed if I go in to comfort him. Which is fine with me because I never really learned how to comfort someone. That kind of stuff didn't happen when I was growing up. I learned from a young age to deal with my own shit and keep my nose out of others'.

So, I back up down the hallway, but stop before I get too far away. "Lane! What are you doing? My food's going to go to waste if it gets to room temperature," I shout as I head down the hallway. When I reach his door, I peek into the room. He has his back to me, but he's pulling on his clothes. "One pile of cat shit rolled in litter waiting for you."

"Sounds better than what you made last night," he says.

"I hate you."

"The feeling is mutual," he says as he covers up the other emotions with a smile.

"Glad to know we agree on one thing," I say.

CHAPTER FOUR

Anxiety jerks me awake, but as soon as my eyes open I recognize it as an old feeling that tastes stale. Its tendrils drip off me as I look around the room and remind myself that I've made it to this point in my life. I am doing just fine. I roll over and look at my phone to see what time it is, but it's not yet three-thirty. I close my eyes and will my body to sleep, but nothing comes for me but the slow hour of four.

By four-fifteen, I'm as awake as one can be, so I give up and pull some clothes on. I quietly walk down the hallway and into the spare bedroom where Lane's computer is set up. I turn it on and wait for it to boot up. As I do, I rummage around his stuff. I flip through his bills and open every desk drawer, but everything is so boring it almost puts me back to sleep. My fingers ache to dig deeper, to find his little secrets and make them my own, but I force myself to turn away from that.

To kill some time, I play on the computer for a few hours, but by the time I'm bored of that, I can't stop the itch to nose through his room. After having already combed through the desk, the only spot left is the closet. When I open it, I notice there are a lot of blankets neatly folded. I mean, there's nothing else in the house, why the heck does he have so many blankets? I push them over and notice that it's not quite all blankets but a safe hidden beneath them. I kneel and look at the safe and the tantalizing key lock. I instantly want to know what's inside of it, but I know not to snoop. I *force* myself not to snoop, but it's really quite hard.

To distract myself, I head to the living room and turn on the TV. For hours I laze around until I hear Lane getting up. The sound of movement is like a starting gun going off and has me up and rushing into his bedroom without knocking.

"Lane?"

"Oh, come right in. No sense in knocking."

"What's in that safe?" I ask.

"What safe?"

"The one in your spare bedroom. What's in there?"

"Don't know. Haven't seen it."

"Please tell me," I say, absolutely dying to know. It's probably just a birth certificate or social security card, but I feel like there *has* to be something better in there than that.

"Why do you need to know?" he asks as I pull open the dresser and grab some clothes for him.

"Because I want to," I say stubbornly.

"You're like a child."

"So? Just tell me."

"Make me something to eat."

"You'll tell me if I do?"

"No...that definitely wasn't even in the equation. I'm just hungry and really confused about where the food is."

I sigh and toss his clothes at him. They hit his chest and he manages to grab the shirt in time, but the pants fall to the ground.

"Why won't you let me snoop? You're so mean!"

"Says the person that is getting paid to help a blind man, but instead just *chucks* clothes at him."

"I'm teaching you independence. You don't want anyone to dote on you, so I'm respecting your wishes."

"Oh! Well, thank you for your care," he says, making me smile.

I plop down on his bed so I can watch the view while he gets dressed. "You're welcome. Flex your arm a little when you put your shirt on."

"You want to see them up close? Come here. I'll bench press you."

"You can't lift me," I say with a snort. I refuse to go over to him because I really don't feel like I need that much embarrassment at eight in the morning.

As soon as he's dressed and his teeth are brushed, I grab him by the hand.

"What are you doing?" he asks.

"Showing you around," I say as I lead him to the entrance of his bedroom. "You were never in this house before you were blind, were you?"

He ignores my question, so I take that as confirmation.

"Okay, so starting from your bedroom, we have a left and a right. Let's go left," I say as I pull him after me. "Let's see, four steps down the hallway—"

"Are those dwarf steps or regular steps?" Lane asks.

I snort. I'm sure it was a very attractive sound. "I am not a *dwarf*."

"So?"

I sigh dramatically. "Four *regular* steps or eight dwarf steps and you reach the doorway," I say as I take his hand and press it against the doorway. "Room on the left is mine, the right is the spare bedroom with the super secretive safe inside." I pull him into my bedroom and set his hand on my dresser. "Dresser…there's a chair here…and the bed. The rest of the room is pretty bare," I say as we head out into the next room until we've gone through every single room. I make sure to run his hand over every piece of furniture and never once does he say anything, but he goes along with me.

"Let's do it again," I say once we're back to the spot we'd started. "If we turn left, where do we go?"

He ignores me, so I pinch his nipple that is showing too clearly through his tight shirt. I feel like I should make fun of him, but then again, I probably just feel bad about myself since the last push-up I did was back in high school. "I'm talking to you."

"Why do I have to narrate it?" he asks.

"It'll help you remember. Now come on or I'm done helping you."

He stops close to my room and waves his hand through the air. "This is the dwarf's room."

"Good," I say as he slowly steps through the door and feels around.

"And the dwarf's dresser."

"Yep."

Then he reaches back and hits me in the face in an attempt to grab me. "And this the dwarf!"

"Funny," I sarcastically say, but I continue to follow him around the house.

After I feel like he's gotten the hang of it, I head back to the kitchen and start making him breakfast. Which I slave over, by sticking a waffle in the toaster.

While he's eating breakfast, I head into his bedroom and throw all his clothes onto his bed. There, I begin putting safety pins on the tags of each shirt and pair of colored pants until I have them all done. Then I retrieve Lane and drag him into his bedroom.

"Alright," I say. "I put safety pins on the tags of your shirts."

"So they'll poke me?" he guesses.

"Close," I say. "It's so you can figure out what color they are without me. One small pin is red, one large pin is blue, two small pins are green…get it?"

He grabs a shirt off the bed and feels around for a moment until he finds the tag. "So, this is red?"

"Yes," I say with a smile. "Why do you sound so skeptical? Do you really not trust me that much?"

"No, I trust you as far as I can throw you. Oh, wait…I could probably throw you pretty far. Basically, I just don't trust you."

I watch as he picks up another shirt.

"This one is green?"

"Yes."

"I'm trying really hard to trust you, and I just can't."

"Good," I say when I hear the doorbell. "I like keeping you on your toes. I'll be back."

I walk up to the front door and notice James standing outside. I pull it open and smile at him. "Hey! I didn't know you were swinging by."

"Hey, kiddo. How are things going?"

"Wonderfully," I say, and he looks at me like I'm suddenly very suspicious.

"Who is it?" Lane calls from within his bedroom.

"It's the blow-up doll you ordered!" I yell back then turn to James with a smile. "We get along splendidly, if that's what you came here to ask."

He laughs. "I see," he says with a shake of his head. "Is he in his bedroom?"

"Yeah."

"Mind if I go have a word with him?"

"Of course not. Would you like to stay for supper?" I ask.

"Don't do it!" Lane yells from in the back.

"Shut up, Lane!" I yell in response.

"I'd love to," James says with a smile before heading to Lane's bedroom.

Like the saintly human being I am, I at least wait until he's closed the door to Lane's room before sneaking up to it and eavesdropping.

"You just made the biggest mistake of your life," Lane says.

"What's that?" James asks.

"Eating that kid's food."

He's even mean when I'm not around! Although…my food really is quite awful.

"Can't be that bad," James says. "Do you have a moment?"

"What do you think?" Lane grumbles. It's clearly not a topic he likes to bring up.

"I think we have a lead, but that's about as much as we have," James says.

I press harder against the door, so I can hear everything they're saying. What do they have a lead on? Is this some soap opera drama? Are they cops? Or are they the bad guys?

"Is this green?" Lane asks, clearing not caring as much about the "lead" as I am.

"The shirt? Yes, it is…" James says, sounding confused.

"Huh," he says. "And this one is blue?"

"It is blue…how do you know that?" James asks curiously.

"Felix put safety pins inside to color coordinate them. So, what have you figured out?" Lane asks.

"Not a lot. Just have an idea of someone that may be working with them."

"Hmm…name?"

"Jonah Robertson."

"Doesn't sound familiar. Criminal record?"

"None, but this guy has reportedly been seen with Red."

"Anything else?"

"Nothing."

"Shit."

"I know, I'm working on it," James says.

They're silent for a moment, making me question if I should back away from the door and actually head toward the kitchen, so it looks like I'm doing something when they come out.

"How are you doing?" James asks.

"I'm so sick of this. I want to be out there, doing something."

"I know. We have to take this slow. Is Felix at least entertaining you?"

"Yeah…He's honestly helped quite a bit. Makes this place a little less boring."

"That's good. He seems like a good kid."

"What's Felix look like? He doesn't tell me much when I ask him. Just says he's plain," Lane says.

James snorts.

"What?"

"Oh nothing, I just wouldn't say he's plain. When I asked Dani why she hired him over the lady that had the experience she told me it was because Felix was, and I quote, 'so adorable, I just wanted to take him home.'"

Lane laughs. "I just…dammit, James, you don't understand how hard it is not being able to see anything. I want to know what he looks like."

"Why don't you ask him?"

"I did, he won't tell me much."

"He's being modest. He's better looking than any of the guys I've seen you with. Let's see…he has hazel eyes. At first, I thought his eyes were brown, but they have a touch of green to them. He has dark blond hair that's…got this messy thing going on, like where it looks good even though it looks like he doesn't do anything with it. Almost…fluffy. Like if I let my hair do that, I'd look like an idiot. He also has this charming smile that I'm pretty sure has gotten him just about everything he's ever wanted in life. Happier now?"

"Slightly," he says reluctantly. "This is getting old, fast."

"It looks like you're doing good. He has some good tricks to help you."

I didn't know dismissing his question about my appearance had been bothering him so much. I prefer him thinking of me as plain, not at all like James described me. Men only ever see my outward appearance, they don't give a shit as long as I'm attractive. No one ever seems to look beyond my face. Or maybe there's nothing beyond it worth looking for. I wouldn't blame them if that's everyone's reasoning for never getting close to me.

When I hear them coming, I quickly rush away from the door and head back into the kitchen where I tear the fridge door open and hunt for something that will make me look like I've been busy. I grab the package of mushrooms and toss them onto the counter. Quickly, I unwrap them and wash them so that by the time James and Lane walk in I've already started cutting them.

"Lane, you're getting pretty good at navigating this place," James says with a smile.

"Self-taught," Lane says with an evil smirk.

"Well, if that's the thanks I'm going to get, I'm going to start moving things around and laughing when you fall," I say.

"See what I said? He's evil."

James laughs. "I don't know, I think someone has to be to put up with you."

I laugh harder at the look on Lane's face than anything. "He told you."

I set the dishes out and listen to the men talk as I finish up supper. I set it all on the table and everyone takes a seat.

"Smells good," James says.

"Don't lie to him," Lane whispers as if I won't hear him.

I slop the food onto his plate and shove it at him. "I hope you choke."

"The smell alone is enough to make me do so," he says with a grin as he reaches for the spot I always put his fork. I debate moving it before he can get ahold of it, but I decide that would require too much effort on my part.

James takes a bite of the food and chews as Lane and I focus on him, waiting eagerly for any reaction.

"I so wish I could see right now. James, how are you enjoying it?" Lane asks.

"This isn't bad at all…it's pretty good," he says. "You actually had me kind of worried."

"It's spaghetti, how can you screw up spaghetti?" I ask as I sit down.

"Says the man that ruined oatmeal."

I give him that one.

***

"Guess where we are going?" I ask as I grab onto Lane's recliner and shake it as hard as I can. He reaches out and flails his arm around as he tries to hit me away from him, but he can't reach me, so I laugh maniacally as I keep shaking his recliner.

"Hell, because I'm going to beat you," he says as I keep just out of his reach.

"*Wrong*! The MALL!"

"Fuck no."

"Yes!" I say as I let go of his chair. "Come on, get up."

"Why do I have to go with you?"

"Because you *want to!*"

"Why do you like me so much?"

"I don't know!" I realize. "I think it's your muscles. I can't look away from them. I want to take you with me and parade you around, so everyone can be jealous of what I get to look at all day."

He laughs. "What do you like more about me? My personality or my muscles?" he asks.

I stare at him for a moment. "Please…please don't make me do this."

"I'm going to stop exercising and see how far your friendship goes."

"Please don't," I say, and he laughs. "Now get up. Come on. Yip yip!"

"Fine," he says as he gets up. He heads toward the door without even waiting for me, so I grab his long cane and rush after him. He refuses to use it around the house, but I could see everything becoming a hassle once in the mall. I follow him out to the car as he gets inside. I open my door, toss the folded-up cane in the back, and sit down.

"You ready?" I ask eagerly.

"You act like we're going to Disney World," he says.

"We might be. You won't know the difference," I say.

"I think I'll know the difference between the mall and Disney."

"Really? Kids screaming, creepers everywhere, people in animal suits dragging you off into quiet rooms. They sound the same to me," I say.

"I'm not sure what kind of mall you've been going to, but maybe you need to start shopping elsewhere."

I laugh as I start the car. "Shut up, you're blind, you don't know anything," I say.

"Yes, mental capacity degrades steadily as one loses eyesight," he retorts sarcastically.

"I knew it!"

"Just drive and make this day end," he says as he buckles his seatbelt.

"Want to play a driving game?" I ask.

"What game?" he asks suspiciously.

"What about I-spy?" I ask.

"I spy with my little eye a cruel asshole who thinks he's funny."

"Me?" I guess.

"Congrats," he says.

I laugh as I pull out onto the road and start driving. "Do you really dislike me, Lane?"

"Very much so," he says.

"That kind of hurts my feelings," I say.

"Does it? And asking a blind man if he wants to play I-spy isn't mean?" he asks.

I think about it for a moment. "When you put it that way...it is horribly mean." When I look over at him, I notice he's grinning but trying to hide it by looking out the window.

"I mean, of *all* the people in the world, how did they end up hiring you? Do you even have experience with this kind of stuff?"

"No, not at all," I say as I merge onto the highway. This time of day the traffic is just starting to get heavy, but it's not as bad as it will be in a few hours. "They just said they'd pay me like a lot, and I told them I'd take half, so they just hired me."

"You are pretty cheap."

"Yeah, I like to think so," I say.

"What are we getting at the mall?"

"Handcuffs, whips, and ball-gags," I say.

"Why didn't you say so sooner?"

I start laughing as Lane chuckles.

The parking lot is already nearly full when I pull in, so I have to drive up and down a few rows before giving in and parking way out back.

"Are we here?" he asks. "I swear to god, if we're at a stop sign again and you tell me we are here like when we went to the pharmacy, I will beat you within an inch of your life."

I grin as I shut the car off. "Not a joke this time," I say as I get out and grab his cane. A car pulls in next to us, so I wait while she parks. Then, I head around my car to catch up to Lane before he rushes off in whatever direction he insists the mall is in because he despises help. "Here's your cane," I say as I push it into his hand.

He clutches onto it and lifts it up. "Oh right...the 'probing' cane. Only probing cane I need is the one in my pants," he says as he tosses it.

I look over at the mother that is staring at me with wide eyes as she pulls her three-year-old out of the car.

"There are children around," I say.

"Can't see them so they must not exist," he says as he starts walking.

I scoop up his cane and run after him. He is following behind two girls much closer than a man should ever follow two girls he doesn't know. They nervously look back at him but with the sunglasses and the bulging muscles, they start to question if their end is near. They whisper something before moving quicker, and because Lane is following the sound of them, he follows along even faster.

"Lane, you're stalking people," I say as I jog to catch up to him. "Take the cane."

I stuff it into his hand and he swings it, smacking the ankle of the girl directly in front of him. She yelps and looks back at him in fear.

"Told you that you were too close," I say before turning to her. "I'm really sorry about that, he just got the cane and doesn't really understand how to use it yet."

Their expressions soften when they see the cane. "That's okay, I'm fine," she says nicely.

"I don't want this thing," Lane says as he collapses it. "Where's the trash?"

"Lane, you are the most stubborn man I've ever met!" I say as I take the cane before he can chuck it.

"Good," he says as the girl he'd been stalking holds the door open for him.

Lane, hearing the door, holds his arm out until he feels it and touches his way in through it. I follow behind him while holding the cane in both hands like a club. It'd just be like clubbing a baby seal.

He wouldn't see it coming until it was too late. I sigh but follow him inside where he's stopped. There are people milling all around us, the noise growing louder as Lane slowly turns his head.

"Lane, just use the cane," I say as I shove it into his hand for the third time.

"I'm getting a seeing-eye horse," he decides. "Like one of those miniature horses with the boots on their feet."

"You'll look real badass then," I say.

He nods. "Thank you."

"Get a dog. Those seeing-eye dogs are awesome. I'd have one just because they're awesome."

"If you got one you'd need like a Chihuahua or the thing would look massive next to you."

"That's fine. If it's a dog, I'll take it."

I grab his wrist and pull him into a store as he swings his cane back and forth, smacking my ankles with each pass. By the fifth hit, I begin to realize that he was right, we should trash the thing.

As I leaf through the clearance rack, he wanders around hitting everything with his cane as people give him a wide berth. I think he's getting enjoyment out of it in some messed-up way.

"Lane, I think you're supposed to tap, not swing it like a broadsword you're aiming at someone's ankles."

He cocks his head at me like what I said was super confusing. "I don't think so."

"Lane, get over here," I say as I pick up a shirt. I hold it up to me, but I'm not sure I like it for me. So, I pick up a larger size that would fit Lane and press it against him. "I think this would look sexy on you."

He reaches out and touches the fabric. "What is it?"

"Two dogs screwing."

"Funny."

"It's a dark blue button-up with gray stripes," I say. "I'm getting it for you, with your credit card of course."

I grab his arm and pull him around a shelf and pick up another shirt.

"Hmm…I like this one. I think this one would look better on me," I decide.

He reaches out, so I put it in his path. I watch as he runs his fingers down the fabric, trying to "see" it in the only way he can. I can't imagine how awful it would be to not even see the color of this shirt.

"Will it be easy to rip off you?" he asks, and all sympathy I held for him is gone.

I laugh and shake my head. "I suppose."

"Then you can get it."

"Great," I say. "I thank you for your permission."

He hits me with his cane. "Oops, sorry."

"I'm sure," I say as I walk up to the cashier with my bruised ankles and toss the clothing onto the counter.

"Good afternoon," the woman behind the counter says with a smile.

"Hi," I say.

"Did you find everything alright?" she asks.

"Yep, everything's good."

She picks up the blue shirt. "Ooh, I love this shirt. The color will look gorgeous on you," she says with a smile.

"Thanks," I say.

I pay for the shirts and grab my bag. As I turn I grab Lane's arm and pull him after me.

"What was that?" he asks.

"What?"

"That girl. What do you think you're doing?"

"Are you jealous she was flirting with me?" I ask. "Are you're jealous that you have too rancid an attitude to flirt with someone?"

"No, I just couldn't imagine someone would flirt with you. Did she have a tip jar out front or something?" he asks as we step out of the store.

I notice a guy in tan pass by me, his eyes briefly catching mine. "That's weird," I mutter as I look behind me, but the guy isn't looking at me any longer. He's walking away from me, looking at his phone.

"What?" Lane asks.

I turn my attention back to where I'm walking. "I swear, I've seen that guy before."

"Like you know him?"

"No…I feel like he's been following me. I think I saw him at the grocery store earlier in the week or something…I don't know."

"You think someone is following you?" he asks as he turns his head like he wants to look back at who I am talking about.

"I'm just being paranoid," I say.

"I'm sure it's not the same guy. Why would someone actually want you?"

I laugh. "That's not what you were saying last night."

"Sometimes, I suffer from a lapse of judgment."

CHAPTER FIVE

When I wake, it's only two in the morning, but I know my insomnia has already settled in. For a while, I lie there as if I can convince my mind that sleep really is needed. But I'm wide awake, so I get up and head into the computer room. I play on Lane's laptop for a bit, but he doesn't have any games on it, and I am not too much into social media. All the while, the safe in the closet taunts me again. After about an hour of refusing to give in, I decide that I should do a sweep of the room and make sure everything is in perfect order.

Okay, maybe I just tore the room apart to find the key, but I had to know.

After finding the key tucked away in a box of junk, I turn on the closet light and crawl inside.

It's like opening Pandora's Box, and as I think that, I try to remind myself that I have tried really hard to not give into this nosy-ass desire I have always carried around with me. But it is like a sickness, so technically it isn't my fault. Honestly, it is in my nature. I have opened the lock, which is half of the fun, and now I should close it and turn away.

The door slowly swings open.

On top are two guns and I know that the angel on my shoulder just lost as the devil on the other rubs his hands together in anticipation.

I hesitate, then pick one up as I admire it. I'm surprised by how heavy it is, but I guess I had no reason to think it would be light. I have never shot a gun, even though I've been around them more than I would like. I set them beside me before picking up a leather case. Flipping it open, I lean over it to see what it has in store for me.

It's a police badge.

So, Lane was a police officer? I could see that. He is athletic and seems to carry around an idea of justice.

I grab another, but this one is from the military. So...he must have been in the military when he was young. But when I pick up the next thing, I'm starting to wonder what exactly Lane did since it is a badge for a man named Mark Hopkins. Under that is a driver's license belonging to a Tom Reinz and another is for a Pete Walker.

Well, Lane isn't who he is claiming to be. Maybe he had been working with the police and had to work undercover. Or maybe he is the bad guy, all these are forged, and I am the fool. But I don't feel any threat from him, so I'm not sure it bothers me either way. If he was the bad guy it might bother me, depending on what he had done, but I just don't get those vibes from him. I quietly put everything back and debate whether to ask him or not in the morning.

Probably shouldn't since I *did* break into his safe. Maybe I'd just ask him what job he had before the accident and see if I can get him to talk.

It's now three-thirty, and I'm no closer to falling asleep, so I close everything up and leave the room. I walk past my bedroom and push open the door to Lane's bedroom. Once I'm in the room, I shut the door quietly behind me, but when I look over at the bed I see that Lane is sitting up.

"Felix?" Lane asks.

"Yeah."

"What are you waking me up for?" he grumbles before lying back down.

"It's only three and I can't sleep," I say.

"I was sleeping very soundly, in case you were wondering."

I crawl onto his bed and sit at the foot of it. He tries to pretend I'm nonexistent by closing his eyes and turning away from me.

"Lane," I whine.

"What? Are you trying to be sexy? Because I don't find much sexy at three in the morning," he mumbles.

"I want you to suffer with me," I admit.

"I don't like suffering. I like to sleep."

"You're a grump," I say as I pull the covers back and crawl under them.

"You want sex?"

"No."

"Then what do you want?"

"I dunno," I admit as I pull the blankets up to my chest. "To sleep."

He grumbles something under his breath that I can't hear. "You're not just going to leave, are you?" He rolls over to face me and I smile, glad he's finally taking this seriously.

"It's not likely," I admit.

"Why can't you sleep?" he asks, clearly submitting to the idea of not going back to sleep any time soon.

"I don't know...I have bouts of insomnia."

"You stressed about something?" he asks.

"No."

"What were you thinking about before you went to bed?"

"How hot Robert Downey Jr. is and how I wish you looked like him," I say.

"I am so glad I stopped sleeping for you," he says.

I laugh and roll onto my side so I'm facing him. With just the dim light of a nearby street lamp shining through the window, I can see him watching me. He may not see me, but he is focused on me as if he can.

"Do you ever wonder what your purpose in life is?"

"What do you mean?"

"Like…why were we born?" I ask.

"Because your mother screwed your father without a condom," he says.

"Ew, gross. You know what I mean."

"I had a purpose until the accident. It's not my fault you've never had a purpose."

He rolls onto his back and grows quiet like he's thinking of something. He's staring up at the ceiling, but I wish he'd look over here again. It feels so much more real when he is focused on me, but I don't know why I even care, I certainly don't want anything to come of this. "What was your purpose?" I ask.

"To help people."

"Do what?"

"I don't want to talk about it," he says. "Do you feel like you need to find your purpose or something? Is that what's bothering you?"

"I don't know," I admit as I pick at the edge of his pillow.

I've never tried too hard to find my purpose in life. Instead, I've just sat back and watched my life unfold, trying to care about where it was heading. Sometimes that's so damn difficult to do that I can't imagine trying harder than I already am. Life felt rough enough as it is.

We are both quiet for a while, and I question if he's already gone back to sleep when he speaks. "Some people don't figure out their purpose until much later. I wouldn't worry about it."

"Yeah…that'd be nice because sometimes I wonder why I'm even here," I say. "Sorry to wake you up, I'm going to try to go back to bed."

"There's a reason you're here, Felix. Even if you can't see it yet. You can sleep in here," he says as he rolls onto his stomach. I watch his bare back for a while, wondering what he didn't wish to tell me.

***

I need to get milk, but Lane is sound asleep on the couch. I was going to wait, and then make him go with me, but it's now seven o'clock and if I wait any later, it'll be dark before I get back. So, I leave the house, wondering if he's even going to notice I'm gone.

The store isn't too far away, and it would probably take me longer to drive the car and find a place to park than if I just walked, so I head off on foot. The wind is just cool enough that it rustles my hair and keeps me from sweating. The houses begin to fade away as businesses fill in the spaces until the road is thick with them. As soon as I turn onto Main Street, I get distracted by the bookstore and head inside.

On the bestseller's shelf is a book from one of my favorite authors, so I grab it and flip through it to see if I would be willing to spend the twenty-eight bucks for the hardcover. But then I notice another book that I may want more and now I can't decide. Before long I'm reading the first chapter of both to make sure I figure out which one would be the best. In the end, I grab the first one I'd picked up and pay for it before heading back down the street to get milk. It's already dark out, and I wonder if I should have left earlier.

My phone rings, so I dig it out of my pocket. "Hello?"

"What are you doing?" Lane asks, sounding slightly annoyed for some reason.

"Getting milk. I see your beauty sleep did nothing to help your personality."

"I was worried. This is the third time I've called you."

"Really? I'm surprised I didn't notice." It must have been because I had set my phone on the armrest of the chair I had been sitting on.

"Why are you getting milk at nine at night?"

"Is it really that late?" I ask, surprised.

"Yes. Where were you?"

"I stopped at the bookstore and was distracted."

"Come on, get back home. Didn't you say someone was freaking you out the other day?"

Hmm…that did happen. "Yeah, that was like a week ago, I kind of forgot about it. I think I made it up because I haven't seen anyone since."

"Come on, I'm hungry, forget the milk."

"I'm almost there, and I already had supper, you just slept through it. There's a plate in the fridge with plastic wrap on it. Heat it up for a couple of minutes."

"You don't need to be wandering around after dark. Come on home."

"I'll be there in ten minutes," I say before issuing my goodbye. I check my phone and see that he had indeed called me three times. Trying to figure out how absorbed I had been in reading, I slide the phone into my pocket. But now that he's mentioned the man that I thought had been following me, I get an uneasy feeling in my stomach. I'd honestly forgotten about him since I hadn't seen him in over a week.

I walk into the store and grab the milk before quickly paying for it. Once back outside, the city is already falling dark as I head down the quiet street. Even though it is Friday, this side of town went to sleep early since there aren't any bars or much nightlife.

Sudden pain overwhelms me as something makes an impact with the back of my head. The force sends me forward, but my feet don't follow, and I begin to fall. I drop the milk and book onto the ground as someone wraps their arms around me and begins to drag me. As soon as I realize what's happening, I get my legs under me and open my mouth to scream for help. Before I can utter a sound, a hand clamps down over my mouth as two men drag me into the dark alleyway.

CHAPTER SIX

"Let me go!" I yell against the hand held tightly over my mouth.

They stop dragging me once we're hidden from view, but the men don't let go of me or remove the clamped hand.

The man that clearly *had* been following me, steps in front of me. He's wearing a black suit jacket and a pair of dark blue pants. He looks to be in his late thirties or early forties with dark brown hair cropped military short. His narrowed eyes watch me as he lowers a cigarette from his lips. He blows the smoke into my face as he grins at me. His teeth are oddly white and for a moment, I don't understand why I would even notice that.

He leans over a little bit so he's at my height and presses his face right up close to mine. His breath smells like cigarettes as I stare at him with wide eyes.

"This is what's going on," he says as he holds up a roll of duct tape.

A big guy to his right takes it from him and starts to pull a strip free. The sound of it tearing is deafening in the quiet alleyway as panic settles into my stomach. The big man reaches out for me and slaps the piece over my mouth. I fight against them as two of the six men force my hands together, allowing him to tape them to each other. I struggle and scream and fight, but I can't budge against them.

The man in the suit smiles at me. "It's a pleasure to meet you. My name is Victor Red, and I want you to remember that, alright? Can you do that for me?"

Quickly, I bring my leg up and kick the man behind me in the dick. He stumbles back but never loosens his grip enough for me to run. Instead, a man on my right with bright red hair smacks my face. Startled, I jerk back. My cheek stings as my eye waters.

"I'm sure you're curious why you are here; let me tell you. You've been hanging around Mr. Price quite a bit, and let's just say he and I don't get along. At the moment, I'm quite upset with him. The thing is, I was going to leave him alone, I was just going to forget he even existed, but there's someone sniffing around my business and I need it to stop. So, I'm going to have you tell him that, alright?" he asks. His voice is so steady and casual that my brain is trying to trick me into believing that this man isn't bad.

I realize I need to just go along with what he says so I just nod eagerly.

"Good," he says with a smile. "Are you going to remember my name?"

I nod again, and he claps his hands together in applause. I jump at the noise and lean away from him.

"Great." He waves his hand and the man with red hair holds out a baseball bat. I have the slightest suspicion that it is what they'd hit me over the head with when I had been walking down the road. "Alright, let's make sure he remembers that." He takes a step back, making my stomach tighten in fear. I watch the baseball bat with wide eyes, wanting to tell him that I'll listen, that I don't need to be threatened, but I can't say anything through the tape.

"Yes, sir," the red-haired man says as he raises the bat in the air and brings it down on my side.

The blow is devastating. It knocks my air out, making me gasp, but the tape makes me feel like all air has been cut off. I begin to jerk against them harder as the pain eats up into my side. I thrash and kick as the hands on my arms squeeze tighter, painfully holding me in place. I can't even get the men to move as the man hits me across the arm with the bat. It feels like my bones are screaming as the blow reverberates up into my arm.

"Let him go, boys, he's not going anywhere," Red says like I'm a timid animal with no chance of escape.

They drop their hold on me, and I'm surprised by the sudden release. I'd been fighting so hard that when their hands leave me I stumble forward. As soon as my balance has been gathered, I try to run. Panic settles in me, but the red-haired man hits me hard across the side. He draws back and swings again. I bring my arms up to protect myself, but the blow breaks right through my block, before smashing into my head. White light bursts before my eyes as I drop to the ground. Light and darkness dance before my eyes as I struggle to my knees. I'm barely up when someone kicks me back down and suddenly they're all kicking and hitting me. I jerk against them and try to crawl away from their circle, but I can't get anywhere. I curl up into a ball, trying to protect my head until it stops. Suddenly there are hands on me, drawing my arms down as the man kneels beside me.

I can feel blood wetting my clothes as he looks at me. I'm terrified he's going to kill me. I'm panting, but with the tape over my mouth, I feel like I can't breathe. Each gasp of air pulls at the tape as my chest compresses. The man is just leering down at me as I pray he'll tell them to stop and just go away.

"You remember my name, right?" he asks, and I nod quickly. Anything to just let me go. As I breathe, blood is bubbling out of my nose. "You tell him exactly what I did to you and tell him that if he doesn't make it stop, I'll do something else to you. Got it? I asked if you understood!" he yells, but he hadn't given me time to react.

I nod quickly, and he smiles.

"Good. Cut the tape off his hands."

The red-haired man to my right pulls a knife out and cuts the tape off my shaking arms. Refusing to move in case they change their minds, I watch as they leave me lying there in the dirty alleyway. I'm shaking as they leave, scared to draw their attention. As soon as they are out of sight, I quickly reach up and grab the tape, pulling it off my mouth. Nausea hits me hard, forcing me to lean over and throw up as my body shakes. I'm gasping for breath as blood runs out of my nose, dripping onto the ground. I watch each drop hit and spread across the dirty ground. The taste in my mouth is making me more nauseous and I fear I'll throw up again. My head is pounding, and each move makes it hurt as I try to steady myself.

My entire body is aching as I slowly roll onto my hands and knees. It causes my vision to blur, and for a moment, I can't tell which direction I'm facing. As soon as it clears, I wipe at my face and my fingers return wet with blood. I close my eyes and drop my head, trying to calm my breathing. Slowly I crawl up onto my feet, causing pain to course down my entire body as dizziness rushes me. I lean against the wall and try to calm myself, so I can make it home. As soon as I can take a breath, I walk toward the road, holding my stomach. As I walk, I begin to calm enough that I stop shaking and I can finally take a steady breath.

About halfway home, I realize I don't have any of the stuff I'd bought, and I wonder if I even give a shit. When I reach for the door, I've pulled all composure back to myself. Taking a deep breath, I pull open the door only to find Lane standing there.

"Felix?"

"What?" I ask as I look up at him. I'm surprised by how steady my voice is, but it isn't like I haven't had practice at this before. I kick my shoes off into the corner.

"Where the fuck have you been? You said you were headed home over forty-five minutes ago," he says.

"Oh," I say as I walk past him. He reaches out and catches my wrist before I can move past. I wince and try to pull it back from his vise-like grip.

"Felix, what the hell?" he asks. "You weren't answering your phone *again*."

I look down at his fingers that are touching my bloody sleeve. "Oh," I repeat as I pull my hand back and turn away from him. "Are you a police officer?"

"What?"

"I broke into your safe a few nights ago," I say.

"How'd you do that?" he asks.

"Are you?"

"…Not exactly. Felix, are you okay?" he asks.

"Fine," I say as I head for the bathroom.

"Felix?"

"Hm?"

"My hand's wet and it smells like blood."

"Oh…"

"Did that guy that was following you, stop you?"

"Yes."

"And you weren't going to say anything to me about it?" he asks, surprised.

"I don't know," I realize. I'm not sure why I wasn't going to say anything. All I seem to know anymore is that my head hurts. Every step causes my head to pound.

"What did they say to you?"

"To tell you to stay out of their business."

"How badly are you hurt?"

"I'm fine," I say.

He stands there, uncertain of what to do, so I turn from him and head into the bathroom. I grab onto the sink and try to figure out what's going on. My head really hurts, and I just want to curl up in my bed until it stops. Even the light in here seems too bright as my brain threatens to explode.

I reach for the light switch when suddenly there's a knock on the door. The noise makes me jump. "Felix, it's James. Lane called me when he couldn't get a hold of you earlier and told me that you weren't home yet, and he was worried about you. I'm glad to see you made it home. Can I come in?"

"Why?" I ask as I turn the faucet on and stick my hands under it. They are red with blood from my nose, but the blood is already drying. As soon as the water hits it, I realize that my left hand is aching horribly and can't understand how I hadn't noticed it before.

"Because I want to check to make sure you're alright."

"I'm fine."

He pushes the door open and walks in against my reply. "What happened?" he asks as he looks me over, but I continue to stare at my throbbing hand.

"Some guys stopped me, said what I already told Lane and roughed me up a bit. It's fine. I'm a big boy, I can handle it."

He grabs my wrist and pulls me away from the sink. "Come on, we're going to the hospital."

I stare at him like he's insane as I try to wrap my mind around why he would want to take me to the hospital. "I'm fine," I say. I just want everything to go away so my head stops hurting.

"You're acting confused, and you're bleeding everywhere, Felix. Come on."

I try to jerk away from him, but his grip tightens. "I am *fine*," I snap.

"Either you can go with me, or I'll drag you there."

"But I'm fine. There's no sense in going to the hospital when I'm not seriously hurt anywhere."

He ignores me and continues to pull me after him into the foyer where Lane is still standing.

"Can I change out of these clothes? They're all dirty, I'll get your car dirty," I say as I suddenly realize just how dirty I am.

"No, come on," he says as he grabs my shoes and kneels. He steadies me with one hand as he pushes my shoe on and ties it before helping me into my other shoe.

"How badly is he hurt?" Lane asks.

"He probably has a concussion. We'll see what the doctors say."

"This is why I told you I didn't want anyone here. I told you not to bring anyone here and now he's hurt because of me. He wasn't fucking answering and there was nothing I could do but fucking sit here!"

"Lane, we'll deal with this later. They won't come here with the security cameras," James says. "You okay here? Can you contact Walsh for me?"

"Yeah."

"I'll be back when we're done at the hospital and take you to a hotel."

"Okay," Lane says, and James pushes me out the door. He opens the car door for me and helps me inside. Pain touches me as I cradle my hand to my chest while my head throbs mercilessly. I lean to the side as I hold my stomach.

James gets into the driver's seat and looks over at me. "You okay?" he asks as he takes a wash rag he must have grabbed and holds it against the side of my head. "Can you hold that there?"

I nod and take it from him.

He begins to drive, and I slowly lean back. "Can you tell me who it was? Did he give you a name?"

"Red…something."

"Victor?"

I nod before instantly regretting the movement.

"Where were you at?"

"I was…heading home from the store."

"Did he just come up and confront you or did he take you somewhere?"

I'm silent for a moment as I try to think about what he is asking. "He pulled me into an alley. Why's this matter?"

"Because I want to know what happened, and you're being very stubborn. So then did he talk to you?"

"Yeah." I just want him to shut up, so I can close my eyes and sink into the nothingness.

"Did he say anything other than what you'd already told me?"

"No…just to stay away from him."

"What'd his men hit you with? It looks like a blunt object. Was it a pipe or a baseball bat?"

"Bat."

"Anything else?"

I shake my head and it makes my vision swim, so I stop. "I want to go home. I'm fine."

"You're not fine, Felix, you're hurt."

"It's not like it hasn't happened to me before. I'm fine," I snap and instantly regret my choice of words.

"What do you mean, 'happened to you before'?"

"Nothing, forget I said anything. Just take me back home, you're pissing me off."

"Someone has beaten you around before?" he asks quietly.

"No, and I'm fine, so take me home."

When we arrive at the hospital, I grudgingly follow James inside. The nurse smiles at me kindly as she leads us to a small room.

"The doctor will be right in to get you all cleaned up, okay?" she asks as she takes my blood pressure. I try to ignore her, but she never stops smiling, even when she lays out a gown.

"We're going to go ahead and put a gown on. Do you need me to help?" she asks.

"Nope," I say.

"I can help him if he needs it, thanks," James says softly, and the woman nods before leaving the room. He walks over to where I'm sitting on the bed and begins to unbutton my shirt. He has it nearly off before I realize what he's doing.

"I can get it," I say as I take the last button from him. I look up at him. "James, I'm fine, really. It's not a big deal. My head just hurts so I want to lie down and sleep it off."

"Okay," he says with a nod as he pulls up the gown and helps me into it before pushing my pants down.

I kick them off my feet just as the doctor comes in.

The man walks up to me and smiles. "Hi there, I'm Dr. Troy Keppler. Let's get you cleaned up, alright?"

"Yeah."

"Anything really painful?"

"No, I'm fine."

"You're favoring your left hand. Can I see it?" he asks as he reaches for me.

"No, I'm fine," I say.

"I think he has a concussion. He's being very obstinate," James says.

"Alright, we'll prepare for a scan," he says as he gently takes my hand. It hurts, and I immediately want to pull it back. "We'll also get an x-ray of your hand, alright?"

"Can I go home?" I ask as I stand up and head for the door. The doctor blocks me before I get too far, and I stare at him as he smiles at me.

"As soon as we are done, alright?" he asks as he urges me back to the table. "Have you thrown up at all?"

"No," I lie as I sit back down.

He keeps talking to me and asking me questions as he starts cleaning me up. I become more and more impatient as they run scans, x-rays, and stitch me up.

"I'm back, how are you doing?" James asks.

"You left?" I ask, confused.

"Yes, remember me telling you that I was taking Lane to a hotel?" he asks.

"Hmm…yeah," I say even though I don't.

"So, what's the prognosis?" he asks me since the doctor had left the room.

"Uh…I'm fine."

"Is that why your hand is wrapped up?"

"It's not broken. Just really effing achy."

"And that's why you have your head and arm stitched up?"

"Yeah."

"Do you have a concussion?"

"I don't think so."

"Yes, you do," the nurse says as she walks in.

"Hmm…Can I go now?"

"As soon as the doctor gives the okay."

"Fantastic. He gave the okay, let's go," I say as I stand up and head for the door. James blocks me and proceeds to deter me until the doctor actually gives us the okay and allows us to leave.

I follow James over to his car and watch as he pulls the door open. I'm on enough pain medication that not much seems to hurt although I feel like I could just sleep right here in the parking lot. Slowly, I slide into the seat and pull the door closed.

James sits down in the driver's seat and looks over at me. "I'm going to take you to my house. Is there anything you need at Lane's house for the night?"

"Where's Lane?" I ask.

"He's at a hotel."

"Why can't I go there?" I ask.

"We don't think it's in your best interest to continue working with Lane. We don't want anything else to happen to you."

I stare at him for a moment as I try to wrap my mind around what he's saying. "You're firing me?"

"No, not…firing. Just…you could get hurt again if you continue working with Lane."

"So, you're firing me," I say, pissed. They seriously just want to push me away?

"No, I'm not. If you want another job, I can find you another one. Okay?"

"No," I say stubbornly. "I'm happy with my job. Take me to the hotel."

"Lane agrees with me, he thinks that you'll be safer in a different job."

I stare at him in shock, not wanting to believe that Lane is in on this as well. I am fine, I don't have to leave. "I think I'm quite happy with what I'm doing."

"And the next time someone could kill you."

"I'll take my chances," I snap.

"Why are you being so stubborn?"

I shrug, and he sighs.

"I might listen to you a little better if I hear your own reasoning. Why do you want to go back to Lane so badly?"

Why *do* I want to go back to Lane? It's not like we're dating. It's not like we've confessed our love to each other. How much do I even like him? Fuck…I don't know. I'm not good with this shit. I just…don't want to be alone. I never realized how hard it is to walk into a house and have no one there until I moved in with Lane. And now all that would go away? I mean, that's fine, right? I can handle that. I've been alone my entire life. I don't *need* someone there. I never have! But…I still don't want to go. "I don't know…I just…I don't have anywhere else to go or anyone else."

James just watches me for a moment and I feel like he's studying me. "You understand how unsafe it is?"

"Yes," I say, and he sighs.

"I'll take you to the hotel, but I'm only promising you tonight. I'll decide what to do with you tomorrow, okay?"

I nod and sink back into the seat as he drives. It takes him fifteen minutes to get to the hotel and get parked. I get out and he leads me through the door and up to the elevator.

"Are you doing okay?" he asks as he steps into the elevator.

"I'm fine."

"Are you still in a lot of pain?"

"I'm fine."

"Okay," he says as he presses the number five and the elevator heads up. I grab onto the wall to steady myself and am glad when the elevator finally stops moving. He leads me down the hallway and up to room 512. He swipes the card and waits a moment before the red light on the door turns green. He slides the door open and heads inside.

The hotel room is small with one queen-sized bed taking up most of the room.

Lane is sitting in a chair by the small table. He looks up at us as I follow James inside.

"Why's Felix with you?"

"He's going to stay here tonight."

"Why? I thought we agreed that he shouldn't be associated with me again after this," Lane says.

"I understand, but he's going to stay here just for tonight. He's exhausted and it's still an hour drive to my house. We'll deal with it tomorrow."

"Okay."

James sets a hand on my back and leads me over to the bed. "Now, he has a concussion, so if he starts acting weird or talking funny, let me know."

"I'm fine," I say.

"Okay. I'll check in with both of you tomorrow," James says.

"You'll pick him up tomorrow?" Lane says.

"Yes, of course. If you need anything, don't hesitate to call."

I watch James go before turning to Lane.

"I don't know why James brought you here, but you're going to have to leave," Lane says as he stands up.

"Why?" I ask as I watch him.

"There's no sense in you being here. You were already hurt once, it could happen again."

"I'm fine."

"No, you're not. I told James to find a different place for you," Lane says, sounding exasperated. He isn't the one that just spent hours being poked and prodded!

I frown as I watch him walk toward me. "You don't want me here at all? I mean...I'm fine, it's not going to happen again—"

"Please just leave, the only reason I let you stay was to fuck you."

I'm honestly kind of surprised that his words hurt. I'm not sure why, when I know there isn't anything even going on between us. "I know. I've never met anyone that ever likes me for who I am. I should have known you were no different...but I have no one else. So...I want to keep working for you..." I swallow hard. Noticing my cheeks are wet, I angrily wipe them. I refuse to cry about this asshole. It's just because my head hurts, my body hurts, and I'm tired. "I'm going to lie down."

"Felix...I'm sorry, I didn't mean that," he says, sounding devastated.

I ignore him as I walk over to the bed and throw the sheets back. I slide my shoes off and crawl into the bed as I grit against the pain. I feel like I already have bruises everywhere. I pull the blanket up until it's against my neck. Exhausted, I close my eyes and wait for the pounding in my head to subside.

I mean, I know that I don't like Lane...it's not that I want to be here because of him. It's the job...it's having something to do. It's the ability to have someone to talk to.

Suddenly the bed dips. I open my eyes and look over at Lane, who is sitting on the edge. He sets his hand down to the bed and slides it over until he's moved up farther onto the bed. He reaches out to me, but I can tell he's hesitant. He doesn't know where I'm at and doesn't want to hit me.

"Felix...I'm so sorry," Lane says. "I'm just...frustrated and overwhelmed. You know that I didn't mean what I said."

"I don't care, Lane. I know you don't like me. It doesn't bother me."

"I just don't want you to get hurt again. They could have easily killed you instead of what they did, so when James comes tomorrow you are going to go with him." He lowers his hand until he gently brushes my arm, but I think he's scared he's going to touch somewhere I'm hurt because he pulls his hand back and sighs. "I'm scared you'll be hurt again and there is nothing I can do. Understand?"

"Yes."

"Good. It'll be fine, alright?"

"Yeah." I've always been moved from one place to the next. I know how to deal with it. "You can stop trying to make me feel better now. I'm fine."

"Felix…fuck…I'm so sorry for what I said. I didn't mean it. I just don't want you hurt."

"I said I heard you!" I yell. "Leave me alone. James can come back in the morning and I can go back to wherever the fuck I want to go."

I turn my back to him as I thank God he can't see the tears threatening to escape my eyes. I don't even know why they're there. They're stupid tears that don't even mean anything when I don't even care about him or any of his shit. Quickly, I blink them away.

I feel him lie down behind me and his hand bumps into my arm. It slowly moves over my side and down my arm until he grabs my hand. Then he pulls me toward him until my back is against his chest. He sets his face against my hair as he holds onto me. He never says anything, but I'm almost thankful for it.

***

When I wake, it's around six in the morning. Which means that I have only been asleep for about an hour, if that. I look beside me to where Lane is sleeping with the pillow over his head. I quietly sit up and wince in pain. It crawls up and down my body as I force myself to my feet and wonder if I can even walk to the bathroom, I'm so sore. I close the door quietly and lean against the sink for a moment to compose myself. I grab the washrag and stick it into the sink. I turn the water on hot until the washrag is soaked and only then do I look at myself in the mirror. There's dried blood on my face so I rub at the blood until it's gone. My shirt is stuck to my arm where I had been cut, so I pull it off and clean the blood off it. There are already bruises forming over the side of my face as well as my stomach and abdomen.

Since I don't have any other clothes, I put them back on and toss the rag on the counter. I grab a card and head out the door and down to the elevator. The trek is rough, but the more I walk, the better I feel. The sore muscles begin to loosen up even if just a bit. Down onto the first floor, I head out to the parking garage to where James's car is. I'd assumed he had stayed at the hotel as well, and my hypothesis is proven correct when I see his car. He must have a habit of locking his keys in his car because I had noticed that he kept a spare in a magnetic box above his rear tire. I pull it out and get into the car.

From what the hotel clerk had told me I am in a town about thirty miles from Lane's home, so I start driving.

CHAPTER SEVEN

When I reach the house, I head inside. It's light enough now that I can see without having to turn any lights on. I grab a duffel bag out of my room and begin filling it with my things. Once that's done, I pull a small suitcase out of the closet before dragging it to Lane's room. I take out his nicest clothes and toss them into it before filling the remaining space with necessities. As I zip it up, I debate getting anything out of the safe, but I know James can take care of that. With everything I need, I head out to the car, tossing both bags into the back seat before driving back to the hotel.

When I pull into the parking garage James is by the hotel entrance with a very impatient look on his face. Ignoring him, I get out of the car and grab the suitcase out of the back seat.

"Mind telling me where you took my car?" he asks.

"To Lane's house," I say.

"What's in the suitcase?"

"Some of his stuff."

"Do you want to get killed?"

I shrug. "Why? Was there someone there to kill me?" I ask.

"There could have been."

"I doubt it. You have officers watching the house," I say.

He looks slightly surprised but quickly covers it up. "What makes you say that?"

"There were two men in a parked car in the alleyway. I noticed one got out of the car as soon as I arrived. He was also on the phone, so I'm assuming he was talking to you."

"Yes, he was. Now don't do that shit again."

"Okay, I won't. I'm fired, remember? I was just getting some shit. How long's Lane going to be here?"

"I don't know."

"A while?"

"Depends."

"Okay," I say. "Let me drop this off, and I'll meet you in the lobby in half an hour."

"Fine."

I nod and drag it over to the elevator. Inside the elevator, I lean against the wall as I rub my aching head. Even though I felt better getting up and moving, my head is still pounding. The door opens, and I head over to the room before swiping the card and letting myself in. Lane is sitting on the bed and looks up quickly when I walk in.

"Where did you go? You're supposed to be resting."

"I brought some of your stuff," I say as I open the suitcase. I pull his clothes out, still on hangers, and hang them up. Shirts on the left, pants on the right.

"What are you doing?" he asks.

"I just told you," I say. "Are you getting deaf in your old age?"

"You should either be lying down or leaving with James. You're not safe with me."

"Yeah, I'm meeting him in the lobby in half an hour," I say as I grab his toiletries and set them on the bathroom counter in the same order they were at home. When I'm finally finished putting things away I notice Lane has not moved nor said anything.

I walk over to him and grab his arm. "Get up." I tug at him and he gets to his feet. I lead him over to the door and turn him around, so his back is against it. "Alright...walk two feet and here's the door to the bathroom," I say as I take his hand and press it against the door. I use his hand to push it open. I pull him inside. "Directly right is the sink," I say as I lead him over to it. "Your stuff's over here," I say. "Toothbrush, toothpaste, pretty much everything is just as it is at home," I say as I set his hand against each one. I turn him straight again. "Left is the bathtub, the sink is on the right, which is the opposite of home and in front of you is the toilet. Above the toilet are the washrags and towels," I say as I walk him out of the bathroom. "Straight ahead is the closet. Pants on the right, shirts on the left. Turn left...if you walk straight you'll run into the bed, so you have to do a bit of an angle here," I say as I pull him. "Then the TV is to the left, bed to the right. Straight ahead is the window. Got it?"

"Yes."

"Good. I put my MP3 player on the nightstand. You can have it. I downloaded that new book you like. See ya," I say as I let go of his arm and head toward the door.

"I'm sorry...about what I said last night," he says.

I snort. "Yeah, I heard you last night. Sorry all I'm good for is a fuck. Now have a good life," I say as I pull open the door and slam into James

"Is that what Lane said to you?" he asks.

"What?" I ask as I look up at him. "No, I'm going out to the car. I have a headache."

James pushes past me, into the room.

"Lane," James growls.

"What?" he asks.

"Did you tell him that all he was good for was a *fuck?*" James asks.

"I already apologized. I didn't fucking mean it! I was frustrated!"

Suddenly James has ahold of his shirt and yanks him toward himself. "The kid was seriously hurt because of you and that's what you tell him? Lane, sometimes you're just so damn stupid."

"I apologized to him, now get off me."

"You shouldn't have said it in the first place!" James yells.

"I didn't mean to, I was angry."

"Angry at Felix? He did nothing wrong!" James says.

"No, I was angry at myself. Angry that I let this happen. And I said that shit to him because I wanted him to leave so he can't get hurt again. I didn't mean it."

"I'm leaving now, Lane. I'll find some place for you to go, but in the meantime, you have my number if you need me," James says briskly, almost in a businesslike manner.

I try to pretend that I hadn't been watching and head toward the elevator, but my head really hurts.

"You alright?" James asks. "You look pale."

"Fine," I lie.

"Why don't we just get some sleep in my room? We can leave in a few hours," he says.

I don't want to agree with him, but right now I just want a dark room away from light and noise. So, when he heads to his room next to Lane's, I follow right behind him.

***

"Felix?"

"Hmm?" I mumble as I slowly open my eyes.

"I just got an important call. I have to run down to Marrion. Will you be okay for a few hours alone?" James asks.

"Perfectly fine," I say as I slowly stretch my achy limbs.

He nods and leaves the room, leaving me alone. It doesn't take long for me to drift back to sleep. I don't wake again until it's nearing night and my phone is ringing.

"Hello?" I mumble into it.

"Felix?"

"Hmm?"

"I've run into an issue, I won't be able to be back until morning. Are you going to be alright?"

"Fine," I say as I sit up and inspect my bruises. I feel like they should look worse than they do to match how achy I am.

"If you need anything, please don't hesitate to call me."

"Okay."

I get up and check myself in the bathroom mirror to make sure I look appropriate enough to step out in public. I pull open the door and instantly notice that Lane is leaning against the wall almost opposite of my door. Honestly, I'm not sure if I'm surprised or irritated or maybe it made me feel a little happy…but just a little. I begin to walk quietly toward the elevator as his head follows me.

"Felix?"

I ignore him.

"Felix, I know that's you," he says.

In perfect Spanish, I say, *"Go away, you old hag."* I don't know a ton of Spanish, and that line is probably the only line I am fluent saying. Mostly because my mom said it almost every day to the homeless lady that lived on the corner of our street when I was a kid.

But I have heard enough Spanish to understand some of it when it is spoken to me.

He hesitates, but he must really trust his ears because he rushes after me. I slip into the elevator and quickly hit the close button as many times as I can, but he slips in before the doors shut. "Felix, can I talk to you for a moment?"

"Why are you so fast for a guy that's blind?"

"Can I talk to you?"

"You can talk, but I'm going to refuse to listen," I say as the door opens. Quickly, I get out. He rushes after me, but in the noise of the lobby he greatly slows down.

"Felix?" he asks as he turns his head, searching for a single sound from me.

"I told you I don't want to listen to you," I say so he can follow my voice. I don't know why. Do I feel bad for him? "So, don't talk."

He reaches out and grabs a handful of my shirt as I head off, dragging him along. I walk through the lobby to the small restaurant that's connected. It's busy with people looking for a beer after a long day. I walk up to the counter and the woman smiles at me before looking curiously at Lane who is still hanging onto me.

"What can I get for you?" she asks.

"I'll take a grilled chicken sandwich with no mayonnaise to go."

"Would you like fries?"

"Sure," I say.

"Okay, and what would you like?" she asks Lane.

"He doesn't want anything," I decide. Lane doesn't say anything, but he tips his head toward me. I glare at him. "What do you want?"

"Whatever is fine."

I sigh and look at the menu. "Cheeseburger with extra, extra mustard and fries," I say, knowing that Lane hates mustard.

He doesn't say anything to stop her and for some reason, I feel slightly guilty.

"Never mind, no mustard on that," I say with a sigh.

She types it in and tells me the price, which I pay with Lane's card. After I'm done paying, she has us step to the side as they make the order to go. We're silent as we wait, but I wish they would hurry up because the loud noise of the bar is making my head pound. Thankfully, the lights are dimmed.

After a while, I see the chef pass a bag through the open window and the cashier reaches back to grab it. Hoping it's ours, I step up toward her as she turns toward me.

"Here you go," she says, and I take it.

I notice her eyes linger on the bruise around my wrist from being restrained, so I quickly grab the bag and go. Lane continues to follow me into the elevator that quickly fills up with the smell of food. My stomach growls as the door opens, and I finally escape the confines.

I stop by his door. "Here's your door. Where's your key?"

"I-I can't find it."

"What?" I ask.

"I had to leave it inside because I couldn't find it."

"Why'd you come out here?"

"To talk to you!"

"And if I never came out of my room?"

"I don't know," he says.

I grit my teeth in annoyance. "So, there's the wall, I'll send James a text when I think about it."

"Felix—"

"Don't try to make me feel bad for you," I say as I swipe my card. I yank the door open and push him inside in annoyance. I walk over to my bed and sit at the foot of it as I pull out my sandwich.

"Are you feeling okay?" he asks. The sound of his voice and the look on his face tells me that he really does care. It makes me feel like I'm repeatedly kicking down an innocent dog.

"I'm fine," I say.

"I'm sorry."

"I heard."

He's still standing by the door, unsure of where to go or where I'm at. "Felix…I really am sorry I said that stuff."

"I heard you!" I say. "Sit down."

He slowly walks over to the bed and sits, so I toss the box on his lap. He fiddles with it for a moment before getting it open and pulling out the sandwich. In order to fill up the silence of the room, I turn the television on and watch it while I eat. When I'm finished, I toss all the boxes and wrappers onto Lane's lap since I'm not interested in getting off the bed to find the trash can.

"Clean that up. I'm not getting paid anymore, so you might as well do it." I lie down on my side and close my eyes since there's nothing good on TV. "You can sleep in the tub."

"You know it's only seven?"

"Obviously, but I'm tired."

"Not even going to brush your teeth?"

"No."

"That's healthy."

"I know," I say as I look over at him. He tosses the trash onto the floor. "Turn the light out."

"Where's the light?"

"I don't know, by the door," I say as I watch him get up. He stumbles around, running his hand along the wall until he finally figures out where the light is and flips it off. He walks back to the bed and sits down.

"You want the TV on?"

"You can watch it if you want, otherwise I can turn it off."

"You can turn it off," he says so I hit the power button on the remote and set it next to the alarm clock.

I watch as Lane undresses before lying down next to me.

He reaches out to me, hand stopping short of me. "I know…saying anything won't help, but…a man I'd been working with was killed not that long ago. It was really hard to deal with. When you didn't come home right away, I just couldn't stop thinking about that, and there was nothing I could do. I couldn't go out and find you. Even if I found you, how would I even help you? I can't do anything, Felix. And I had to sit in that house and just wonder if you would even come home. If you were lying dead somewhere because of *me*. When you said someone was following you at the mall, I should have done something. I didn't think…I didn't think he would have found me this quickly, so I didn't think anything of your comment. It was stupid of me. All of this was stupid of me, and I'm sorry, but I just can't handle getting another person killed. So, it's not that I want you to leave because I don't like you or that I'm sick of you, I want you to leave because he could have killed you. You could be dead right now and it would be my fault. I just can't have that happen again. Okay? So please, please believe me when I say I didn't mean what I said. I said it because I was angry at myself. I said it because I hoped it would make you leave because I don't know that I can force you to leave. This new place I've found myself in since the accident is so different, and I don't like it.

But you've helped me more than you'll ever know. So...will you leave? No matter how much I don't want you to, I *need* you to. When James comes back...please leave so I don't have to see you get hurt again."

I watch him for a moment. I never imagined seeing such raw honesty coming from Lane. His words are so real and for some reason, it makes me feel wanted. Like he really didn't want to make me go. It makes the thought of leaving all that much harder. "Okay...I'll leave with James in the morning."

"Thank you," he says as he reaches for me, but before I can take his hand, he pulls it back to himself and rolls away from me.

CHAPTER EIGHT

When I wake, the clock reads 3:24. I'm not quite sure what has woken me, but my bladder is pressuring me to get to my feet, so I grudgingly get up and walk toward the bathroom. My foot catches on something, so I reach down to see what it is. It feels like Lane's pants, but I notice there's something in the pocket. Even in the dark of the room, I realize that it is the keycard to his room, telling me that he had lied to me. I stick the keycard back into his pocket and toss the pants.

Half asleep, I head to the toilet and release my bladder before flushing the toilet.

As I step toward the door, I hear a rustling noise. Quickly, I turn in time to see someone step up beside me. The man reaches for me, so I bolt from him, rushing back into the bathroom to get away. He grabs onto me, hand snaking around to clamp over my mouth as he presses a gun against my head.

"Scream, and I'll blow your brains out," the man says right into my ear.

I swallow hard as he pulls me against him and in the light of the bathroom I see that it is the red-haired man that had been with Victor Red.

He pushes me forward, but my foot catches on the jeans I'd tossed. Stumbling forward, my shin slams into the edge of the tub as I grab onto the shower curtain to keep myself from falling. The sudden movement must startle him because I feel his grip loosen. Twisting away from him, I run for the door, but not before he grabs me around the waist and presses the gun harder against my head. What startles me even more, is another gun pointed in my direction.

Lane is holding this one from where he's at in the bed.

"Let him go," Lane growls.

"Let him go? Cute. You killed my brother, and I'm supposed to just 'let him go'? What are you going to do with that gun? You're blind! I might have been a little nervous before, but now you can't tell the difference between me and him. I think before I kill you, I'll let you listen to me torturing him. What do you say? Do you like that idea?"

"I don't," I say.

"Shut up," he says as he hits me on the side of the head with the gun.

My head screams at me, reminding me that it still is very angry about the last time I'd run into this guy.

Lane is holding the gun steady, but quite frankly I agree with my captor on this one. I don't want to be shot, especially by Lane.

In perfect Spanish, Lane says, *"Down. Hit the floor when you're down. One, two, three."* Clearly, he'd known exactly what I'd spat at him on the way to the elevator.

I drop down quickly and hit the floor as a muffled shot fills the room. I hear the man behind me fall back as I jump to my feet and run for Lane.

"Did I hit him?" he asks.

"Yes," I say as I look back at the man choking on his own blood in the light of the bathroom. The bullet had torn right into his chest and blood was blossoming out as he gasped for breath.

"Come on, I'm sure he's not the only one," he says as he grabs my hand.

I nod. "Where?"

"We need to find a car."

"We need clothes," I say, realizing that I have underwear on and that is it.

"We don't have time, just put your shoes on so we can run if we have to."

I stuff my shoes on as I shove his at him, then I pull open the door as I grab his wrist, sliding my hand down until our fingers are intertwined. I drag him after me toward the elevator, but they're both already headed up. "Elevators are headed up."

"Get to the stairs."

I nod and yank a door open. We begin to rush down them until Lane's arm snaps me to a stop. My foot slips and if I hadn't been holding onto Lane, I probably would have fallen. Then again, if I hadn't been holding onto Lane, I wouldn't have been snapped backward.

"I don't like this," he warns me. "I feel like I'm going to fall."

"Sorry! Two feet and then a step."

He nods and inches forward until his foot dips over the edge, but once he has a rhythm, he descends quickly as long as I tell him every time it levels out. As we near the last door leading out, I hear a commotion beyond it.

"Someone's coming," I say as the shouting on the other side of the door increases.

"Is there anywhere to hide?" he asks as we reach the first floor.

I look around and pull him back behind the stairs, where it is shadowed enough that we can tuck ourselves into the corner. I pull him close to me and he wraps his arms around me, holding me against him. My heart is beating so loudly that I feel it in my ears, but as I lean against him, I notice he's completely steady. There's not even a tremor in his body as he holds the gun casually at his side. His arm is keeping me pressed against him, like a barrier to protect me.

The door leading to the stairs slams open and I jump, but Lane's arm tightens around me. And for some reason, I take that moment to remember that we are both wearing nothing but our underwear.

Perfect.

I can't see them, but I can hear them as they rush up the stairs, and with the pounding of their feet, my heart races. I dig my fingers into Lane's arm, trusting the security of it.

"Okay, let's go," Lane says as he pushes me forward.

I take his hand and lead him to the door the men had just come in through. I pull it open and look down the hallway, but it appears to be empty of life. As we step into the hallway, I see signs for a tunnel that leads to the parking garage. I quickly take the first right and rush down the hall as I follow the signs.

"Look casual, Felix. You feel like you're anxious and if anyone sees you, they'll know something is up," he says, voice even like we are having a regular conversation.

"Look casual?" I hiss. "Someone's trying to kill us! And just in case you forgot…we're in our underwear. Real damn casual."

"Stop it. Calm down. We are fine."

I want to say that we're not, but he sounds like some monk trying to teach tranquility, so I just take a deep breath.

I reach the door to the parking garage and push it open.

"Where are we?" Lane asks.

"Parking garage."

"Find a car that has keys in it," he says as we step into the darkened garage. The lights are dim and the air smells dense and dirty like car exhaust.

"You're kidding. There isn't going to be a car sitting here with keys in it!" I hiss.

"Well, you better hurry, I hear someone."

"I need some way to break in."

I rush up to a car with a thin antenna and break it off before rushing up to an older car. I have honestly never picked a car lock before. I am not even positive if it's possible. When breaking into cars, I usually went under the door's seal and just hit the unlock button with a long rod. But, I guess there is only one way to find out if it is as easy as picking other locks.

"Found them!" someone yells, and I hear the sound of cement crumbling behind me where a bullet had struck a pillar. Lane yanks me down.

"Move!" he says as he drags me away from the car I'd crouched next to.

"But—"

"Now!" he snaps as he pushes me down into a crouch. He runs one hand along the side of the car as he begins to move.

I can't see anyone, but I can tell that they're far too close to us. I shuffle on my hands and knees as Lane pulls me after him. When we reach the hood of the car, Lane feels his way over to the next car.

"Where'd they go?" a man asks.

"They're near the blue car," another says.

I stop as I realize that we've run out of cars in this aisle to hide behind.

"There's nowhere else to go," I whisper.

Lane seems to be concentrating as he keeps his head bowed. "Break the window, get the car open."

I slip the thin antenna in the key lock as I notice Lane stands up and begins shooting.

What the hell is he shooting at?

I jiggle it as Lane reaches over and touches the car window a moment before he shoots it. I jump, startled as he breaks away the jagged glass with the butt of his gun.

"Door is unlocked," he says.

"Uh…great."

"You've been arrested before for stealing cars. You can start it, I assume?" he asks.

"And you know that why?" I ask as I slip my hand through the busted window, careful of the glass still attached. I pull the lock up and climb inside. I reach for the paneling when I see a toolkit on the floor and right in the middle is a drill. I pick it up and pull the trigger. It revs to life and I am pleased to see it has full power. I set it against the ignition and start drilling. The bit screams as I ram it into the ignition until it gives. Then I grab a screwdriver and shove it inside. I turn it like I would a key and the car roars to life.

"Let me in," Lane says as he ducks in through the driver's door. I pull him as he scrambles over top of me and into the passenger seat.

The moment he's sitting, I shove the car into reverse and press down on the gas. We lunge out of the parking spot and into the aisle. I quickly shove the car into drive, but I'm not sure I had to be too quick because as I head for the exit I see a man lying on the ground clutching onto a very precise bullet wound.

"You hit him?" I ask, astounded. I mean, I would have probably been less surprised if they had shot themselves.

"I did? I mean…of course."

"Of course?" I ask skeptically.

He hesitates. "I don't know, Felix, they had to have walked into the bullet or maybe it ricocheted. Let's just narrow it down to luck."

"Uh huh, sure. Luck. Well, let's hope your luck doesn't run out. Where am I going?"

"I don't care, just go somewhere," he says as I reach the garage's automatic gate. The arm is down, but it doesn't stand a chance against the car. It breaks the moment we hit it and Lane jumps.

"What was that?"

"The gate…arm…thingy," I say. "I didn't think we had time to pay for parking while driving a stolen vehicle."

"Probably not," he says.

I glance both ways before rushing out onto the road. A car blares its horn at me, but I'm gone before they can even get a good look at me. I drive quickly as I bite my lip in nervousness. My heart is pounding in my chest as I tighten my grip on the steering wheel. I'm assessing each red light as we come upon it. If it is red, I leap into the right lane, so I can keep moving, if it's green, I plow on through.

"Hey," Lane says as he sets his hand on my leg. "You need to calm down. You're driving recklessly."

Is he insane? Of course I'm driving *recklessly*! I would like to live! "We were just being shot at! Of course I'm fucking driving recklessly!"

"Felix," he says, completely calm. His voice is steadier than it usually is. Like this whole thing has calmed him down. Like he's meditating and has just found his happy place. "You're just drawing attention to yourself. So, take a deep breath and slow the car down."

Praying Lane hasn't lost his mind and actually knows what he is doing, I nod and slow the car from eighty-two to sixty-five. Which is still fast when the speed limit is forty-five.

"Good," he says. "Now, just head out of town but keep an eye out if anyone is following. You'll be able to tell better once we're on the highway."

"Okay." I start focusing on road signs, following the ones pointing me toward the highway.

"Do you have your phone?" he asks.

I'd left mine in the hotel room. I hadn't even thought of grabbing it after Lane shot that man. "No, should I stop somewhere?"

"No, just drive."

I reach the southbound lane first, so I take it. The tires squeal as I descend the ramp far too quickly, but we make it out onto the highway where it is at least logical for me to be running over seventy.

"Are you okay? Did he hurt you?" he asks.

"I'm fine," I say.

"Are you sure?"

"Yes, I'm fine," I say, but honestly my head is aching again from that man hitting me with the gun. "Did you kill him?"

"I don't know," he says.

"Oh…why is he after you?"

"For confidential reasons."

I almost look away from the road to stare at him like he's an idiot. "I'm pretty sure I deserve to be told," I snap.

"I should not share information from my work."

"*Seriously?* Who am I going to tell? I don't have a family." That's when it dawns on me. "Oh my God! Is that why I was *hired?* If I was killed off or something happened to me there's no one that would notice! No one to care. Right?"

He hesitates, but I'm not sure why when I already know. "Yeah…pretty much."

I stare at him for a moment then laugh. I'm not sure why I'm laughing. Maybe I have brain damage. Maybe I've finally lost it. "Seriously?"

"Seriously," he says with a grimace. "Sorry."

"I hate you and the people you work with. I was excited that I got a good job and it was all just because I am expendable!"

"Well…I mean, if you think about it, would it be better for someone who doesn't have anyone to be murdered or a woman with three children, a loving husband, and parents who still have her over for supper every Sunday?"

"I'm so glad my life means less because I didn't get knocked up in high school and marry a man I despise," I reply snidely.

"Felix, that is not what I'm saying, and you know it. I'm not trying to be mean. And don't forget, I didn't ask you to put your life in danger."

I look in the rearview mirror. "Hey…well…I'm sorry to ruin you bashing my life, but I think we're being followed."

"What kind of car?"

I look in the rearview mirror. "A black and white one with sirens on top."

He sighs. "I told you that you were driving erratically."

"You don't think perchance it was because you *shot two people and I hijacked a car?*" I ask as I look back again. The lights aren't on yet, so I try to keep to the speed limit without losing my mind.

"Yeah, but they probably found you quicker because you were driving like a maniac."

"Aren't you a cop? Isn't this like…no big deal, right?"

"Sure," he says as I see the lights flash on and the sirens start.

For a split second, I want to push the car faster, just get away from all of this, but I know that won't help the situation. So, I take a deep breath and pull the car over onto the side of the road. I glance at Lane, hoping for some type of support. "Lane?"

"Yes?" he asks like none of this is a big deal at all. Like he does this every day. Maybe he does. Maybe he gets off on this shit and thinks I'll be interested in this bizarre fetish of his. God, I'm going to die today, aren't I?

"Are we going to be shot to death by a police officer?" I ask as I look over at him.

"It's not real likely," he says as he pulls his gun out and tosses it onto the floor.

"Great. I love when things are just 'not likely.' And…just in case you forgot, we are still in our underwear."

"Then if you're as hot as you claim you are, they definitely won't want to shoot you," he says.

He thinks now is a good time to joke? Of course he does. "I never claimed that I am hot!" I say. "We're going to die."

Another police car pulls up in front of the other, kind of boxing us in, but neither are coming up to our car.

"GET OUT OF THE CAR WITH YOUR HANDS UP!" the man says through a speaker.

"Yup, we're going to die," I say as I turn the car off.

"Just get out, tell them nothing. If they ask what happened, you say you don't know. You don't know anything, understood?"

"I'm supposed to lie?"

"Anything they ask say, 'I don't know.'"

"Okay," I say as I push the car door open and step out with my hands up. There are blinding lights on me, making me cringe back.

"Come around to this side of the vehicle and keep your hands where we can see them!" a man shouts, gun trained on us. And I realize that within the past hour I've had three guns pointed at my head.

I don't get paid enough for this shit.

Lane slowly walks around to my side of the vehicle, his hands in the air. He walks with his hip touching the car, so he can easily find his way around.

"Get on your knees, hands behind your head!" someone shouts.

Stones dig into my bare knees when I drop down to them and slowly put my hands behind my head. Lane does the same as I see two more cop cars pull up. The police officers then rush us; one of them grabs my arm and yanks it behind my back.

"Ow, that hurts!" I cry, but they don't seem to mind nor care as they snap the handcuffs in place.

The officer holding onto me begins stating my rights as I'm pulled up to my feet. They shout in my face while I wonder when Lane is going to come forth with the information that he is a man of the law, so we can just walk out of this place. As I'm taken over to the police car, I start to wonder not *when* but *if* Lane is going to say anything at all. The man sets a hand on my head as he pushes me through the open door. I slide in as I look back to see if Lane is doing *anything* to get us out of this mess, but the officer just slams the door shut in my face.

They drag Lane off to another car, and I am taken for a ride in a police car for the third time in my life.

CHAPTER NINE

"What's your name?" the woman interrogating me asks. She had introduced herself to me a while ago, but I can't remember what she said her name is. I blame it on the raging headache.

"I don't know," I say, wondering if this is the part where I am supposed to start my new mantra or if that is supposed to come in later.

"Were you staying at the Renaissance Hotel?"

She's an older lady that looks like she could beat the bad right out of me with just a look. I bet she is also the kind of lady that looks hard as hell, yet cries when an animal dies in a movie. Then again, only a heathen wouldn't.

"I don't know," I say.

"Do you want a lawyer or something? Is that what you're waiting for?"

"I don't know," I admit. "That one I really don't know. What I *do* know is that my wrist *really* hurts, so can you take these handcuffs off?"

She stares at me for a long moment. "I don't know," she says in a mocking tone.

I grin. "I like you," I say.

"How'd you get hurt?"

"I don't know," I say.

"This is a waste of time," she says as she gets up and leaves the interrogation room.

I expect her to return right away, but after a while of sitting in that room and contemplating my life, I begin to wonder if she ever will. To pass time, I decide to just take a nap. So, I lay my head down on the table and close my eyes, but I can't sleep.

Thankfully, a minute later the door opens, so I quickly sit up.

It's the same lady as before and she looks none too pleased to see me.

"Well, Felix Wake, there's someone here to pick you up."

"There is? Is that like a euphemism for like Satan or something? You going to send me to hell if I don't answer?" I ask.

"Here, I brought you some clothes," she says as she tosses them on the table.

"Oh? You're tired of seeing me half-naked?"

"Just leave," she says as she walks over to me and undoes my handcuffs. "Please. Just clothe yourself and leave."

"I'll take it," I say as I rub my aching wrists.

I pick up the shirt and see that I clearly pissed off the wrong lady because it's a woman's shirt. I pull it on and tug on the bottom, but it seems to be missing the second half of it.

"Is this a belly shirt?" I ask. "Great, I'm wearing some diseased hooker's clothes. There should be a rule against that."

"They're my daughter's clothes. You should feel lucky I didn't go digging through the clothes that get left behind. Now put them on and leave."

"Nothing a bit more…covering in your car?"

"Just be happy I'm helping you."

I pull the sweats on that are bright pink and match the bejeweled top. Then I follow her out of the room and into a different one where Lane is waiting with a man I don't recognize.

"This him?" the man says. "Oh…sorry, I forgot you can't see him."

"This is ridiculous," I say. I'm not sure if I'm talking about my clothes or the situation or basically my life in general since meeting Lane.

"Yeah, that's him. Let's go," he says as he turns his head in the other man's direction.

The man starts walking, and Lane quickly follows close behind. I wave to my new favorite interrogator before rushing after them.

When we step outside, I can't believe it's already light out. Then again, it felt like I'd been in that dungeon for years. The man walks up to a red, four-door car and gets in.

I grab Lane's wrist, so I can help him to his door, but he starts to pull away. "What's wrong?" I ask.

"I can do it myself," he says, but he doesn't pull his hand from me, so I keep guiding him. It's almost like he's embarrassed to be helped in front of this guy. Like he's lost all the confidence he had earlier. "Are you okay?"

"Yeah, I'm fine. You?" I ask.

"Yeah…took them far too long, but I'm fine," he says as he reaches out and feels along the car door. I slide his hand over to the door handle and he pulls it open and gets in. I get into the back seat and buckle up before sinking into the cushion. At this point, it feels like my bruises have bruises.

"So…I'm Felix," I say as I look at the man in the driver's seat.

He glances back at me and smiles before holding a hand out. "Sorry for not introducing myself in the police station but they were making me furious and I just wanted to get out." His grip is tight as he shakes my hand. "Mick Reed."

"Nice to meet you," I say.

He's a man in his early forties with dark brown hair and a round face that gives him a young appearance. He's tall and lanky, causing his sports hoodie to look too short in the sleeves but too big everywhere else.

"This was my partner for my last job on the force," Lane says.

Finally, I'm given some confirmation that Lane did work in law enforcement. Honestly, I'm surprised he's finally opening up, but I can tell the secrets don't end there.

"We were relatively new partners, but I learned a lot from Price," he says as he nods at Lane.

"I can't imagine what you would learn from Lane other than how not to act toward people," I say.

He laughs as he looks over at Lane for his reaction.

"You can drop Felix off on any street corner. If you can find a cardboard box, I can write 'Free' on it," Lane says with a grin.

"You're stuck with me, buddy. The moment you aimed a gun at my head you burnt that bridge of pawning me off," I say.

"You seriously still want to hang around?" Lane asks in disbelief.

"Of course," I say. Maybe it's feeling that same thrill I got as a kid when I stole shit, or maybe it's feeling like someone cared, but I don't want to go anywhere.

"What I'm confused about is if they sent a threat your way, why would they not wait to see where the threat went before just trying to kill you?" Mick asks.

"Red didn't come to the hotel. He's the one that sent the threat. I'm not quite sure, but it sounded like Carter was the one at the hotel. He said I killed his brother and that's the only one I could think of. He was in it for revenge. Red wants us to back off and he knows that killing me isn't the way to make that happen. That would have just made the police work harder to find him and his group. Red sends a threat and there's really nothing we can do about it. They beat up Felix, but Red didn't touch him so we can't arrest him. Felix's word against Red's isn't going to fly in court and Red knows it."

"So...are they like the mafia? Or like a street gang or something exciting?" I ask.

"You don't need to worry about it. The less you know the better," Lane says.

"Seriously?" I ask as I lean forward so I'm right next to his ear. "*Seriously?*"

He sighs, and I know that I have finally broken him down. "Victor Red owns a successful business handing out loans to anyone that will take them. It's a perfectly legal business, but a while back a police officer was killed while associating with them. There wasn't any proof that Red or any of his men had anything to do with it, but there were rumors. There were also speculations about drug trafficking going on, but again no proof. Pinning them down isn't easy, though, and the department needed proof. They wanted to dig a little deeper, which is where I came in. They brought me in from out of state to work undercover and try to piece things together. That is all you need to know."

"Did you get caught?" I ask.

"That is *all* you need to know," he says sternly.

"Yes, papa!" I say sarcastically.

"For now, we'll just get you both back to Chicago, and we'll go from there," Mick says to Lane. "You guys can stay with me for a few days until we figure out where to put you."

"Alright," Lane says. "We can stay at a hotel if that works better. I don't want to be intruding."

"Not at all," Mick says with a smile. "Honestly, it's fine."

"Alright, thanks again. We won't stay long."

They begin to talk about mundane things and my headache is back, so I lie down on the back seat and close my eyes. Mick is talking about some café his sister opened as I slowly drift away.

CHAPTER TEN

"We're stopping for breakfast," Lane says, startling me awake. "Are you hungry?"

"Huh?" I mutter as I try to get my brain to comprehend his first comment.

"Come on," he says.

I stretch and stuff my feet back into my shoes as I wipe the drool off my cheek. When I push the door open, I notice Lane is standing outside of the car as Mick waits for us. He's staring at Lane, clearly uncertain on what to do with him. I think he wants to help him but doesn't know what to say or do about it.

As I walk up, I notice that Lane's shirt is pushed up in the back and can see just the edge of his underwear peeking out from his pants. I grab it and tug up, making him yelp as he tries to push me away. I laugh as I watch him try to dig it out of his butt crack.

"Your underwear is showing, Lane," I say.

"I have realized that. Thank you."

"You're very welcome," I say while trying not to laugh. I reach out and grab his wrist. "Where'd you get those clothes?" Unlike my bright pink, bejeweled sweat outfit, he is wearing a pair of jeans and a plain gray T-shirt.

"They're Reed's," he says.

I look over at Mick. "You don't have anything else in that car, do you?"

"Sorry," Mick says as he grimaces at my clothes.

"Feels like I'm wearing a thong now, thanks to you," Lane growls as he tries to pull his underwear out of his ass crack.

I grin and tug him after me. "Ooh, sexy," I say as Mick laughs. He holds the door open, and I direct Lane through to where a hostess is waiting for us.

"How many?" the hostess asks.

"Three," Mick says.

"Right this way," she says as she leads us after her.

I haven't taken Lane out to a restaurant before because he absolutely refused to go anywhere other than fast food. I can tell this is Mick's suggestion and Lane went along with it because he didn't want to refuse. I pull Lane behind me so, as we are walking between the thin aisles, we aren't bumping into people. When the hostess eventually stops at a booth, I push him in first before sitting next to him.

"Your waitress will be right with you," she says with a smile before leaving.

A moment later the waitress comes and sets the menus down in front of us. Lane touches the edge of his absently but doesn't open it.

"What drink can I get you started off with?" she asks as she stares at us.

I'm sure we are quite the sight. My face is the color of violets, daisies, and a black hole. I'm wearing clothes supplied to me by a sweatpants-wearing hooker. Lane's clothes are so tight they appear to have been spray painted on. And Mick just smiles at her.

"Do you want chocolate milk?" I ask.

"Coffee."

"I hate the smell of coffee," I say. "So, you'll have chocolate milk or water."

"Is that a rule now? Has the coffee machine at home really not been broken this entire time?"

"I don't know what you're talking about," I lie. "He'll have chocolate milk."

"No, I'll take a coffee."

I glare at him before turning to the woman. "Chocolate milk," I say.

She glances at me before turning to Mick. "Alright, and you?"

"I'll take milk as well," Mick says.

"I'll get your drinks and take your orders when you're ready," she says with a smile before leaving.

"Alright…menu. What do you want?" I ask Lane as I flip my menu open.

"I'm not hungry," he says.

"Seriously? This will be the first edible food you've had since I moved in," I say. "Omelet? Sausage? Biscuits? Toast?"

"I'm fine," he says, and I realize that Lane has to be the most stubborn human being that was ever conceived. He thinks he looks like an idiot or something. Or doesn't want people to pity him or some stupid shit. It just makes me want to smack some sense into him. The only thing I pity about him is how he can't see how amazing I look right now in my belly shirt.

The waitress returns with our drinks and sets them down. "Alright, are you ready to order?"

"Yeah, I'll have eggs, bacon, and home fries, and he'll have the same," I say and since he doesn't complain I decide that it must be up to his standards.

When we have finished ordering, she leaves, and Mick turns his attention to me. "So how has it been going living with Lane?"

"He's like a sweet, innocent child. Just so much fun to be around," I say. "But sometimes I feel like I'm living in God's sacred house. It's hard keeping all my thoughts and actions as innocent as Lane's."

Mick is grinning as he stares at me while Lane laughs.

"If you hear of a job opening, Felix is looking for something," Lane says.

"Why is that? I like him," Mick says.

Lane snorts. "The thing is *everyone* says that, and I don't get it. It's because all of you aren't living with him that you like him."

"It's my charming personality," I say. "Oh, and this awesome belly shirt I'm wearing."

"You're wearing a belly shirt?" he asks as he reaches over to touch me.

"Yes, the officer dealing with me loved me and gave it to me," I say.

Lane laughs and shakes his head. "Nice."

When we are finished eating, we get back in the car but drive only another fifteen minutes before Mick pulls up to a two-story house in the suburbs of Chicago.

"Are you sure we aren't bothering you, Reed?" Lane asks as Mick parks the car in the two-car garage. There's another car next to it, but it's hidden under a cover.

Mick shakes his head as he turns the car off. "No, not at all. I only have one guest bed though."

"I can sleep on the couch," I say as I push the door open before grabbing for Lane's door. Lane pushes it open and slams the door into my bruised side.

"Ow!" I snap.

"What happened?" Lane asks as he gets out.

"You just hit me as hard as you could with your car door!"

"I thought I felt some resistance," he says. "I didn't think you'd be standing next to my door. You alright?"

"I'm fine," I grumble as I grab his hand and pull him over to where Mick is fumbling with the house door.

There's a keypad on the door that Mick punches a few numbers into before pulling the door open. Just inside, a dog is patiently waiting for us. He's wiggling in excitement as we come through the door, and I nearly melt as I'm overcome with the desire to pet it. The dog looks like a German Shepherd with long, silky black hair and large, brown eyes.

"Oh my God, your dog!" I say as I reach for him just as Mick bumps into me. I suppose he didn't expect me to dive in front of him to get to his dog.

Mick lifts his hand quickly to steady himself on the wall, but I see the dog duck and scamper back. Quickly, my eyes flicker over to Mick who is lowering his hand from where he had it placed on the wall. I watch him for a moment before stepping back to give him room to pass.

"Sorry," I say as I glance at the dog hovering in the background. His tail is down and tucked as he watches Mick closely. "I have a weakness for cute dogs."

"That's Copper. He's a bit shy, but he'll warm up to you," he says. "He used to be a police dog, but he never learned how to enjoy the fun life."

"Oh, I see," I say. "Can I pet him?"

"Sure," he says as I walk over to the dog and kneel down.

"Hey Copper," I coo as I hold my hand out. He walks up to me and sniffs my hand, so I reach out a bit farther and pet his head. "Oh…Lane, I want a dog!"

"Go get one. I'll buy it for you, then maybe you won't bug me to do so much with you. I mean, if you force me to go any more places with you, I'm going to be standing in the bathroom next to you while you take a piss," he says.

"Funny," I say as I stroke the silky black hair.

The dog slowly starts to wag his tail, but I notice Lane is hovering around, unsure of where to go. I give the dog one more pat before standing up and taking Lane's wrist.

"Kick your shoes off to the right," I say as I do the same.

"I'm assuming you guys are exhausted, so I'll get your beds made and then I'm going to head to work for a few," he says, clearly not realizing that I have slept for close to twenty-four hours straight at this point. With a little bit of being held at gunpoint and arrested by the cops in between.

"Alright," Lane says since he hasn't slept as much as I have.

Holding Lane's hand, I lead him into the kitchen as Mick shows me the way. Everything is simple but nice. He clearly didn't put much time into decorating, but everything out is neat and orderly. He cuts through the living room and waves to the left. "The bathroom is here; towels and stuff are in this cupboard. Feel free to use whatever you need. Same with the kitchen, help yourself," he says before reaching the stairs. He leads us up them and down a hallway before pushing open a closed door. "Here's the guest room. Are you alright with this, Lane?"

"Yeah, it's fine," he says.

"There's a bathroom right off of it," Mick says as he shows us. "Just…don't forget about the stairs. Want me to put something in front of them?"

"No, I'm fine," Lane says.

"Alright, I'll go get some blankets for Felix. If you need anything, let me know," Mick says before leaving the room.

I take Lane into the bathroom and show him where everything is, before doing the same in the bedroom. "And if you need anything, just holler, I'll hear you if I feel like it."

"I wouldn't expect anything else," he says. "Makes me feel special the few times you listen."

I grin. "Good. I like to leave you wanting more. Well, good night, even though it's not night."

Lane grabs my wrist, making me look back at him. "Are you alright?" he asks as he reaches out with his other hand. I set my other hand into his and he holds them together.

"Yeah, I'm fine," I say.

"Are you hurting?" he asks.

"I have a headache and am a little sore, but I'm fine," I say.

"Okay…" he says as he drops my hands. "You're not lying, right?"

"Nope, I promise," I say.

He looks like he wants to say something else, and for some reason, I find myself wishing he'd tell me to stay in here with him, but he doesn't. "Get some sleep so you can heal up. I hope you feel better when you wake up. If you need me, let me know."

"Thanks, good night," I say.

"Night."

I watch him for a moment before turning toward the door. As I walk through the hallway and down the stairs, I can't help but wonder what he had been wanting to say to me. When I reach the living room, I see that Mick has the couch pulled out into a bed and is tossing blankets onto it.

"I put a change of clothes in the bathroom for you. Do you need anything else?" he asks.

"No, I'm good, thank you," I say as I head to the bathroom.

By the time I come out, Mick is gone, and the dog is staring at me with his sad brown eyes. I give him a pat on the head as I pass by. He jumps up to follow me. I walk over to the pullout bed and slowly lie down on it to keep from angering my bruises. The dog is still staring at me, so I pat the bed, but he doesn't jump up next to me.

The room is so orderly that I feel like I'm already making a mess by leaving the sweat outfit on the floor next to the couch. There is a large, flat-screen TV facing me with shelves along both sides. The bed is comfortable, but the sheets smell like they had been in the closet for a while. Mind buzzing, I lie there and stare at Copper who is lying on a rug near the couch.

Suddenly there's a bang, and I jump, before realizing it was probably someone out on the street. But my heart is pounding as I stare at the locked door because what if it was someone else? I get up and walk up the stairs as Copper follows me. I continue down the hallway to Lane's door. I knock once before letting myself in.

"Lane?"

"Is something wrong?" he asks as he sits up.

I realize the bedroom lights are still on and turn them off.

"How well do you know Mick?" I ask as I walk up to the queen-sized bed. Lane relaxes as I crawl up onto the bed and sit down next to him.

"I've known him for close to a year, but we didn't become partners until a few months before the accident," he says.

"There's something about him I don't like," I admit.

He raises an eyebrow. "You've known him like two hours. He bought you breakfast and made you a bed on his couch. Why don't you like him?"

"When I was a kid, I rarely stayed in the same house for very long. My mom would drag me off to whichever boyfriend's house she was staying with at the time. Or I was tossed between foster homes...and I learned that you can judge the personality of a person by how their animal acts around them. One of the guys my mom stayed with had this mixed breed dog. It was always walking around like it was walking on glass. Always dodging and ducking everything. I thought it was because the dog was timid and didn't know me. But soon enough he was beating on the dog and would smack me around whenever I didn't do something perfect enough. I started judging the homes I went into by how their animals acted because if a person is bad, they're generally worse to their pet."

"I don't...really get what this has to do with Mick. You're talking about how Copper acts? He has always acted timidly. He was part of the K9 unit, but he was too timid to be used, so Mick adopted him. Trust me, Mick is not a bad person. I'm sure your childhood wasn't a good one, but you can trust people sometimes. Alright? I promise that I will keep you safe."

I debate saying more, but I know that I'm not always the best at giving people a chance. "Yeah...you're right...I'm just tired," I say. "I should go back downstairs."

"I want you to sleep in here," he says.

I look at him in surprise. "You sure? Won't Mick find it weird?"

"Oh well," he says, so I push the blanket back and crawl under the covers. "Felix…I'm sorry all of this happened to you. I'm really sorry you were hurt because of me."

"I'm fine, really," I assure him.

"Okay," he says as he reaches out to me.

I press myself up against him and he wraps a strong arm around me. It feels like safety and I have to remind myself that Lane is just a person I work for. That I shouldn't allow anything between us because he'll leave me just like everyone else does. But that's alright because I am fine alone.

"Are you sure you're alright?" he whispers into my hair. "You're acting surprisingly calm for having been beaten up, held at gunpoint, seen a man get shot, steal a car, get arrested at gunpoint, and get interrogated."

I press my face against his chest as I close my eyes. "It's just because you can't see. If you could see my expression right now, you'd realize that I am freaking the fuck out."

He laughs, and it makes me smile. "I'm being serious."

"I've actually been held at gunpoint before by a drug dealer my mom was beating with her purse."

"She was trying to save you?"

"Oh God, no. He was trying to get her to back the fuck off and was using me as a hostage, but she didn't much care. I think when you grow up with a mother like mine, you just go along with everything life throws at you. You're like 'oh, there's some meth where the cereal is supposed to be? alright, push that to the side.'"

"When did you go into foster care?"

"When I was fifteen," I say. "Because I guess you can't hijack a policeman's car. I mean, come on. How stuck up can you be?"

"You seriously broke into a police officer's car?" he asks as he looks at me in disbelief.

I grin at the thought. "They came in and were raiding the house I was in, so I thought it would be fun," I say. "I was a dumb kid, alright? It definitely wasn't the best thing I've ever done, but I did feel like a badass." For a short amount of time. But I didn't care. I was feeling something and sometimes that was all I needed.

"Did you have a foster family?"

"Not really. I was in juvie a while after that stunt, then kind of passed around a bit until I was eighteen and realized that if I didn't want to end up like my mom shooting poison into my veins then I needed to do something worthwhile with my life."

"You haven't done it yet, so what are you waiting for?" he jokes.

I grin. Most people wouldn't have turned this around to make fun of me, but I think he knows that I needed that. Sometimes I feel like I am so close to falling into that pit of nothingness, where I feel like nothing matters anymore. But this? This makes me smile. "Fuck off, you mean old prick," I say. "Now I'm tired, so good night."

"Haven't you slept a ton? You sure your brain is alright?"

"It was never alright, Lane."

"That's true. Good night, Felix."

His arms tighten around me, so his body is flush against mine. He kisses my forehead, and I'm slightly surprised by the gentle gesture.

***

"Are you doing alright?" Mick asks as I stuff my face with his delicious cooking. Which probably isn't a good thing because when I have to go back to eating the trash I make, it'll taste worse. It is kind of like when you're freezing outside so you go inside to warm up, but then when you go back outside it feels ten times colder. That kind of thing.

"God yes," I say. "This is so good. How'd you make this?"

"It's my mother's recipe. Pretty simple, really," he says.

"Felix is just impressed because he can't make oatmeal," Lane says as he slowly walks into the room. He was in the bathroom, and I suppose I could have waited for him, but I really didn't care to after I got a whiff of some bacon.

"Lane, you're going to run into something, step to your right," I say.

Lane, trusting me like the good man he is, steps to the right and bumps into the counter.

"Fuck," he growls as I start laughing.

"That's what you get for being mean to me," I say.

"Oh, I'll get you back for that," he promises.

"You mean getting me arrested wasn't enough?"

"I guess I'll let it slide," he says, and I laugh.

Mick is looking at me with wide eyes like he can't believe I'd torture a man that's blind. I just feel like it would be worse to treat him differently because he's blind. Lane doesn't want pity and he is definitely not going to get any from me. I think he secretly loves it.

When Lane reaches the table, he slowly slides the chair out and sits down cautiously, like he's expecting another trick. Mick sets a plate in front of him.

"Lane, you mind talking for a bit after this?" Mick asks.

"Yeah, of course. I should probably go to the office at some point as well," he says.

"Yeah, we can deal with that later," Mick says.

"Whatcha guys gonna talk about?" I ask curiously.

"Does not pertain to you," Lane says as he takes his first bite of the sandwich. "This is really good."

"Thanks," Mick says.

After they finish eating, Mick and Lane head to another room, leaving Copper and me alone. Which just means that I have to try harder to eavesdrop. So, I get up and creep down the hallway. They're in the last room on the left, but I can't hear much of anything as I stand outside of the door. No crazy secrets or spy talk that I can hear. Disappointed, I eventually head back to the living room.

After they're done with their super-secret meeting, Mick goes to work. I leave Lane in the living room with the TV and head into the room Lane and Mick had been in. It's set up like an office with a desk in the middle and filing cabinets off to the side. The moment I walk in, I start snooping. The desk is uneventful with its sticky notes, paper clips, and bills. The closet is crammed full of boxes holding junk and the laptop is password locked.

"What are you doing?"

I jump and look up at Lane. "Why are you so sneaky?"

"I literally just followed the sound of your scurrying," he says. "What are you doing?"

I would have assumed at this point he knew me well enough to figure that out. "Being nosy, of course."

"Is this a habit of yours?"

"Well…yes…"

"Just every time you come into someone's house, you just rifle through all of their personal belongings after they've graciously let you stay in the house?" he asks.

"You're making me sound like a dick, but yes," I say. "I just…wanted to be nosy. Sue me."

"Screw you?"

"No. Sue."

"I'd rather screw you," he says.

"Ha! No. I'm sore as hell. But you can suck my cock."

"Can I?" he asks as if he's excited.

I take a step toward him and lean against him. "You sure can," I say as my cock seems to realize I'm talking about it.

"I never thought you'd ask," he jokes as I watch him bite his bottom lip absently. It makes me want to suck it and lick it and my cock starts to harden at the thought. "Whenever I think about kissing you, I'm just not sure where to go. It's like…you're so far down it's hard to find you." He demonstrates by patting the air much closer to my stomach than my head and all desire for him dissipates.

"You're not as funny as you think you are."

He grins, and I lean up on the balls of my feet and gently press my lips against his. Lane's hand slides into my hair, pulling me closer to him until I can feel his body through his clothes and can tell that his cock is just as interested as mine. I wrap my arm around his shoulders as I try to pull him a little closer to my level.

When he gives in and lowers himself, I let my hand slide down his stubbly cheek. His lips part and I feel the touch of his tongue against my lip before sliding against mine. I can taste mint and a hint of coffee on his lips as his tongue dances against my own. I pull back and nip his lip where he'd licked earlier. I want to touch him, touch more of him, but I can tell he's being tentative touching me. He doesn't want to hit my bruises or hurt me, but at this moment I'm not sure I care.

Lane pushes me back against the desk and a picture sitting on it teeters for a moment. Lane's mouth is harsh and addicting against my own as we fight for dominance.

Suddenly, Lane jerks back.

"What?" I ask, but he holds up a hand to shush me.

"I heard something. I think Reed's home," he says as he withdraws from me, causing me to let out a disappointed groan.

I quickly close the drawer I had been peeping in and rush after him into the hallway. Copper watches me with accusing eyes so I pet his ears and he quickly forgives me for being nosy.

When I walk into the living room, Mick is standing with his iPad and is flicking through it. I have to keep myself from glaring at him in anger since he had interrupted us.

"What are you guys up to?" he asks.

"I accidentally paused the show, and now I'm trying to force Felix to be of some help and fix it," Lane says. "I had to find him first."

Mick looks up from his iPad as I stare at what he's doing on it. It looks like he's looking at mail, but I can't see it very well from this angle.

"I see. James wants to meet with you tonight at the department. He has your suitcase and stuff as well," Mick says as he sets his iPad down on the footstool.

"Great," Lane says. "I'll go get a shower."

"Can I go with you guys?" I ask, already knowing the answer.

"No," Lane says before heading toward the bathroom.

Grumbling, I slump down on the couch and pick up the remote.

Mick returns with a beer and sits down in the recliner. "You want one?" he asks as he nods at his beer.

"No, thanks," I say.

"Are you and Lane dating?" he asks curiously.

"No, I don't think I could date him. His charming personality would be too much," I say. "Too sickeningly sweet."

Mick laughs. "Yeah…sure…" His grin falls. "I hate seeing him like this."

"He's fine," I say. "He's just paranoid that everyone is judging him or feeling sorry for him or something."

"Yeah…it's just hard *not* to, I guess," he says.

"I know," I say as Copper walks up to me. I scratch his ear. "He's not allowed on the couch?"

"No," he says as he picks his iPad back up. From this angle, I can see the screen as he types his password in with practiced motion.

"But he's a cutie pie. How can you say no to this sweet little face?"

"Easily," he says as he looks over at me.

I stare at him for a moment and watch as his serious expression shifts to a smile. The smile is quite genuine, but there's still something about it.

"He chewed up my last couch. This one he can just stay off," he says as he tips his beer back against his lips.

"I'm sure it was an accident," I say.

He laughs as he lowers his beer. "Sure."

I start watching a movie as Lane comes down and the two get ready to go.

"If you get hungry, feel free to eat whatever you'd like for supper," Mick says.

"Alright, thanks," I say as I watch them leave. As soon as they're gone I pat the couch. "Come up here, Copper."

The dog stares at me with his big brown eyes.

"Come on. He's mean," I say.

The dog uncertainly watches me before setting a foot up on the couch. But as soon as I reach for him, he quickly withdraws it. I reach down to him when I hear a ding. I look around for the source of the noise before noticing Mick's iPad. I pick it up, but nothing shows on the main screen, so I try to open it. It needs a password, but since I'm nosy as hell, I'd seen him type the password in earlier.

8214

As soon as the iPad opens, I click on Messages. He must have his phone connected to his iPad because he has an entire list of messages. There's one unread one from a number he doesn't have in his contacts. I click it open and read the most recent text.

I'll have someone take care of the kid.

Kid? Does he have a kid?

I scroll up to the previous text that was sent from Mick.

What do I do with the kid still at my house?

Oh…*I'm* the kid.

I scroll up to the start of the conversation from today.

Mick: *I'm not getting any information out of Price. You sure he knows?*

Unknown: *He knows. Bring him tonight.*

Mick: *Where?*

Unknown: *512 Queens Street. Come around back. We'll make something happen.*

Mick: *What about the kid?*

"Fucking told you so!" I yell, and Copper flees in terror. "Copper. I told Lane that Mick was a dick but no! No one listens to me. Let's go," I say as I check the iPad. It has 3G, so I input the address into the maps and run for the door. I stuff my feet into my shoes and grab the dog leash hanging by the door. There's a set of keys hanging near the dog leash, so I grab them before snapping the leash onto Copper's collar. "You can come with me, baby."

He wags his tail and follows me outside. I rush over to the garage and let myself through the man door. I head over to the car hidden beneath a cover while praying that it runs. I pull the cover off and look at the beauty beneath.

"Bet he'll have a fit with your dog hair all in here," I say as I open the car door and direct him inside.

He hops in eagerly and wags his tail as he looks over at me. I toss the iPad on the dashboard as I realize that I have to get out of the car to open the garage door. After searching the garage over, I finally find the button and press it. It slowly opens as I climb back into the sports car and start it. The noise of it roaring to life startles me. I couldn't sneak up on a deaf grandpa with this thing!

I press down on the gas and we shoot out of the garage so quickly, I nearly wipe out the mailbox. We leap the curb and jump out onto the road as the dog claws onto the seat.

"Sorry, bud," I say as I reach over him and grab the seat belt. I yank it over his body and strap him in as he stares at me like I'm crazy. "I feel kind of like a badass," I tell Copper. "I'm just so excited to shout, 'I told you so' at Lane's face, you know?"

Copper doesn't know because he's too busy trying to figure out how to get out of the seatbelt.

I follow the GPS that is telling me that I'll be at my destination in thirty minutes. I'm driving above the speed limit, but they have a good fifteen to twenty minutes head start on me.

I quickly slow down as I see a cop heading my way and pretend to be a normal civilian until he passes before pushing the car up to seventy. The engine roars like a lion, and I feel like a predator.

As I near the destination, I realize that I haven't caught up to them as I had hoped. I'm not sure if they're taking the same path or if I've flown right by them at some point since I can't quite remember what color Mick's car is. Now I am only three minutes from my destination *and* I'm starting to feel a bit queasy. My prior moment of badassery is starting to drift away now that I realize that I don't know what the hell I am doing.

I mean, seriously? I'm just going to go in and do what? I didn't even grab a knife! I have a paranoid dog that looks like it's going to be carsick, a car that costs way too much money for any man just working in law enforcement, and an iPad.

Wait a minute…

The glove compartment! In all action movies, there is a requirement for a fully loaded gun to be inside.

I pop open the glove compartment praying there is at least a rocket launcher in there or something, but no! Some Arby's napkins and a *Now That's What I Call Music!* CD that must have been from the Stone Age because there's no possible way people still listen to those things.

"We're going to die, Copper," I say.

He wags his tail in agreement.

CHAPTER ELEVEN

I see Mick's car pulling up to the building and know that there's only one weapon I currently have.

His car.

I shed a tear at what I must do.

I push the car up to sixty as I turn into the parking lot of what looks like an abandoned factory. Deciding that I don't want to die, I slow down quite a bit as I grab Copper and hold him against me as I run the car right into the back of Mick's.

By the time I actually hit him, I am not going too fast since I really don't want to kill myself and Copper. Oh, and Lane. Thankfully, it isn't enough to deploy the airbags, so I hop out and run for the passenger door of Mick's car.

Lane and Mick are still trying to recover from the hit as I grab the door handle, but it's locked. Their airbags had gone off and they're trying to battle them as I beat on the door.

"Lane, he's a bad guy!" I yell.

Lane turns his head in my direction as Mick turns to me. I quickly duck down but keep hitting on the door until Lane unlocks it.

"Lane, he's lying to you," I say as Mick comes around the side of the car with his gun drawn. I hadn't even seen him get out, but now I'm quite concerned. "Hi…"

"What the fuck did you do to my car?" he growls, clearly horrified when he sees the damage. I am slightly mortified, and it isn't even my car.

"I'm sorry about that but...you know...?"

Lane steps out of the car and grabs onto Mick, sliding his hand over his neck as he draws it tight. In just as fluent of a movement, Mick brings his gun up and aims it at me.

"If you do anything stupid, I will shoot Felix," he says.

"So, you're working for them," Lane states.

Mick laughs, and I question when this became a comedy. I see nothing funny about having a gun aimed at me *again*. "Didn't you wonder how your cover got blown?" Mick asks.

"I knew someone within the department blew my cover, I just couldn't figure out who it was," Lane says.

"We can stand here all night, but I'm sure Red's men have heard the mess and are already headed here," Mick says. "Let me go or I'll shoot Felix."

I look up at him from where I am crouching on the ground. I can't help but question what I can do to help the situation since everything I have done so far has been very helpful. Suddenly, there's a flash of movement and Mick looks up. It's only Copper, but Lane must have heard it as well because he drops his weight down. With Lane's arm around Mick's neck, it throws Mick's balance completely off and his shooting arm goes up as he stumbles back, and then falls. Mick lands on top of Lane, but Lane's grip never loosens.

"Fass!" Mick struggles to get out and Copper's ears perk up. He bolts as I leap for the leash, but it slides right between my fingertips as the dog launches himself at Lane. He grabs the arm that's not around Mick's neck and yanks at it. Lane howls out as I realize that *just maybe* I shouldn't have brought a police dog to a fight against his owner.

Mick has stopped fighting by the time I race over, and Lane is being surprisingly calm with a dog attached to his arm.

"Aus!" Lane shouts and the dog hesitates. "Aus! Fuss!"

Copper releases and whines as he looks between the three of us nervously.

"You okay?" I ask hesitantly.

"Good idea, Felix. Bring the police dog," he says as he pushes Mick's unconscious body off him.

"He's really sorry," I say with a grimace as I pet Copper's ears back. "It's good you knew the words to stop him, though!"

"I was just shouting shit at him. Thank God I've worked with him before or he probably wouldn't have listened to me. I don't even remember if those are the right words. Now let's go."

I look at his torn hoodie. "Your arm alright?"

"It's fine," he says.

I grab Copper's leash and Lane's hand as I rush for the car Mick had been driving. It appears to have had the least amount of damage, so all three of us pile into it.

As I get in, I see that the key is not in the ignition.

"Lane, the keys are gone," I say.

"Go check his body."

I start to get out of the car when I see a handful of people coming out of the old factory. They're walking with a whole lot more confidence than I am currently feeling. A large percentage of that confidence probably comes from the guns quite a few are holding.

"Lane…there are currently about six people with really large guns heading this way. What do we do?"

"Where are they at?"

"Like...three o'clock."

"Okay, get out. Can they shoot you if you're on that side?"

"I suppose not," I say as I push the car door open and crawl out. I tug Copper after me while Lane crawls over the middle console. I hear a bullet hit the window and Lane grabs for me.

"Lane, we're going to die," I realize as he pushes my head down.

His arm is protectively wrapped around me as he ushers me forward. I know it's supposed to make me feel safe, but I still feel like I'm going to die.

"No, we're not. We're fine," he says, so completely calm. Just like he hadn't been betrayed by his partner, choked him out, been chewed on by a dog, and been shot at. Just like this is an everyday thing.

God, I hope this isn't an everyday thing with Lane.

"Lane…I'm kind of scared," I say.

"It's okay," he says. "Just scoot on over to the next car, and we'll try to get it going, alright?"

I nod and shimmy my way along the side of the car. I open the car door before reaching in and grabbing the key. I turn it and the car screams. Not to life. It just screams.

"I think I ruined it."

"Okay. New plan. What's closest to us?"

I look around, but my attention is completely focused on the men heading our way. "The men trying to kill us."

"Felix."

I look to my left, away from the men promising pain and death, and scan the grounds. I see a small building, maybe a maintenance building, just to the side. "Building thirty feet from us."

"Okay. We can handle that," he says.

"We can?" I ask because I'm pretty sure we can get shot up pretty good in thirty feet.

"Yes. Now, they're not going to want to kill me. They think I know something that they need to know. So, they're going to try and catch us. I'm going to shield you with my body because they probably won't care if you die or not."

"Splendid," I say.

"We'll be fine," he says. He's so confident that I almost believe him. *Almost.*

"Lane, you might as well just give up. Where do you think you're going to run to?" a man says. It sounds like Red, but I am not too eager to stick my head up to see if it is.

"Ready?" Lane asks, completely calm.

"Sure," I say. "Please don't let me die."

"I won't."

I take his hand in my right hand and Copper's leash in the other. "What's going to keep them from like…shooting our legs?"

"Luck," he says. "Ready? Go."

I take off running, pulling him after me as I wait for the pain of being shot and then, ultimately, murdered. It wouldn't be long now.

I hear a few shots as Lane pushes me forward. We slip around the corner of the building where I look over at Lane. "We're alive."

"For the moment, yes. Now tell me what you see?"

"Um…a fence surrounding the property."

"You're joking."

"No. No, I'm not."

"Okay," he says much more calmly than he should be when death was literally right around the corner. "Is there a door to get into this place?"

"Yes."

"Open it."

I run over to it, dragging him and the dog with me. The door is locked, but it has a glass pane, so I grab a rock and smash the window. The glass shatters, and I wrap my hand in my sleeve to knock the glass away. I reach in and feel for the handle before unlocking it. Quickly, I yank the door open and look around inside.

It's clearly used for storing things that no one seems to ever want access to again. The only thing not in a box or shoved on a shelf is a lawn mower sitting by the garage door.

"Um…just…like a mower and stuff."

"Okay, I want you to go inside and start it. Then run back out here."

"What? Why?"

"Distraction. They'll think you're planning a getaway with something. They won't realize it's a lawnmower. Go."

I run inside and jump on top of the lawn mower. I turn the key and thank God it starts. I pull the lock off it and push the levers forward. As it begins to move, I jump off it and race back to the door while the lawnmower runs into everything in its path.

"Okay," I say as I grab Lane's hand.

"We're just going to move to the next side of the building," he says.

"Alright," I say as I pull him with me so we slip around the side. I hear shouting behind us as I slow down, just out of sight.

"Move slowly until you can see the area where they had been standing," he says. "Keep your back pressed against the building and slowly move forward."

I do, but I'm terrified the distraction inside isn't going to be enough and they'll know we're just fucking with them. My heart is pounding so loudly I'm positive I won't hear anyone over the sound, even if they banged a gong right next to my ear. I slow when I see the area they had been, but it's clear. So, I keep moving until I see one man standing watch next to Mick's cars.

"There's one man standing next to Mick's car."

"Just one?"

"Yes."

"Which way is he looking?"

"Away from us. The way we ran."

"Perfect," he says as he pulls Mick's gun out. "Have you used a gun before?"

"What? NO! Not going to happen!"

"Okay," he says. "Then I need you to be my eyes. If I can't hear him then I can't tell where he's at," he says as he steps up behind me, his chest pressed against my back as he wraps his arms around my front and holds the gun with both hands.

"Put your hand on mine," he says. I slowly set my hand on top of his and wrap my fingers around them.

"Wait…if we shoot this, won't someone hear?"

"Not with the noise of the lawnmower. There's a suppressor on this gun that will make it a little quieter. Give me your other hand."

I reach out and take his left hand. He moves my hand around until he has set it on the top of the gun, then slides my fingers forward until I feel a little hump in the barrel.

"This is called the front sight and…" He moves my hand back until I feel two more humps. "This is the rear sight. The front sight will settle between the rear sight. I want you to aim at the target and then line the sights up with each other, alright?"

"Okay," I say. "Where do you want me to aim?"

"Chest. It's a wider area to hit. May cause us more issues in the long run, but it'll at least put him down."

"Okay," I say as I slowly push the gun to the right and aim it at the man's chest. The man is casually looking around like none of this is very concerning to him. He stretches as he leans back against the car. I can feel Lane's hand steady and calm beneath mine as I tip the gun, so I can look through the sights. I think they're right, but I'm nervous they're not. I'm scared I'll fuck this up.

"You kind of need to hurry up," Lane says calmly.

"Okay…I think they're right," I say.

"Alright," he says. "Pull your hand back."

I do, but I don't move out from where his arms are around me, gun in front of me.

"Still good?" he says as he slides his finger against the trigger.

"Yes," I say.

He pulls the trigger, making me jump, but my eyes never leave the target. The bullet strikes the man right in the chest, causing him to fall back against the car. I stare at the man with wide eyes as he slides down the side of the car and onto the ground.

"We're going to run for the car. You get the keys, alright?"

"Yeah…will it work with the airbags deployed?"

"It's an old enough car, the fuel line probably didn't shut off. We're going to try."

Snapped out of my trance, I nod and start running. Lane is right behind me and Copper is racing ahead as I near the car. The man is groaning on the ground as we grow closer. There's blood sprayed out over the side of the car and I quickly look away. Lane moves over to him as I rush around the side of the car to reach Mick's unconscious body. As I slip my hand into his pocket, I hear a thump.

I jump and look over at Lane, but he's leaning over the shot man, so I continue my search. I slide my hand into Mick's other pocket and feel the metal of the keys. Quickly, I yank them out just as a hand closes around mine. Mick's eyes open as I jerk back, but he reaches for me with his other hand. I hit him in the head without even thinking about it, before jumping up and running for the other side of the car.

"Got them, get in!" I say as Lane wastes no time climbing in through the driver's seat. I push Copper in and clamber in after him.

The airbags are in the way, so I bat them out of my face before ramming the keys into the ignition. It roars to life, so I quickly put it in drive. I press down on the accelerator as a horrible noise tears through the air. It must have been the scraping of the car bumper pulling free of the other car, but when we start rolling, I realize that the other car is kind of attached.

"What is that noise?" Lane asks. He turns his head as if it'll allow him to see.

"Um..." I look back in the rearview mirror as I press against the gas. The tires squeal as the car starts to slowly drag the other vehicle. "That...may...be the other car...stuck to it?" I say.

"The car is stuck?" he asks.

"Correct," I say as we proceed to drag the car that isn't smoothly rolling along behind us. It also must have been heavier than this car because we aren't going anywhere fast.

"Throw it in reverse."

"What?"

"Slam into the other car, try to get it unstuck."

"Okay, sure," I say as I push the airbag bag back and put the car in reverse. I accelerate and the grinding of metal on metal fills the car as Copper whines. Then I throw it back in drive and gun it. The other car is still stuck as it accelerates, dragging along behind us. Then with a screaming of plastic, metal, and whatever else cars are made of, the car lunges forward. I turn the wheel quickly as I see the men running around the corner of the building.

"They're running toward us."

"Get down," Lane says as he reaches for me to push my head down. Instead of protecting my head like my knight in shining armor, he jabs me right in the eyeball.

"Ow, fuck," I say as my eye instantly tears up, making it hard for me to see.

"Was that your eye?"

"Yes! It was!" My eye waters as I try to blink away the pain.

Lane pushes my head down, which makes it even harder to see since the tearing eyes didn't make it hard enough. I peek over the steering wheel just enough to see where I am going as I hear gunshots.

A bullet strikes the back window and suddenly the car jerks.

"What was that?" I ask.

"They probably shot out a tire. Just go," he says.

"What'd you think I was going to do? Jump out and change it?" I ask sarcastically.

"Maybe you should go back and feed them some of your food and we wouldn't have to even fight them," he suggests.

I reach over and pinch his nipple, making him yelp.

"What? Did you think you got shot in the tit?" I ask. "I mean I know that I feel like I got shot in my eye."

"Just drive!"

"I am! We're dragging half the car, the tire is blown, and we're being chased by serial killers."

"They're not serial killers…they're just…bad guys."

I check my rearview mirror, but they haven't come out of the parking lot yet. Without bothering to stop, I turn out onto a road as the car squeals. I can hear the *thud thudding* of the flat tire as I push it forward.

"What's that noise?" Lane asks.

"The car dying?" I suggest.

"No…listen," he says, and I listen while anxiously glancing behind us. Maybe he has some Daredevil-like hearing and can hear the bad guys coming upon us. "Is that a train?"

"Um…" I look around and see a train racing up on my left-hand side. "Yes?"

"Follow it, stop at the next station, we're getting on it."

"Okay…sure…" I say.

There's a car going the speed limit in front of me, so I rush around it and push our car up as fast as it will struggle to go.

"I swear to God if I have survived through all of this week, just to get shot up in let's say…an hour from now, I'm going to haunt your ass until you die," I threaten.

"That's alright, ghosts aren't as scary if you can't see them," he says before holding his arms up to protect his nipples.

"What are you doing, Lane?"

"Thought for sure that would end with a pinch," he says.

"Should have," I say as I see the parking lot for the train station. "We're here. Do I park?" I ask as I see a car turn onto the street. "Are the bad guys' cars all black?"

"I haven't asked," he says.

"Well, they are in movies, and there's a black car following us," I say as I drive right up to the train station door. A couple leaps out of the way like I would actually hit them as I drive the car up onto the sidewalk. "Let's go."

CHAPTER TWELVE

I jump out of the car and grab Copper's leash as Lane makes his way to my side of the car. I grab his hand and run inside but am instantly stopped by people milling about like they're out for a leisurely day. "We need a ticket."

"Jump the turnstile," he says.

"Okay…sure. Let's stage a getaway with a blind man and a dog," I say as I push some guy out of the way and jump up onto the turnstile. "Come on." I tug on Lane's arm.

He clambers up as Copper leaps up and over, instead of going under like I thought he would.

"Hey!" someone shouts as I pull Lane off it and onto the other side.

"Which train?" I ask as I look at the signs. They're pointing every which way and I don't understand any of it.

"Any."

"I've never been to Chicago, this is so confusing," I say as I look at the arrows and the colors.

"Just pick one and run."

I nod and yank him up the stairs as I hear someone screaming behind us. "Is that the 'bad guys with guns are here' signal?" I ask.

"It's highly likely," he says as he slows on the stairs. I can tell he's trying to concentrate and my tugging probably isn't helping, but I'd really like to live through this. "They're probably not carrying their guns, but I'm sure they're being none too gentle with pushing people out of their way."

A woman carrying fifteen tons of bags is coming down at us and Lane plows into her bags, nearly sending them all flying

"Sorry!" I say. "He's blind! And not the cool kind of blind like Daredevil!"

She just stares at us as we rush past and up onto the platform.

"Did we have to add that last part?" Lane asks.

"Well…yeah," I say as we reach the platform. "What now?"

"Which train is coming next?"

I look around, curious about how I am supposed to figure that out. Unlike the movies, there isn't a train already sitting, door open. Instead, there are people spread out, sitting on benches, or waiting. Then I see a little screen hanging from the ceiling.

"Says eight minutes." There are a few people staring at us, telling me that we aren't being too inconspicuous.

"What about the other side?" Lane asks.

I look to my left and see that there's nothing but a fence there before realizing he means *the other side of the tracks*. "Um…death?"

"How long?"

I catch sight of the sign from this angle. "Two minutes."

"Let's go," he says as he turns right sharply. "Where's the drop off?"

"NO!" The man has clearly lost his mind. There's no way he *actually* intends on jumping the tracks.

"Come on."

"TWO MINUTES," I remind him in case he has forgotten how to tell time. But his expression is completely steady like he is trying to talk me into trying a new restaurant, or maybe getting water instead of drowning my worries away with alcohol. Which I plan to do after this.

"It'll be one if you don't hurry up," he says as he slides his feet along the ground until he feels the drop-off. He tests it with his toe like he's testing the temperature in a pool. Then he just jumps right down onto the track like a fucking madman. Because I'm still holding his hand, it yanks me forward, but I persist. My feet lock and I look down at the man that I could have grown to really like, but now he was going to die.

I'm still standing on the platform, bent over because his grasp on my hand is keeping me from fleeing. "Lane, really?"

Copper leaps in and now I know that I *have* to go. I can't let the dog die.

"Hey! What are you doing!" a man shouts as I lean forward and jump down.

Lane yanks me forward and stumbles on the track but keeps moving. He reaches the other end, grabs me around the waist and pushes me up like I weigh nothing. I grab onto the edge as I hear shouting on the other side. I clamber my way up as Copper rears up onto the wall.

"Get the dog!" I demand.

"He can jump," he says.

"If the dog dies, I will force him to haunt you."

He feels around for the dog before grabbing him and tossing him like he's a rag doll. I catch him as his feet flail and bear hug him. He looks slightly alarmed as I drop him onto his feet and turn my attention back to Lane. It's then that I feel the floor begin to rattle.

"Get your ass up here, Lane," I say as I grab for him. I catch his shirt in one hand and slide my fingers around his wrist as I tug. He hoists himself up with his arms as I see some commotion on the other side. I see some of the men that had been in the alleyway four nights ago rush out onto the platform just as Lane pulls himself up next to me. I tug him as hard as I can, and he rolls up onto the platform.

"Hurry, hurry!" I say.

"Sorry, I had to save the *dog* that has the training to scale up *walls*," he says sarcastically as he climbs to his feet.

I can hear them shouting something as I start dragging Lane. I keep my eyes trained on the men as I move until the train turns the corner and cuts away my view. We keep moving until it stops next to us and the doors open. I rush inside with Lane's wrist in one hand and Copper's leash in the other. As I'm barging my way in, someone bumps into me as they try to get out. Ignoring the shove, I drag Lane to the middle and turn my attention to the two doors that are open in this car.

"Come on, close, close, close," I chant, now wishing I was Magneto so I could force the doors to work to my will. Or you know, just like destroy everything because I would be Magneto and I would be awesome, but obviously a less dicky version of him.

The doors close and I let out a deep breath a moment before the train lurches forward and I nearly fall. Lane catches me with a steady hand and pulls me toward him as he wraps a strong arm around me. He's clearly used to these death machines because he stands rock still. I take the opportunity to cling to his muscular upper arm like there isn't a more appropriate area to hang onto, but I needed a little fix to calm me down. Sue me.

"Any open seats?" he asks.

The train car is about half full and about half of them are staring at us like we're an oddity to be watched. Or maybe they are jealous of Lane's muscular arm that I get to cling onto.

"Yeah...sure," I say as I slowly shuffle over to some seats in the middle. I slump down into them as he sits down next to me.

I'm breathing ridiculously hard as I realize that I need to start exercising. Or stop hanging around Lane. That would probably be the wiser option. I have never been very wise, though. Especially when it comes to hot, mysterious, and dangerous men.

"How are you doing?" Lane asks.

"Lane?" I ask as I reach out and gently squeeze his hand, almost in a caring gesture.

"Hmm?"

"OH...*LANE*."

"What's up?" he asks like he isn't too concerned.

"I want to tell you something. Something very important. Something that could change everything as you know it—"

"I told you so?" he guesses.

"I *fucking* told you so," I say as I shake his hand violently. "I. TOLD. YOU. *SO*."

He snorts like he really doesn't care about all that. "I know you did. I'm sorry for not listening."

All the fight leaves me then and I sink against his shoulder. It's kind of hard and not as comfy as it looked, but it still feels so damn good. He wraps an arm around my side and pulls me against him as I close my eyes and just sink into him.

"You did good," he says.

For some reason the approval makes me feel good. It isn't often someone tells me that I did something right. "Did I? 'Cause it really seemed like everything I tried to do turned into a bigger mess."

He laughs, and I can feel the vibrations of it and it makes me smile. "How'd you figure out what was going on with Reed?" he asks as I feel the steady rise and fall of his chest.

"I broke into his iPad and read his text messages," I say.

He snorts. "You nosy little bastard," he says. "Good job."

"Am I still not worthy to know what the hell is going on?" I ask.

"I'll tell you, just not here," he says. "See if you can borrow someone's phone."

"I can't. I'm too exhausted." Right now, I want nothing more than to just lie here against him and not move for maybe a couple of days. I don't even care about the strange smell permeating the train car we are in.

"Can I borrow someone's phone? It's an emergency," Lane says, disrupting my moment of paradise.

I open my eyes as a woman sitting near us holds her phone out. Taking her phone, I thank her since it seems like I don't have much of a choice in the matter.

I look down at the keypad that she has up for us. "Who are you calling?"

"James."

"Okay," I say as I type in the numbers as he lists them. As soon as I'm done, he holds his hand out, so I reach out and set the phone into it. His hand closes over it before bringing it up to his ear. I notice the woman whose phone it is watching us very closely.

For a moment he just listens, then he hands it to me. "He's not answering. I need to call the department."

I end the call. "What's the number?"

He tells me, so I type it in before handing it to him. He at least gets someone to answer this time.

"Hey, it's Lane Price. Reed is working with Victor Red. Yeah…no…I'm positive. He took me to an abandoned factory where…Yeah, I can get you the address…Felix, what was the address?" he asks.

I look over at him, surprised he'd ask such a thing. "Uh…I don't know."

"Road?"

Is he crazy? I can't even tell him the road he lives on. "I…don't know?"

"Think…"

Think…think… "Queens Street!" I shout and quite a few people in the train car look over at us. I don't know train car protocol, but it clearly doesn't involve shouting.

"He said it was on Queens Street. Who? Felix…my babysitter. Yeah, I'm not sure if they're still there. I think some of them followed us over to the station. Felix, which station were we at?"

"I don't know."

"The closest station to that location," Lane says. "Yeah…yeah…alright, I'll be there as soon as I can."

He hands the phone to me, so I end the call before passing the phone over to the lady. "Thanks," I tell her.

She nods slowly, probably questioning exactly what kind of call had been made on her phone.

"Felix, what's the next stop?"

"I don't know. How do you tell?"

"Look above the door," he says.

"Uh…" I look at the minuscule map above the door that I guess I'm supposed to be able to read and decipher. It just looks like a bunch of crazy lines to me.

I look around and finally realize we're on the red line. "Redline, next stop is…"

"Chinatown," the woman who we'd borrowed the phone from says.

"Thanks," Lane says.

"Ohhhh, I want some Chinese food," I say, suddenly very excited. That would be a perfect end to this nightmare. Just go into a Chinese food coma after stuffing my face with all the wondrous delights.

"I think…we have more pressing matters to attend to. First of which is that we are headed the wrong way," he says.

As the train starts to slow he stands up. I get up and nearly fall on my face as the train lurches before stopping. Lane must sense my imminent demise because he grabs my shoulder.

I reach out and take Lane's hand, mostly to keep myself from dying but partly to keep him from dying as well. Who knows when he will decide to leap onto the track again? I lead him through the open door as people try to cram in. "So…do we go get a ticket? Or do we just climb through the track again?"

"We can just go to the other side like normal people," he says.

***

I walk into the department as my head moves on a swivel. "I feel important."

"Yeah, you are. You're…there to keep me from stubbing my toe," he says.

"'You are very important, Felix. You have saved my ass multiple times. I'm so lucky to have you,'" I say as I try to talk like Lane. It's nowhere close and it just makes me sound like I'm a heavy smoker.

He snorts. "Take us over to the elevator."

I lead him with me over to the elevator and hit the up button as I watch people move about. The door opens, and a woman looks at us in surprise.

"Lane!" she says.

"Hey Jenny," Lane says before quickly stepping past her even though it looks like she's interested in talking more.

He's acting calm and collected, but I can tell he's a little upset. He doesn't like people seeing him like this, but he's going to have to get used to it.

"Would you rather hold Copper's leash? He probably won't lead you into anything," I say as I squeeze his hand.

"Sure," he says as he lets go of my hand and holds his out.

As soon as I set Copper's leash into his hand, he wraps his fingers around the leather. I watch as he gathers the leash up as the elevator dings. The door slides open and I step out, instinctively wanting to reach for him to pull him after me, but Copper starts walking, and Lane follows.

"Where are we going?" I ask, but I don't have to wait for an answer because a man in a button-up and dress pants is walking toward us.

"Hey, Price," he says when he sees Lane.

He looks to be in his sixties with eyes that I can only describe as birdlike. I feel like with those eyes he could catch me doing anything even if his back was turned to me. He's wearing a button-up that is pulled tight over his gut. Two of the buttons should win an Oscar for how hard they're working at keeping it together.

"Sir," Lane says with a respectful nod. "Did you send anyone out there?"

"Yeah, let's talk," he says.

He starts walking before he seems to remember that Lane is blind and looks back at him like he's unsure of what to do with him. I'm so glad Lane can't sense these looks he gets from people because I think it would make him upset or angry or a combination of both.

So, I start following the man, and Copper follows me.

"Whose dog is that?" the man asks curiously.

"Reed's. I'm not quite sure why we have it," Lane admits.

"Because Mick was treating him poorly and because Mick is a dick," I say.

The older man nods slowly like he's not sure how to confirm that information. "And this is?"

"I'm Felix," I say with a smile.

"The babysitter James hired," Lane says.

"I see. Aaron Walsh," he says as he holds out a hand.

I reach out and take it. He gives it a solid, bone-crushing shake like he has to prove his masculinity and I glare at him, but he doesn't seem to notice. I'm just glad my right hand isn't the one that had been bruised.

"He can sit out here and wait while we talk," Walsh says.

"I think he's fine to hear what's going on. He's already aware of everything happening," Lane says. "And he could prove helpful in case he noticed something that I didn't."

Walsh looks back at me and it's clear he's not very keen on the idea, but he doesn't say anything as he leads us through a door and into a small, conference-style room. "I'm going to go find García, I'll be right back."

He leaves, so I take Lane's arm and lead him over to a chair. He sits down and by the time I sit, Walsh is back with a Latino man.

"Hey Lane!" he says as he rushes over to our side of the table. He reaches out to Lane and instead of shaking his hand like I thought, he grabs him in a big bear hug. The man is almost as short as me but is built. His shirt is so tight over his muscles that I can't help but admire them. Not that Lane doesn't have nice muscles, but my God this García man looked nice. Even with his shirt on, I can see every outline of muscle which has me wondering how exactly he gets that shirt on and if he has to cut it off at night.

"How have you been, García?" Lane asks, *actually* hugging him back. Is there something going on here that I should be jealous about? But then I think about how hot it would be to have a threesome with García included. *That* I could handle.

Bad thoughts, Felix. Bad thoughts.

I really didn't need a hard-on in the middle of the seemingly important meeting.

"I've been good! Real good! I've missed you around here!" García says a bit too loudly.

"What?" I ask. "Lane, someone could actually…miss you?"

García starts laughing as he looks over at me. "James told me Lane scared away the first person assigned to helping him, but I see you have prevailed."

"I have. I've just been locking him in the bathroom. He can't find the door without his sight and I just toss some food at him once a day," I say.

García laughs. "That's cruel."

"Felix also thinks he's funnier than he is."

"Alright, have a seat, García," Mr. No Fun Allowed says.

García sits down next to Lane and we turn our attention to Walsh.

"After your call, we sent a few people out to the location. When they got there, there was no one still around. You said they had followed you to the station, right? I had them check the station out and suggested they look at the footage to kind of get an idea of who all was involved, but we already have a pretty good idea of who they were. The larger issue is that we haven't heard from Dixon in a few days."

Lane leans forward. "What? What do you mean you haven't heard from James? When's the last time?"

"Wednesday."

"That was when we were at the hotel," I say as I try to think about it. My days are a bit of a jumble, but we'd stayed at Mick's for a few days, not aware that James had been missing the entire time.

"He returned from the job we sent him out on, but we haven't heard from him since."

"Reed said he had been talking to him," Lane says.

"Well, Mick the Dick clearly wasn't being real honest with most of what he was talking about," I say snidely.

Lane nods slowly like he's thinking about something more. "So, Reed knows where he's at."

Walsh shakes his head. "We don't know that. We can't jump to conclusions. That's how mistakes are made."

"Well, we can't just sit here. Have you talked to his wife? Want me to go talk to her?" Lane asks.

There's a noticeable moment of hesitation as Walsh leans back in his chair. He glances over at García before looking back at Lane. "Lane…we're going to have someone come to pick you two up and take you to a safe location."

Lane seems to sink into his chair, and I can see the surprise on his face. García looks a little upset about it, and I realize what this is. And know that it will *not* go over well.

"You think I can't help?" Lane asks.

"I think it would be best for you to go someplace safe," Walsh says. "You have already been targeted multiple times."

Lane snorts in disbelief. "You think I can't help." It's not a question this time.

"Lane, you're blind, I think this is a bit…too much for you. I'd like to place you someplace safe until this whole thing blows over. I have talked with your department, and they agree with me. It will just be until we can figure something else out."

Lane nods. "Okay."

"Great," Walsh says with a relieved smile. "I'll call them right now."

Yeah, I know there is no way Lane would have agreed that quickly.

"Felix, let's go," Lane says as he stands up.

Walsh looks surprised, but I'm not sure why. He clearly hadn't worked with Lane a whole lot if he thought he was going to take all this in stride. "What do you mean?" Walsh asks. "Lane, you can't honestly think it would be wise for me to put you on this case."

"Of course not," Lane says as he heads in the general area of the door. "I don't need you to protect me. I'm leaving. I'm not dealing with this shit. Come on, Felix."

I rush for him, but García reaches him first.

"Hey, we'll figure something out," he says as he gives him a hearty one-armed hug.

"Thanks," Lane says.

I step in front of García and smile at him. It's not often I chance upon someone as short as me, so I feel an instant connection with him. "I like you. Mostly your muscles. But I like you," I say.

He laughs. "Do you need a hug too?"

"I'd love one," I say as I wrap my arms around him. He's gentle, but I still feel the soreness of my ribs as he hugs me. I slide my hand up under his shirt and feel his badge. I pull it free as I draw away from the hug. I jab a finger at Walsh, drawing attention away from my right hand that is sliding the badge into my back pocket. He had moved over to the door in order to pull it open for Lane. "And you…I hope you're involved in this because you're a real ass," I say as I bump into him. I slide my fingers into his back pocket and pluck his wallet out with practiced fingers.

I rush over to Lane and grab his wrist as I pull him out the door. He doesn't say anything as I lead him over to the elevator, and when the door closes, I look up at his face. His expression is hard set and completely unreadable, but I can feel the anger bristling under his skin.

"So…what's our next step?" I ask.

"Go find a hotel and sit on my ass. Twiddle my thumbs, maybe. Eat fast food and become fat."

I stare at him in surprise before quickly covering it up with disgust. "What? Then you'll lose your muscles, and that's not sexy or badass in any way."

Lane's frown deepens. "Yeah, and what the hell can a blind man even do to help besides getting in the fucking way?"

I look at him in confusion as the elevator door opens. "Seriously, Lane? Just because some a-hole thinks you're incapable of helping doesn't mean you are. Look at all of the shit you just did today." I pull him from the elevator. "If I had stopped every time someone told me I was useless, I wouldn't have made it past age six."

"You're not blind, Felix. You were poor and had a shitty upbringing. I think it's different. You had options."

"And you don't?" I ask as I pull him out through the door. "So, it ends here? Everything ends here? That's just it. Toss in the…rag? Is it rag? Is that how that saying goes?"

"Towel."

"Oh…right. So…you're going to toss in the towel?"

Lane stops suddenly and a woman who'd been walking behind us nearly runs into us since she'd been staring at her phone. I grab Lane's arms and aim him toward me.

"Lane."

He refuses to turn his head anywhere in my direction.

"So, this is it? Just…screw James. Let someone kill him because you're blind."

"Yep," he says stubbornly.

I glare at him, really wishing he could see my annoyance. "Lane, you're an idiot. An absolute idiot. Think about everything that happened today. Now, *a normal* person couldn't do that shit, yet we lived through it because of you."

"You don't understand, Felix."

"The only thing I don't understand is how damn stubborn you are. Do you trust me?"

"Not in the slightest," he says, and I know I'm winning this conversation. He wouldn't joke with me if he wasn't starting to teeter on the edge.

"Alright…well…how about this time you try? We'll just…find James. Then we can go hide under a rock where you can roll around and scurry to your heart's content *and* if you keep your muscles, I promise to always stay by your side."

The upset expression on his face changes to a grin that I can tell he's fighting. "Fine. But we have nothing," he says. "We don't have money, we don't have a car. We're still wearing Reed's clothes."

"What are you talking about, silly?" I ask as I pull the badge out and smack his cheek with it. "I have a detective's badge right here, so we can get in anywhere we want to go."

His hand shoots up to mine and stops the badge from smacking his cheek again. "Where did you get this?"

He takes it from me and feels it over, probably making sure I am telling the truth.

"I stole it from García," I say before smacking his other cheek with Walsh's wallet. "And I stole this wallet from your good buddy Walsh."

"You stole a badge and a wallet from two *detectives?*"

"Correct," I say with a smile.

"Are you an idiot?" he asks skeptically.

"Hmm…" I say as if I'm thinking really hard about it. "I don't think so."

Lane just starts laughing and I'm relieved. I've pulled him back over to my side where I like him.

"Walsh is going to lose his mind when he realizes it's missing."

"So, *Detective,* where are we off to first?" I ask as I pass him the badge.

"Away from here before they realize we have their wallet and badge. How much money is in there?"

I flip open the wallet and am instantly shocked by the amount. "We're rich."

"How much?"

I pull the money out before realizing that doing so is a good way to get mugged. I am usually not so careless, but I have never seen so much cash, so I am not quite sure how a rich human interacts with it. Probably not by waving it around on a busy Chicago street. "I don't know…close to five hundred," I say as I flip through the bills.

"So, let's head to James's house. See if we can talk to his wife," Lane says. "I may not have known James a long time, but he has been very kind and helpful to me. When I lost my eyesight, he was there to help me. I want to be able to help him."

"Alright, where's he live?"

"Hail a cab," he says.

I eye Lane like he's crazy. "And…I do that how, exactly? I mean, people in movies just like…run out in the middle of the road and cabs just leap off their path to them."

"Wave at one."

"Ooh…that sounds scary. We could just steal one. I'm better at that," I say.

He shakes his head. "Let's just get back on the train, it'll save us some money," he says, so I start walking. When we reach the train station I notice there's an ATM in the corner that a man is leaving.

"Hold on, there's an ATM," I say as I grab his wrist to stop him.

"You have a credit card with you?" he asks.

"Yeah, Walsh's," I say, surprised he has already forgotten that I'd stolen it. "We'll try his birthday for the code. You'd be surprised how many people use their birthday."

Lane looks at me in surprise. "We're not just going to wipe out his savings. You already stole five hundred from him," Lane says like he can't believe I would say such a thing.

"It was a joke." It was not a joke.

"You were seriously going to take it, weren't you?" he asks.

"Sorry, Saint Lane, we can't all be perfect like you. He was a dick to you. Losing a couple more hundred wouldn't have hurt him," I say. Or a thousand.

"Is this a…regular occurrence with you?" he asks.

"Of course not. Now come on," I say as I walk away from the ATM and over to the ticket machine.

But Lane is clearly not done with this conversation. "How much money of mine did you steal?" he asks.

Now it is my turn to look at him in surprise. "None! I've been good! I turned my life around when I became an adult!" I say.

"So, I have made you resort to your old ways?"

"It's fine…we would have paid him back." Maybe. "You're rich."

"Not exactly," he says. "And I'm not paying him back. I can't stand the man."

I stare at the ticket machine. "How do you buy a ticket?"

"Just follow the prompt," he says.

"Uh huh…" I say as I stare at the machine, again wanting to tell him that if he would have just let me steal Walsh's car, we would be at our destination by now. It's not like we *couldn't* return it.

I purchase the tickets and then lead us to the turnstile.

An attendant steps up between me and the turnstile before I can set the ticket against it. He holds a hand up, making me stop so abruptly that Lane slams into me.

"Sorry, dogs have to be in a carrier bag," the attendant says.

"Alright. Do you have a Walmart bag? If you have four, I could put a foot in each," I tell him.

"Felix," Lane says in his "teacher" tone. "He's a service dog, I'm blind."

"Oh, I'm sorry, please go right ahead," the man says.

We get on the train without any more issues and easily make it to James's apartment complex. It is a large building right in the middle of the city. I see a lady passing through the door, so I scoot right up and grab it before the door locks. I hold the door open for Lane and head inside. Directly in front of us is an elevator, which we take up to the third floor.

"What door number?" I ask as I look down the hallway. It reminds me of a hotel with the colorful carpet and wallpapered walls.

"Hmm…I don't remember."

"What do you mean, you don't know the door number?" I ask.

"Well…I usually walk in and recognize the area. I've been here quite a few times and just…know."

"Do I knock on each door?"

"No…it's in this area," he says. "Muscle memory." He walks from the elevator and down the hallway a bit before stopping and turning. "It's right here. This feels right."

I walk over to where Lane is facing a small table with a fake fern on it. I walk up to it and shake the leaf of the fern. "Hi, James's wife, it's nice to meet you," I say before realizing the joke isn't as funny when the recipient can't see. "Here, Lane, she wants to talk to you." I pick it up and move it toward his face until a dusty leaf touches his cheek.

"I will take this plant and shove it up your ass," he says as he bats it away.

"Ooh…you know I like stuff up there, but it's a bit too big," I say.

"Trust me, I'll make it fit," he says before pushing it away.

"Oh Lane, you know how to *turn me on*," I purr as I run a finger over his groin. The startled look on his face excites me and I grin, but a noise stops me from saying anything else.

Someone steps off the elevator, so I put the fern back down. "Hi, where does James live?" I ask the old lady as she hobbles toward us.

"Next door," she says as she jabs at it with her cane.

"Great, thanks," I say.

I knock on the door as the little old lady continues down the hallway and disappears through a door. We wait a few minutes, but there's no response.

"What do you want to do?" I ask.

"Fuck…I don't know. What time is it?"

"I don't know…it's dark outside."

"Let's go get some sleep," he says. "We won't be of any use half asleep. Let's leave her a note. Go knock on that lady's door and ask for a pen and paper."

I go and get the required stationary before writing down the message for James's wife to call the nearby hotel when she gets home and ask for Lane. We then walk to the hotel Lane had mentioned after stopping at a dollar store, to grab some dog food, as well as a burger joint. I leave Lane with the bags of food and stuff from the dollar store as I get us a hotel room. I get a room after a minor issue with me trying to get a hotel room without an ID. I end up saving the day by pulling out my police badge.

Lane snacks on the fries as we ride up to the fourth floor. "Do you feel guilty about that?" he asks curiously.

"Of course not," I admit as the elevator doors open.

"Of course," Lane says with a grin as he eats another fry.

We head down the hallway as I glance at the room number written on the envelope. I find our room at the end of the hall just past the ice machine. Once there, I swipe the keycard and wait for the light to turn green. "Are we going to get murdered?" I ask, trying not to recall my last time in a hotel.

"Hopefully not," he says as he follows me inside. I close the door and lock it. Then I toss the grocery bag on the bathroom counter and wash my face. For a moment, I consider taking a shower, then decide that being on the run is exhausting and I would in the morning instead.

I walk into the bedroom where Lane is sitting on the bed eating his cheeseburger. I reach into the bag and pull out my cheeseburger and start stuffing my face as I hand Copper a piece of it. He scarfs it down then wags his tail as he watches me eat mine.

"So?" I ask.

"So, what?" Lane asks.

"Nothing? You have nothing to say?"

"Good idea getting these burgers," he says with a nod.

"You're so frustrating," I say.

I'm not yet done when he gets up and heads to the bathroom. I sigh but finish eating and let Copper have half my fries. He'll probably get the shits, knowing my current luck.

When I'm finished, I go into the bathroom and push Lane out of the way, so I can brush my teeth. The toothbrushes are small and stiff and feel like they're trying to scrape my gums off instead of cleaning them. I suppose that means that I shouldn't have been so cheap and bought decent ones.

Lane hands me his toothbrush, which I set down so that it's not touching the counter since I'm paranoid about germs.

"So…how do I take these sutures out?" I ask as I examine the small line of sutures just before my hairline.

"Snip them."

"Uh huh."

"Want me to do it?" he asks as his hand smacks the bag that holds the scissors I'd bought. Who needs a doctor anyway?

"Sure," I say as he snips the scissors in the air. I grab them from him before he cuts something important and carefully cut each suture until they're free. The wound on my arm looks decently healed, so I cut them off as well before tossing the scissors onto the counter.

When I'm finished, I walk out and find Lane sitting on the edge of the bed.

"Are you going to bed?" I ask.

"Yeah…in a bit." He looks up in my direction as I walk toward him.

"Do you want to rub my back?" I suggest as I walk up to him and climb onto his lap.

"No," he says. "I can't. I'm blind."

I laugh and watch as he reaches up toward my face. I'm a little worried after he'd tried poking my eyeball out in the car, so I can't help but cringe a bit from the memory of the trauma. His finger touches my cheek and he hesitates but keeps moving it up until his hand is at my hairline. He slides his hand up as his fingers sink into my hair. It's not really a romantic or suggestive gesture, so I just watch.

His hand brushes against my skin as his fingers run down the strand of blond hair.

"Is your hair curly?"

"No, just a little wavy. It has this messy thing perfected," I say.

He lets a finger follow a strand down, and then slides his hand through my hair up to my forehead. He touches the hair, pushing it back, before sliding his fingers down my forehead like he's trying to memorize it. Then his thumb begins to run a line from the middle of my forehead down my nose until he reaches the tip.

"You said you're paler than me?" he asks. He leaves his thumb on the tip of my nose as his fingers span out, sliding over my forehead and down the side of my face.

I look at his slightly tanned skin; he clearly hadn't been afraid of the outdoors before this mess. "Yes," I say.

"Do you have freckles?"

"No."

His finger stops as he touches a small scar just above my eyebrow. Most people don't even notice it since it is barely visible anymore. "What's this?"

"A scar."

"From what?"

I watch the concentration on his face. His eyes not focused at all, yet showing complete concentration like he's truly seeing something.

"Um…I think that was when my brother hit me with a baseball bat," I say.

"Brother? I didn't know you have a brother."

"Yeah…I haven't seen him in a long time."

"Why?"

"I don't know. He got into some bad shit. I guess he took a bit too much after my mom." I sigh. "Anyways, back to my scar, it wouldn't stop bleeding, so he glued it back together with some super glue, but had gotten his finger stuck to it, so when he pulled his finger away, he ripped the wound back open."

"Ow," he says.

"Yeah, it wasn't pleasant."

His finger slides inward, and I close my eyes, a little worried about the proximity of his finger and my eye. His finger slides over my eyelid, then through my eyelashes.

"You said your eyes are brown?"

"Yes."

"What color brown?"

"Uh….I don't know. Kind of hazel, I guess."

"Your eyelashes are long," he says as his fingers slide down my cheek. His thumb dips down my nose to my upper lip, then slides over my cheek as I open my eyes. He traces the edge of my lips as I follow each movement with my eyes.

And I can't help but wonder when everything changed. When did I stop seeing him as just an object of desire? Something to lust after? I never let myself get this close to anyone, so why is it that I am suddenly consumed by him? I can't stand the thought of leaving him. I would rather go through all this shit he's putting me through than to be alone again. I want him near me more than I have ever allowed myself to want anything in my life. He gives me a purpose while also making me feel wanted and needed.

When his fingers touch my chin, he slides his hand down to the bottom of my shirt where he grabs it and pulls it up, over my head. I lift my arms up and the shirt pulls free. Once my top half is bared to him, he quickly tackles the buttons of my pants. Eager to help, I get off his lap and push my pants down, stepping out of them. Using my toes, I slide my socks off. He reaches for me and sets his hands on my hips, wrapping his fingers around them. He lifts me up and lays me down on the bed.

He reaches under me and pulls the top cover up and off before climbing up until his knees are on each side of my waist. I don't reach for his clothes because I'm not quite sure that's what he's wanting. Instead, he picks up where he left off. His fingers dip down my chin to my neck, finding every mole, every dip, everything that makes me who I am, and I just watch him. I have never felt so noticed, so vulnerable before as I lie there. It is like he's seeing every inch of me that no one else has ever taken the time to look at. His hands slide down my chest, his fingertips brushing over my nipples. Then moving from my chest, his fingertips dip over my shoulders and down my arms, only stopping when he finds another scar.

"What's this one from?"

I shift a bit. I'm trying really hard not to get an erection since he clearly just wants to find a way to see me, but his hands are warm and a little rough as they slide down my arms. His finger moves down the scar before drawing a circle around it.

"Where did this scar come from?" he repeats as his finger circles it again.

I'm silent as I watch him, finger still circling the scar.

"Felix?"

"Hmm?" I ask.

"Where'd this scar come from?"

I watch his expression, but he's not giving anything away. "I was fifteen and I stole money from my mom. She was going to spend it on drugs and I just wanted something to eat. Her boyfriend got pissed and started hitting me with a beer bottle. I hated him, and I hated her. I hated everyone. I hated myself. I just…wanted to get away, but I couldn't. When he was finished beating me, I remember just lying in the closet. It was the only place I felt like I could get away from them.

And that's when I heard the sirens. For a split second, I thought my mom called the police. I thought…I thought she was so worried about me that she called the cops. I…didn't care that I ached, that my lip was bleeding, my arm needed stitches. I didn't care because my mom cared! She actually cared!

"I stepped out of the closet and there she was. My mom. And she turned to me and the look wasn't one of concern, it was of anger. She started yelling at me as the cops wrestled her boyfriend. She screamed and yelled at me, blaming me for calling them. Like I could have fucking called them from where I was hiding from that asshole. The cops then moved for her, and I ran. I slipped through the window and stepped outside and there it was, the cop car was just sitting there. There was a cop hovering around it, but he wasn't paying attention to it as I slid into that driver's seat and drove away. I think part of me wanted him to just shoot me down. Just…kill me so all this shit would end. Another part just wanted someone to fucking notice."

"I noticed you the moment I met you," he says.

"No, you didn't. You wanted me to go away," I say.

"I hated my life. I hated my world. But I noticed you, Felix," he says as his hands slide down my sides, over my hips. "I notice every inch of you. Every mark, every mole, I feel it. And I notice it."

"Why?" I ask. "Why do you notice any of it?"

He leans forward and presses his lips against mine. I close my eyes and lean into him. The hard press of his lips, the caress of his tongue. I open my mouth, allowing his tongue to tangle with mine. But then he pulls back and returns to my stomach like he just remembered his original objective. His hand slides over my flesh, making my skin shiver under his gentle touch. I have no control over the desire pent up inside of me. His fingers slide down my thighs, and I ache to touch him.

Ache for him to never stop touching me.

"Lane…"

"What?" he asks as his hands move down to my knees, down to my ankles, down to my feet.

I shake my head because I can't say it. I know he can't see the gesture, but he doesn't ask again. His hands find their way up my thighs, and then between my legs, pushing them apart. He moves his hand up, under my cock as he rubs the area between my testicles and cock. I'm already erect and this just forces me to lose all composure. His fingers trace over my testicles, circling around them, rubbing them, pulling gently.

"There's lubricant in the bag from the dollar store," I say.

"What?" he asks. "You're like, let's stop in here, grab essentials and that was lubricant?"

"That's what I meant by essentials! Do you understand how sexy you are being all badass?" I ask. "You're all 'hand me that gun' then just go badass with it."

"That scenario never even happened." He shakes his head. "Where's it at?"

"I'll get it."

"No, let me," he says. "Just tell me."

"Bathroom counter," I say.

He gets off the bed and now that he's gone I long for his return. For his touch. For his attention. But he's back as soon as he left. He takes his clothes off in a hurry before climbing back onto the bed. I want to reach out, run my fingers over his muscled chest, his hard stomach, his scarred legs, but as soon as I reach for him he pushes my hands down.

"No."

"I can't touch you?"

"No," he says. "Roll over."

"Like…hands and knees?"

"No, on your stomach," he says as he rolls me onto my stomach and straddles me as he reaches up to my head.

"You're squishing my cock," I moan as I shift to try to make it comfortable.

"You shouldn't have an erection then," he says. "I just wanted to see you."

I snort but close my eyes as his fingers run down my neck to my back. They brush down, following the line of my shoulder blade. A single finger traces a line down my spine and between my butt cheeks. His touch is soft. Gentle. Fingers moving and touching every part of me. He kisses the small of my back as his finger travels down over my butt. He rubs his finger around my hole and then presses against it. He has all my nerves on fire. Every touch makes my skin heat up and quiver in anticipation.

His finger pushes in deeper, plunging and moving, making me moan. I want him deep inside of me, yet I don't want this to ever end. These gentle touches, the kisses, the way he's looking at me. The way only he knows how to look anymore.

He pushes another slick finger inside of me as he kisses my hip bone, his other hand running up my side, fingers rubbing and caressing. His fingers thrust inside of me, stretching and rubbing before he pulls them out. He rolls me onto my back before pushing a pillow under my hips. I don't reach out to him, instead, I lie before him and let him work his fingers over me like an artist works clay. I was there for him to do anything he wished to.

His finger brushes the underside of my cock as his other hand moves back to my butt, where he rubs the rim before pushing his fingers inside. I moan as I watch him feel every inch of me. He never stops moving his fingers inside of me as his other hand rubs lubricant over his thick cock. I greedily watch his every move.

He pulls his fingers free, and I feel his cock brush my thigh before settling between my legs. He presses against me, the ring of muscle resisting for a moment before giving in. His thickness fills me, and I finally grab onto him, pulling him closer to me. Lane moves so slowly, it is driving me mad. It makes me ache for him and crave for him to move quicker, to grab me tighter.

But it just makes the moment when he pulls back and thrusts in that much more of a rush. I moan as I dig my nails into his back before realizing what I am doing.

"Harder," I say as I crash my lips against his.

"Shh," he says as he slows as if going against my plea. I nearly whine as his movement is almost to a standstill. He needs to move. There's no way my body can take him moving so slowly inside of me.

"Lane! Harder."

He's grinning as I stare at him desperately. "Shush," he says, quieting me with a hard kiss of his lips. He pulls back until he's out of me before thrusting hard into me. The quick movement makes me arch up into him as I moan. The change in pace makes it that much sweeter as I desperately grab onto him. I have never felt like this before. Never had this heat and desire rushing through my body. The rawness of it almost scares me, but it excites me at the same time. He moves quickly inside of me as my body aches for release. The rhythm pulls me in deeper as his hand slides up my thigh and finds my testicles. He rubs his fingers over the sensitive skin before sliding up my cock, his thumb rubbing the head as I kiss him. He's driving me crazy. His hands, his cock. They're making me go insane, making me feel like it is too much, making me feel like I can never get enough.

His hand rubs my cock and I moan as I let my body give in to him. Ecstasy consumes me as his hand moves over me, making me come. He moans against my neck as he kisses it, moving with quick, shallow thrusts as he reaches his limit.

For a moment we just lie there, settling into the pleasure. I slide my hand up his chest, just touching him and feeling him. He pulls out of me and lies down beside me.

"I'm scared," I say.

"I won't let anyone hurt you," he murmurs into my hair as I press my body up flush against his naked skin.

"I'm not scared of being hurt…I'm scared of being alone," I admit. I feel like I shouldn't tell him. I feel like I'm giving him a part of myself that I can never get back. And if he doesn't accept it, I don't know how I will ever recover. "I'm scared you will leave me."

He's silent for a long moment and my stomach tightens. He's going to tell me I have to go. That I am unsafe with him and the best place for me would be far away. But I know that I could handle it. I always do.

"The moment I realized that I would never see anything again, I felt my world compress. I felt it tighten and tighten like a noose around my neck. I have never noticed how close the walls around me were until I could no longer see them. They were so close that I couldn't even reach out anymore. But…I realized that was wrong. I realized…that I can still see…when someone helps paint the world for me. You have given me sight again, Felix, I am not going to push you away. I am scared something will happen to you but…I won't push you away," he says.

"I can handle that," I say.

Why is it that the first person to ever notice me is a man that can no longer see me?

CHAPTER THIRTEEN

The ringing of a phone wakes me up. For a moment my brain tells me to sleep through it since it isn't my ringtone.

"Felix, the phone," Lane says.

"Hmm?"

"Answer the phone," Lane says as he shakes me awake.

I grudgingly reach over and turn on the light, so I can find the ringing phone. "Hello?"

"Good morning, I have a call from a Janice Dixon, would you like to accept?"

"Yes," I say, trying to piece together who that is as my fuzzy mind slowly clears.

"Hello?" the woman says. Her voice is soft, but there's an element of wariness to it that I can easily hear.

"Hi…hold on, I'll give you to Lane," I say.

"Okay…thank you."

I hold the phone out and push it into Lane's hand. He takes it as I draw myself up against him. Not for the comfort, but because I have to hear what's going on.

"Janice?" Lane says.

"Oh God, Lane. You know how good it is to hear from you? Lane…I'm scared."

"What's going on? The department didn't tell me anything since they don't seem to think I'm of any use," he says.

"On Wednesday, James came home for the night. He had heard all about you guys getting ambushed at the hotel, but by the time he'd heard about it, Mick was already heading out to get you. So, he planned to meet up with you in the morning, but he went out and never came back. I was at work, so I didn't even think anything of it. I assumed that's where he was at. When he's busy it's not unusual for him to not text me or anything, but when he didn't call to tell me he was going to be late for supper, I started to get worried. I called his boss, but he said James hadn't shown up. He didn't find it unusual because he thought he was dealing with your situation. It's been four days now. Why would they want him? He wasn't even involved, was he? Oh God, Lane...what are they going to do to him?"

"Janice, he knows nothing about it. I don't know why they would even want him, okay? I'll find him though. You mind if I come over and take some of James's equipment?"

"No, of course not. Take anything you want," she says.

"Alright, we'll be over in a bit."

"Okay," she says. "Thank you, Lane."

"Of course," he says as he hangs up.

"I'm sure I don't have to retell you any of that," Lane says.

"Nope," I say as I take the phone from him and hang it up. "I'm a superior eavesdropper."

He snorts. "Is that what you're calling it?"

"Yup."

"The really sad thing is that I can tell you're proud of this skill...and it's really not a favorable skill."

"Don't be so jealous, Lane. I'm going to take a shower."

"What time is it?"

"Noon," I say as I glance at the alarm clock that says 6:24.

"What?" he asks, startled.

"I know. You slept a long time, especially when we're all like…in a hurry to not die and stuff," I say.

His surprised expression disappears. "It's not noon," he says. "You're so annoying."

I laugh as I get up. "It's around six-thirty," I say.

"I take back every nice thing I said to you last night," he says.

"Well, I take back all the nice things I said to you as well," I say with a grin. "I regret opening up to you."

He tries to bite back his smile. "I regret asking you to open up for me."

"Good," I say.

"Good," he says with a laugh. "You're such a brat."

"Maybe," I say.

I head into the bathroom and pee before brushing my teeth. Lane just smacks the door open and steps inside without bothering to knock. I spit the toothpaste out in the sink and look up at him. "What if I was taking a shit?"

"Not like I can see anything," he says. "You want to know the worst thing about being blind?"

"Not seeing anything?"

"No, it's not seeing the look on your face when I leave your ass here and never come back," he says.

I laugh as I stare at him in surprise. "That's *harsh*. Alright, alright. What's annoying about it?"

"Sitting down to take a piss so I don't pee on everything. It's so gross in public places because you're like is the toilet seat down? Is there a lid? And you have to feel around and it's disgusting."

"You could just…ask me, you know?" I say. "Here, I'll put the lid up for you."

I reach over and put the toilet lid *and* seat up for him then step back to watch.

"Thanks," he says, and I *almost* feel bad about it, until I watch him sit down and nearly fall into the toilet.

He jumps up as laughter escapes me. "I'm going to murder you," he says as he grabs for me.

I rush through the open door, but I can't stop laughing as the naked man chases me.

"I take back every nice thing I have *ever* said about you," he says as he follows my laughter as I back away. Eventually, he has me cornered against the door leading out into the hallway.

I put my hands up as I am pressed into the corner. "I'm sorry, Lane. It was an accident," I say. "I thought you said you wanted to try standing up to pee."

"No, I didn't say that!" He grabs me around the waist and starts dragging me toward the bathroom.

"You still care about me, right?"

"No! Not at all," he says as I struggle to get away, but the man's arms are like vise grips. I struggle and wiggle, but he's holding me far too tight as he drags me over to the toilet.

"What are you doing?" I ask, suddenly alarmed.

"I'm going to stick your face in the toilet since you find it so funny."

"No! DON'T YOU DARE!" I yell. "I thought you couldn't find the toilet."

"Oh, let me show you how well I can find it," he says as he drags me. I grab onto the bathroom counter and refuse to let go as he tugs me.

"Lane! Please! It was just a joke! Your butt washes off, my face won't! I'll get some disease."

"Good, I hope it's as horrid as your personality," he says as he lets me go.

"No, you don't. You love my personality," I say as I head over to the shower. He is messing with the toilet himself as I climb into the shower.

I adjust the water before sinking back into it. Lane yanks the shower curtain open and feels his way into the bathtub. He grabs me by the shoulders and shoves me out of the way before stepping under the water. I slip my hand around him and turn the knob all the way to cold.

He jumps forward, out of the water, and slams into me. I nearly slip on the edge of the tub but manage to grab onto Lane's arm to steady myself. Before I know it, he's grabbed me and spun me around, holding me under the frigid water.

"Stop! Stop!" I push against him and struggle, but he just smiles at me. The water is like ice pounding down on my head.

"Why? Why are you so mean?"

"I don't know, Lane," I admit as I push against him. "I guess I didn't get enough love as a child." He has planted his feet and my measly weight is doing nothing to move him. "Lane, it's so cold that I can't even admire the flexing of your arms as you pin me in place."

That's when I realize that I can just reach behind me and change the temperature, so I do.

"Alright, Lane, we need to talk."

"About?" he asks as he lets go of me now that I'm not struggling. A compliant victim is never as much fun.

"I don't know...maybe about all this stuff that's going on. This Red guy is doing all this shit, why can't you just arrest him? I mean...isn't that an option?" I ask as I squeeze some shampoo out of the small complimentary bottle.

"Victor Red actually has no felonies. He's never been to jail. He's never been caught with drugs, weapons, nothing. He's never done anything illegal...that we can blame him for. We need to prove that he's involved in the distribution of drugs. That was what I was doing when I was working for him."

"Ooh...are you a bad boy turned good?" I ask as I put the shampoo in my hair before handing him the bottle. "That sounds sexy."

"No, I was working undercover. That was my job. We, of course, have an idea of what is going on, but we can't pin any of the higher-ups because they never do anything wrong. They're running a hundred percent legitimate company dealing with loans. Victor Red is smart, he never does anything illegal, so he can never get anything pinned on him. He has men that work under him *just for that*. If he wants someone shot, he has a man for that. We catch the man, we arrest him, Victor Red is out one man, so he hires another. We weren't accomplishing *anything*. The Chicago Police Department had suspicions he was trafficking drugs. But because there was no solid proof, nothing had come of it until a cop nosing in the area had been murdered. The case was then passed over to homicide, which is where James and García work. As they started digging, they began to suspect that the roots of this organization went much deeper than they could ever imagine. So that's when I was brought in. My job is working as an undercover agent. I do not belong to their department, but I was working with them because it is technically still their case. It was my job to find out more. If it was a drug case, it would move over to the DEA's hands.

"It was hard to get anywhere in Red's organization, but I have a talent with weapons that most don't have. It helped me rise faster than I should have. It also caused me to have more eyes on me. I started in security and slowly started to work my way up. I was careful. I lived that life and it was hard as fuck to live. While working undercover, I didn't associate with anyone from the department other than my handler. I had been involved with the operation for four months when my handler was killed while working another case.

"But I had finally gotten close to Victor Red when things started to go wrong. After my handler died, Walsh put me with good ol' Mick Reed. He was supposed to be my new handler and he was good at it. But looking back now, I should have realized that after my first handler died and Reed became my new partner, I didn't lunge up the hierarchy as I had been before. I think they weren't yet sure what to do with me, but I still worked with them for a couple of weeks. Why I didn't suspect Reed was because he helped me. He helped me look deeper into all of it. I was so close to having all the information I needed. Close enough that if I'd have kept going, it would have ruined Red. It would have given us the proof to put that man away for a long time, but they got to me. When I went too deep they made sure to stop me."

He slips around me to get back into the water where he washes the shampoo out of his hair.

"They tied me up and asked what intel I had. They tried getting the information out of me. How much do the police know? Where was my information? What information did I have? Red stayed out of it. I think he might have come in once, but I'm not sure. He never touched me. The man that did this to me was arrested. They could find absolutely no ties between him and Red. When held in court he wove some tale about this happening because of a case I was on years ago. Again, Red knew just what to do and what to stay to get out any situation he's put into.

"Thankfully...I wasn't with them long. They wouldn't have stopped with my eyes. They'd have kept going until I gave them something they wanted. The only reason that I got away was that they were being lax. I guess when you're dealing with a guy you've just blinded, you tend to think they're helpless. I managed to get out and get far enough away that someone found me. But what the fuck did I gain out of any of it? Nothing. And now everyone sees me as useless."

"So...we go in and get something," I say.

"Don't be an idiot," Lane says as he shuts the shower off and gets out. I'm still covered in the soap since he'd been hogging the water, so I turn it back on and step under it. "Let's take it one step at a time. Right now, we'll stop at James's, talk to his wife, and grab some clothes. Then we'll move forward."

"Okay," I say. "But don't forget your newest asset."

"Which is?"

"Me. I'm really damn good at stealing things," I say.

"I'm not putting you in danger."

I don't fight him because I know that right now, he's not going to agree to anything I say. But I'll get him to see my side of it.

We get dressed in our dirty clothes from yesterday, which are actually Mick's. The shirt is so long on me that I could wear it as a dress and too tight on Lane. Needless to say, we look sexy as we leave the hotel and walk down the street with Copper between us.

When we reach James's apartment, we can at least figure out how to find the right door.

I knock on it and when the door opens, a pretty woman steps out. Her hair is dyed dark brown with blonde roots showing. It's thrown up into a messy bun and her makeup looks like it's been on for a few days at least. She rushes forward and grabs onto Lane, hugging him tightly. He seems a little startled, like he hadn't been expecting it, before wrapping his arms around her.

"Lane, please help me," she says as her voice cracks.

"We'll find him," Lane says as he squeezes her.

She pulls back. "I'm sorry...please come in." She steps into the apartment, but Lane waits for me to lead him inside. "Grab anything you need. I have the keys to his weapons safe," she says as she ushers us into the homey apartment. It's nice and looks well lived in. The kitchen and living room are all one big room and in the middle of it is a table with a cat sitting on top.

The moment the cat sees Copper it flees. Copper's ears perk up, but he doesn't seem to care as the cat runs in place on the linoleum a moment before getting enough grip to propel itself out of the room.

"Right in here," Janice says as she hurries through an open door.

We follow her into a second bedroom. It looks like it is being used for storage, but there is a small futon crammed in the corner. She goes to the closet where she kneels before a safe and sticks the key into it. She pulls it open and steps back, so we can access it.

"Lane...do you need help with any of it?" she asks.

"No, I'm fine," Lane says.

"Are you guys hungry? Have you eaten breakfast?"

"We could eat something," Lane says.

"I'll go make you breakfast." She turns to the door before her eyes catch mine. "I'm sorry, I never introduced myself. I'm Janice."

"Hi," I say. "I'm Felix."

"James has said really good things about you," she says. "I'm glad this arrangement is working out, but I'm sorry you're getting swept up into this mess."

"It's not your fault. It's all Lane's fault," I assure her.

She smiles weakly before leaving the room. I walk over to the safe and pull Lane down next to me. I swing the door open and look in at a really nice collection of guns.

"Ooh."

"Can you tell me what they are?" Lane asks as he hovers over the safe.

"There are some little pew pews and a couple of big pew pews," I say.

"You're useless."

"I don't know what the heck they are! There are a few handguns and a rifle? I don't know."

"Hand me one of the handguns," he says.

I tentatively pick up the heavy object of mass destruction and hand it over to Lane. He holds it in one hand and feels his way down it with the other. After setting it to the side, he holds his hand out for the next one, so I hand it to him. He does the same to this one, and then the last handgun before passing the first one back to me.

"Put that one away," he says so I do. "Ammo?"

I see that there are a couple of boxes at the bottom of the safe. "Yeah."

"Grab it," he says as he holds his hand out.

"Mind me asking why you need *three* guns?" I ask. "I wouldn't think a blind man would need *one*."

"I don't like Reed's gun," he says. "The other is for you."

"HA! Funny, Lane. Funny."

"Thanks," he says as he stands up. "Ask Janice if James has a spare holster around here somewhere."

"Yeah, yeah. Hopefully, it has three spots for all three of your guns," I say. "Because I'm not touching one."

"You want to stay with me?" Lane asks.

I stare at him, knowing this question is going to come back and bite me in the ass. "Yes…"

"Then you're going to carry a gun."

"You *blind* have a better chance of doing something with a gun than I do," I say.

"I know, but sometimes you need it for show."

"Then can I have something awesome? Like a battle axe? I mean, I definitely wouldn't fuck with a guy toting a battle axe around."

"Those noodle arms couldn't lift a battle axe, let alone carry it around all day," he says.

"These noodle arms have saved your ass," I remind him as I get up to find Janice.

When I find her, I almost wish I hadn't. She's sitting on the kitchen floor, sobbing. It's not that I'm heartless, it's that I have no idea how to comfort a human being. My mom would comfort me by calling me a pussy and walking away. I don't think that would work in this situation, so I kind of stop and just stare. But she has already heard me and shows it by looking right at me.

"Hey…" I say quietly. Is that a good way to start? Probably not. I walk over to her and kneel in front of her. "You alright?"

She quickly wipes at her eyes and her running nose. "I'm fine. Sorry."

"You sure? Why don't you stay with someone so you're not here alone?"

She nods. "I will…I just…thought if he came home…I needed to be here. I just…I know what happened to Lane, and I just…James is different than Lane. James isn't as…Lane…he's better at this."

"Hey, it's okay," I say as I wrap my arms around her. "We'll do everything we can to help, okay?"

She nods. "I know you guys will."

"I don't know much about this whole…stuff that's going on, but I think you would be safer somewhere else. Why don't you go to your parents or something? When James comes home, he's not going to just come here and not contact you."

She nods as she wipes her eyes. "I know, I'm being stupid."

"Of course not," I say. "You're worried."

I stand up, and since I can't see any Kleenexes, I grab her a napkin. She wipes her eyes and then blows her nose on it. As she tosses the napkin in the trash, she takes a deep breath, so I hold my hand down to her. She takes it and I pull her up to her feet.

"Did you come out here because you needed something?" she asks.

"Lane wanted to know if James had a holster or anything for his guns?"

"Yeah, let me find them," she says. "Do you guys need clothes as well? You both look a little out of place. Get Lane and meet me in my room."

"Alright, thanks," I say as I head back to retrieve Lane. When I walk in he's standing by the door looking upset. "You alright?" I ask.

"Yeah, just makes it harder to hear Janice cry," he says. "Hard to stay composed, I guess."

"I know," I say as I grab his hand and squeeze it gently. "I've lived in this world long enough to know that not everything always turns out the way you hope and expect, but we are going to try our hardest to make sure it does this time, alright?"

He nods, so I give his hand a tug and pull him after me. We walk into Janice's bedroom where she is tearing clothes out of the closet and tossing them on the bed.

"Lane, you'd fit in James's clothes, wouldn't you?" she asks from where she is buried in the closet.

"Yeah, he's about the same height as me," he says.

"Just…honestly, grab anything, look through the dresser, the closet, whatever you want. And Felix, you'd fit in a pair of my pants, right?"

I want to tell her no. I want to disagree with all my might that I would fit into her pants, but I grudgingly nod. "Yeah…probably," I say in defeat.

She rummages around her drawer and holds up some pants. "These should fit, and grab anything you want from the closet. Honestly anything," she says. "I'm going to make you guys French toast. Do you like French toast?"

"That would be amazing," Lane says, and she quickly leaves.

"What's our plan?" I ask. "Like what kind of clothes are reasonable?"

"We're going to a posh club. Find something nice," he says.

I rummage through the clothes on the bed and hand Lane a pair of dark blue jeans before going over to the closet. I find a nice rich red button-up and a black suit jacket that I grab and head over to Lane. "Is red good?"

"Yeah," he says as he pulls his shirt off. I hold the new shirt up and guide his arm into it. When he pulls it straight in the front, I start buttoning it.

"What time does the club open?"

"Not until tonight, but I'm not sure what else we should do before then. It's not like we can run in guns blazing. Especially when you won't even shoot one."

"True," I say as I move down to the next button. The shirt is a little loose on him, but it fits better than Mick's.

"Arms up," I say as I push one sleeve over his arm.

"What is this?"

"A suit jacket," I say.

"We're not going to a wedding."

"Lane, Lane, Lane. Have you ever watched *Lucifer?*"

"No."

"Yeah, well, you should because he looks damn sexy."

"Are you just…trying to tell me who you have wet dreams about or something?"

"He wears this sexy suit or vest for the whole show. I'm just trying to up your sexiness a bit," I say as I leave it unbuttoned in the front. Then I step back just to eye my masterpiece. "And you do look mighty fine."

I pull on Janice's jeans and die a little inside when they're too long on me, so I pretend that it looks hotter if I roll them up. Then I go to her closet and leaf through it until I find a plain black shirt and pull a gray blazer on. The outfit is a tad feminine, but it's better than most things I've worn lately.

"Go see if a pair of James's sunglasses is on the dresser," he says.

I walk over to the dresser that is very messy. There are books, papers, clothes, but no sunglasses. Instead, I find a winter hat which I grab and head over to Lane. I pull it onto his head and pull it down over his eyes.

"There ya go. Now you're pulling off the Daredevil look," I say with a grin.

"I feel like an idiot," he says.

"Yeah, but you look like a superhero," I say.

"If this is how I have to look to be a superhero, then I have no interest," he says as he tosses the hat in the general direction of the dresser. It misses by a foot, so I pick it up and toss it on top.

"No sunglasses...ooh, look at this cute hat," I say as I pick up a flat cap hat.

"No, I'm not wearing one of James's ridiculous hats. He thinks he's from the twenties or whenever those things were popular."

"We're blending in," I say as I pop it on his head. "Oh...you actually look good with it on."

"Why do you sound surprised? It tells me that your original intention was to put it on because you thought it *wouldn't* look good."

I laugh. "Come on," I say as I pull him after me.

"Did you find everything you need?" Janice asks as she peeks through the open door. She actually smiles when she sees Lane. "Nice hat, Lane."

"Yeah...James would be ecstatic," Lane says.

CHAPTER FOURTEEN

When we're finished eating, Janice drops us off at an indoor shooting range on her way to her parents. A place that we definitely didn't need to go to, but Lane insisted we stop.

"What are we doing here?" I ask.

"García is meeting us here," he says. "And while we wait, I'm going to teach you how to shoot."

"Yay me," I say as I head into the building.

The man at the counter looks up in surprise. "Lane?"

"Hey, Harold," Lane says.

"I'm so sorry about…what happened," he says as he gets up and walks over to us, just so he can hover awkwardly near us.

"Thanks, I'm just gonna mess around a bit."

"Of course, please, go ahead, take as long as you want. You need anything, just holler," he says.

I start walking, a little unsure of where to go as Harold stares at us, unsure of what to do or say.

"I hate this. I hate seeing people that I know," he grumbles once we are out of earshot.

"Well, it's a good thing you're blind then," I say.

He stops walking, and I slowly look over at him as he starts laughing. "Why do I even try with you? It's like I'm bothered about something, I tell you, and you make fun of me."

"But are you upset now? Or are you laughing?"

He shakes his head. "Fine, thanks…I needed that."

I smile as I turn away. "I get what you mean though. It must be hard. I think you need to just try something else," I say. "When they're like 'hey' and you hear that moment of sympathy you go 'I love that new haircut, it looks so much nicer than the last time I saw you!'"

Lane starts laughing. "You imagine if I said that? It would confuse everyone."

"I know," I say. "That's the plan. Then, as they awkwardly try to think of what to say, you give them a high five and head off."

He shakes his head. "I'll try that."

We stop at one of the lanes or whatever shooter people call them. It's like an indoor shooting range, which I thought was a thing only cops visited when they needed to look emotionally dramatic in a movie. But I guess unlike out in the country, it isn't as easy to just set down a shooting range in the middle of a city. Lane gets me set up with protective gear, then steps up to the railing with me. He sets the gun in my hand as I stare at it.

"I'm not supposed to like…sign a waiver or something so that if someone shoots me, I can't sue?"

"I don't know, probably."

"You come here often?" I ask.

"Used to," he says before taking the gun from me and firing it. I look at the hole right in the bullseye. "So much that I can shoot the middle without having to look."

"Well…that was kind of hot," I say. "How about instead of teaching me to shoot, I step back, you take your clothes off, and I watch you shoot while I jerk off?"

He snorts and puts the gun in my hand. "Come on, I won't be distracted," he says as he takes my left hand in his. "You already know where the sights are. Then down here," he says as he slides my finger across the barrel toward the handle, "is the safety. Do not ever take it off unless you plan to shoot something and never shoot unless you're prepared to kill someone."

"Can I have my battle axe now?"

"Nope. You're too stiff," he says as he runs his hands down my arms up to my shoulders. "Relax."

I try to relax my shoulders as I hold the gun steady. He reaches down and taps my thigh with his hand.

"Spread your legs a bit, you're off balance."

"Ooh," I say. "Sounds fun."

"Shut it," he says as he kicks the heel of my foot.

"Ow!"

"Move your foot. Have a solid stance. You should be solid enough that if someone came running at you while you're shooting and hits you, you don't fall."

"Uh huh," I say as I move my foot forward.

Lane pushes me, causing me to stumble and nearly fall into the half wall that keeps people from going on a suicide mission.

"Not solid enough," he says as he barks orders at me until he can push me without sending me stumbling. I'm surprised at how much a little positioning and weight change helps.

"I may not be badass, but I look badass," I decide.

"Take aim," he says, so I do. "Now steady your breath and hold it. See how much steadier you are when you hold your breath? If your frame is not perfect, if it is not still, you will make a mistake. And when dealing with guns, a mistake could cost you your life. Alright, now step back and relax."

I do and look up at him.

"Again. Try to remember that position. Perfect it."

I step up into the position, so he touches my shoulders and hips to try to feel my stance.

"Much better," he says. "Now shoot the target."

I switch the safety off, line the sights, hold my breath and pull the trigger. The gun has a kick that surprises me. I guess I hadn't realized that there would be much of a kick at all. The smell leaving the gun fills the air as I look at the target. Shockingly, I've hit the target. It's about three rings off the middle, but I am still surprised I'd made it that far.

I'm also surprised to find that I like it. It is…empowering. I feel like I am in control of a situation.

"Where'd it hit?"

"I don't know…like the third ring."

"That's good," he says.

"It is?" I ask.

"Yes. Do it again."

I continue to shoot the target until I hear García's voice.

"Hey, Lane! Good shot, Felix!" he says as he claps me on the back.

"Thanks," I say as I switch the safety on. "I think I'll be better than Lane in no time!"

García laughs. "That's the spirit! So, I brought the stuff you wanted. You can also borrow my car since I can use the company car if I need to. But if you get caught doing this *I was not the one that helped*. Got it? Now all your paperwork is under review until they decide what to do with you. What tests you need to take, where you can safely work. Blah blah, you've heard it all before. Speaking of which…I lost my damn badge again. The third time I've lost it this year. Oh well, I just won't tell Walsh, and it'll eventually turn up," he says confidently.

"That's strange," Lane says as I pretend that I am deeply concerned by nodding my head and furrowing my eyebrows.

"That's awful. I'm sure it'll turn up. Until then, you could wave around one of those stripper badges?" I suggest.

He laughs. "But then I'd have to wear the outfit as well or I don't think it would look legit," he says with a grin.

"I'm not sure anyone would complain," I say.

Lane turns his head in my direction and I can see the annoyance. "Really?"

"What? Someone else said that," I say.

"I'm not *deaf*."

"Are you two dating? You two are just perfect together," García says.

"Just give him the keys to the car," Lane says.

***

We have to park the car a mile away from the club, or at least it seems that far. When I shut the car off, Lane sets the gun I had practiced with on my lap. It may have been fun to shoot at the range, but that doesn' mean I am in any way interested in carrying it around and aiming it at people.

"Um…I can't just walk around with a gun!"

"Why can't you?" he asks. "Your jacket will hide it. Secure it and keep your jacket tight. You have García's badge, so if anyone asks, flash it. Simple."

"Hmm…" Simple, he says. Lane's idea of simple is like a high-speed car chase while gunning down fifteen cars.

"Put it *on*," he orders.

"Yes, sir," I say as I pick the gun up and slide it under the driver's seat as he watches me. "It's on."

"You're such a liar," he says as he gets out of the car.

"What are you talking about? It's on!" I say like I am shocked that he would doubt me.

He sticks his head back in the car. "I'm not *deaf!*"

I snort and open the car door. Copper whines from the back seat as he watches us. "Sorry buddy, we won't be long." Poor Copper has to stay in the car since we could probably blend in easier without the dog.

We walk down the sidewalk, away from the apartments, and toward the bright lights of a city not yet asleep. I see the butt end of a line on the other side of the street. As soon as the light flashes for us to pass, we head toward them side-by-side. The line is long and winds around the corner and up to a brightly lit club.

"What's this huge line for?" I ask.

"It's probably the line to get in the club we are going to."

"What?" I ask, slightly alarmed. It doesn't appear like the line ever moves by the way people are sitting on the ground or watching videos on their phone. At this rate, we won't get in until next Sunday. "We should have been here hours ago then."

"No one of importance shows up early. Walk up to the bouncer and ask to go in. If you're hot enough, he'll let you in."

"What? That's not going to work."

"They want attractive, rich people in there," Lane explains as he adjusts the sunglasses he took from García's car.

"Well, then that means I would have to at least be one of those things and I'm not!" At least my bruises aren't as sharp on my face or they probably wouldn't have let me in even if I had waited in the line all day.

"Come on." Lane doesn't sound at all concerned about this, making me question what kind of image he has procured of me in his head.

We walk past the line of impatient people wearing barely any clothes and over to where the bouncer is reaming some guy for trying to get in. He is an attractive guy as well, which just reconfirms my assumption.

"He just turned away a hot guy!" I say.

"Was he hotter than you?"

"Yes!"

"No, he wasn't."

"You don't even know what I look like!"

Lane pushes me forward, and I stumble into the bouncer. It is like hitting a brick wall of pure muscle and raging testosterone.

"Hey there," I say with a smile as the big, hulking man stares down at me. "Will you let me in if I show you a magic trick?"

"No." Not even a moment of hesitation.

"Aw? Really? I was going to do a magic trick where I pulled your wallet out from behind your ear, but now I don't know what to do with your wallet," I say as I hold it up.

When Lane had pushed me, I *probably* didn't need to slam into the man, but it gave me a chance to lift his wallet right out of his back pocket. The man stares at me for a moment, and I know that this will go one of two ways:

1) My face will get smashed in.
2) The man will be impressed.

He stares down at me with his narrowed eyes that look black in the blue hue of the club sign.

"How'd you do that?" he asks as he plucks his wallet out of my hand. He flips it open and checks that everything is in there.

"It's easy," I say. "It's a trick of distracting a person."

I reach up and pat his hand as I slip my other hand in his front pocket and pull out his phone. "Like just now, you were expecting another trick, so you followed my hand while my other hand was busy taking your phone."

I hold it up in front of my face with a grin and the man stares at me in shock.

"That's my phone?" he asks.

"That's your phone," I say as I hand it over. "What do you want me to steal next?"

The big man laughs. "How did I not feel that?"

"You were focused on the hand that was touching you because you thought you could catch something. Simple trick, really. Now the real trick is the next trick I do," I say with a grin.

His eyes are locked onto every move I make. "Alright, alright," he says as he folds his arms over his chest and watches closely.

"Are you paying attention? You won't see this one coming," I say with a wink. "Ready?"

"Oh, you're not getting anything past me," he says defiantly.

I grab Lane's wrist and pull him as I slowly walk by the guy, never breaking eyesight with him as he watches my every move. "Thanks for letting me in."

"What? I didn't tell you that you can go in," he says.

"That was the final trick. Me walking right in. See ya around!" I say as I wave to him before heading in through the door.

I hear the man laugh and he never comes after me, so I continue into the club.

"Magic tricks?" Lane says skeptically.

"It worked."

"Just be glad he didn't punch you in the face," he says.

"Oh, I am," I say as the music drowns out my voice.

The floor and walls feel like they're shaking with the deep bass of the song. The lights are flashing while sweaty, half-clothed bodies move all along the dance floor. Past them are a few steps leading up to a higher level that creates a horseshoe around the dance floor. There are tables and couches hidden in the blue hue of lighting. To the back is a large bar where people are eagerly waiting for drinks.

"What's the plan?"

"We're looking for a man named Ryan Gibson. He works for Red, but he is an informant. His job is to get information on people and he hunts down the ones that don't pay their loans. I don't think he knows me enough to recognize me since we've never met formally. So, we are going to try and locate him, get him alone, and get some information out of him. So be on the lookout for a man that's about six feet tall, late thirties with one of those ponytail bun things. He thinks he's the hottest thing that God ever dropped into this cesspool. I've only ever seen him wearing suits and a ring on each finger."

I walk with him a bit, but this Ryan guy isn't too hard to find. He's sitting in the middle of a couch, feet up on the table, surrounded by men and women. There's just something weird about the way he makes it feel like everyone is sitting before him, instead of next to him, like he's a bright light in their lives.

"Found him," I say as I pull Lane over to a table that just cleared out. I sit down as some woman, who'd been heading for it, glares at me. "Is he gay?"

"Doesn't matter."

"Does too."

"You're not flirting with him."

"So, I'll go flirt with him, get him to take me to a hotel, and you'll be there to get the info out of him."

"I can't see shit, how am I going to meet you anywhere?" he asks.

Oops…forgot about that. "Hmm…what's the closest hotel from here?"

"I don't know…probably the Hilton."

"Alright. So, I talk him into going with me. You wait near the car. I tell him I want to drive us to my room at the Hilton or, if he insists on driving, I tell him that I left something in my car and I need it. Hopefully, he follows me. You could wait outside of the club. Or do you think you could find our car? It's on this road, but you'd have to cross two roads. You could ask someone to help you find it." I find that I'm talking quickly because I'm slightly excited about my idea. I think it will work, and it'll show Lane that I can be helpful.

"No."

"Why?" I ask, slightly disappointed.

"You could get hurt."

"You said he's an informant! To me, an informant is like a…gossiper."

"He beats the shit out of people for information."

Um…okay. "I'll be fine." Hopefully.

"No."

"I'm going," I say. "Have one of these pretty ladies walk you out to your car. Tell them your Seeing Eye dog ran off with another man."

"Goddammit, Felix, don't you dare!"

"Too late," I say as I jump up and rush into the crowd.

"Felix!" he yells, but his voice gets drowned in the noise.

Alright, now for my nonexistent plan.

I hover around the floor a bit before I see Ryan get up and head for the bathroom. When I look back at my table, I see that Lane is gone, so I know that even if Lane is not for it, the plan is in motion.

I pretend to be interested in the dancers as I wait for Ryan to return from the bathroom. When he steps out, instead of turning right toward his table, he turns left, so I assume he's heading for the bar. I'm closer, so I head toward it, arriving just a few seconds before he does. When the bartender looks up, he looks right over my head, like I don't exist.

"Another," Ryan says and since he's so cool he doesn't even have to specify what "another" is.

"Coming right up," the man says as he heads off to make the drink.

I look over at Ryan who is staring at his phone. "Do you usually cut in front of people?" I ask.

He glances up from his phone and looks me over from head to toe. I can almost feel his eyes running down my body as I stare at him. "You are so small, I didn't even see you there."

Oh, buddy. You just fucked up. "Ah, I see. You're so in love with yourself that you don't think anyone else exists?"

Shit. Shit. I'm supposed to be getting him to want me, not hate me!

He looks at me in surprise. "Is that what you think?"

"I'm sorry, I can't hear you from way down here," I say as the bartender sets the drink down. "Oh? You said you bought this for me? How gentlemanly of you." I scoop up his drink and head away with it.

I take a sip of it and nearly gag at how strong it is. I typically avoid alcohol after seeing what it does to people. It doesn't mean that I never have a drink, but this stuff is like pouring rubbing alcohol right into my mouth. I try not to grimace as I swallow it.

Instead of taking another wretched sip, I keep walking. I don't even make it to the wall before he steps in front of me.

"If you wanted a drink, all you had to do was ask," he says with a smirk.

"I apologize, I'm much too small to ask for anything."

He grins, and it lights up his handsome face. "I'm sorry. That was rather rude of me. Would you like something else to drink, or are you content with that?"

"I suppose I'll make do with this trash," I say as I grimace at it.

He laughs. "You don't know what that is, do you?"

"Tastes like piss," I say as I question exactly how much this small glass cost.

A mischievous grin slides over his handsome face, telling me just how easy it is for him to talk people into things. "Oh man, you sure are a hard one to please, aren't you?"

"Just means that you have to be pretty damn good to please me," I say as I reach out and give his tie a tug.

His eyebrows arch as he leans back against the wall and takes a sip of his acid. "Oh, I know I'm good."

"When men say things like that to me, I automatically assume they're just not that good," I say apologetically. "Like...they're trying to make up for something." I make a show of glancing down at his pants.

He shakes his head in disbelief. His attitude tells me that it's not too often someone doesn't worship the ground he walks on. "You are a piece of work. I haven't seen you around here before."

"First time," I say.

"Is it? Who did you come with?" he asks.

"I came alone," I say.

He raises an eyebrow. "And how did you get in?"

"I showed the bouncer a magic trick and walked right in. He was *quite* impressed," I say as I give his tie a flick.

His eyebrows furrow as he glances at the door. "Now my bouncer is letting magicians in? I may need to have a talk with him."

"I'm pretty impressive," I purr.

"I can tell," he says, and I smile at him. He steps up closer to me until his side is pressed against mine. "Would you like me to get you something else to drink? I can have them on it immediately."

"You own this place?" I ask.

"I do. Do you like it?" he asks.

"It's alright," I say. "I've seen better."

He looks down at me in surprise and then starts laughing. "I'd love to see what it takes to impress you."

"I would too because right now it's just not happening," I say apologetically.

"Why don't you come join me and my friends?" he suggests.

I shrug. "I hope they're more exciting than you. Where are they?"

This man clearly isn't used to someone acting like this toward him because his eyes get wide and he gets this half smile on his face like he's not sure whether to laugh it off or just be completely confused.

"Right this way," he says as he starts walking toward the couch I'd first seen him on. It's overflowing with humans and the only spot still open is just the right size for his ass. He takes my hand and leads me between the mass of people and the table, to his spot on the couch. He sits down and pats his knee like he expects me to sit on his lap.

"Seriously? Am I supposed to call you daddy? Or you going to bend me over your knee and spank my ass?" I ask.

He grins at me as he takes a sip of his drink before setting it down on the table. "Come on, sit."

I stare down at him before pouring my drink into his glass and setting the empty one on the table. I place one hand on the couch behind his head, put my knee between his legs, and lean down to him so my mouth is against his ear. "The only way I'm sitting on your lap is if your cock is inside of me. Now have a nice night," I say as I stand up and head for the door.

CHAPTER FIFTEEN

I get about three strides before Ryan grabs my hand and pulls me around to face him. "I can arrange that."

"Can you?" I ask. "Because I'm kind of bored of this place." I look down at the hand holding my wrist. Each finger has a ring on it and I can't help but wonder how hard it would be to steal one or two.

"I have a room in the back," he says.

"Ew, gross. No. I'm going to my hotel. You can join me or not. Your choice," I say as I pull my hand away from him and push my way through the sweaty dancing bodies. I slip through the door as he steps up next to me.

"Do you always get everything you want?" he asks as we step outside.

"More often than not. Just ask this guy. You like me too, don't you?" I ask the bouncer.

"Hey Ryan, you should see this kid's magic!" the man says.

"Yeah…the thing I'm very concerned about is my bouncer being swayed by a magic trick," Ryan says as he follows me down the road. "I can drive."

"No, but thanks."

"You just have to have everything your way, don't you?" he asks, but I can tell he's enjoying it.

"Oh, wait until I have you in bed," I say.

He stares at me for a moment and then grins. "Oh, I can't," he says as he slides his hand around my waist and pulls me tighter against him. My hip presses against his as I grin up at him.

Alright…now I'm putting all my hope in Lane. What if he can't even find the car? He's so damn stubborn that I could see him refusing to ask anyone to help him to the car or, knowing my luck, he was probably hit on the road. If something has gone wrong on his end, what the hell do I do with this guy? Run away?

This is a bad idea. Why do I have such bad ideas? It's because I never think. I *think* I have an idea, but I don't think it through, I just do it.

"Where's your car?" he asks.

Oh my God. What if I don't recognize the car? I don't even remember what color it is!

I'm going to die. I'm going to die.

"Uh…in this area," I say as I keep walking.

Was it green?

No!

Blue…ish…black?

Fuck.

I stop at a crosswalk and look around as I try to remember where we parked. It was along a road, I do know that. The light changes and I step across the road as Ryan starts blabbing about something. It's probably something about how awesome or rich he is, but all I can think about is not letting the panic show on my face.

"What hotel are you staying at?"

"Hilton," I mutter.

"We could have walked there by now," he says as he points behind him.

"Not that Hilton," I say.

"There's another in the area?" he asks as he tries to think.

"Are you questioning my memory?" I ask.

"Of course not," he says as he holds his hands up in mock defense.

Well…I am.

I see a car that *I think* might be the car we borrowed from García, but Copper isn't in the back seat. Did Lane put him somewhere?

I look around to see if Copper is waiting anywhere. I don't see him, so I turn my attention back to the car. It must be the right car.

Please be the right car!

"Is this your car?" he asks.

"Yeah?"

"Yeah? Are you asking me?" he asks as he stares at me like I'm something to be curious about.

"It's a rental…I kind of forget what it looks like," I say.

"Hit the beeper on the keys."

Yeah…those are with Lane.

"No, this is it," I say, trying to sound confident as I walk up to the driver's door.

Please be it, please be it.

He walks around to the passenger door as I look around a bit nervously. What is Lane's plan? Maybe he didn't have a plan because I just jumped up like an idiot because I wanted to prove myself to him. I wanted to prove that I can be useful.

I pull on the door and it gives, so that is a good thing. I'm pretty sure not too many cars in this area are left unlocked. But what now? I don't have the keys and I don't know what I'm doing.

Ryan opens the passenger door and gets inside as he grins at me. "Where are we off to now?" he asks as he sets a hand on my upper thigh before sliding it up until I can feel his fingers brush my cock.

"It's a secret," I whisper as I see something move behind me.

I turn to look, just as Ryan is slammed back against his seat. He jerks his hand away from me and grabs for his throat as Lane holds a thin rope against it.

I just stare in shock as Ryan's body jerks and flails as he digs at his neck, trying to grip the rope enough to pull it away. Then, with one last jerk of his hand, his body stills and he slumps down into the seat. Lane quickly loosens the rope and Ryan's body falls forward. His head slams down onto the dashboard as I slowly look over at Lane.

"You alright?" Lane asks.

"Ha ha!" I say, but I'm not sure why because I'm not sure what part of this is funny. "Oh my *God,* Lane. Why did you let me be such an idiot?"

He looks over at me, alarmed. "Are you alright?" he asks. "Did he hurt you?"

"No! No! I'm fine. I was just…there was no plan. I had no plan. I just jumped up and ran off," I say.

"Yeah. I *know.* And if you ever do that shit again, I'll strangle *you* instead. What if you got hurt?"

"I'm sorry," I say, really meaning it. I should have listened to him.

"Good," he says as he pulls me toward him and kisses my forehead. "But…if I'm being honest, this worked out really well."

"How long will he be out for?"

"As long as I didn't kill him, probably not long," he says nonchalantly.

"What?" I ask in alarm as I reach over to Ryan, but when I press my fingers under his nose, I can feel his breath. "Okay, what's the plan?"

"Oh, you're going to ask for a plan this time? You're not just going to jump out of the car and do it? It's kind of weird to ask about a plan with a man who has dedicated *years* of his life to this kind of work. You're going to ask him?"

"No…I just thought I'd give you a chance to make a plan, so you would feel better about yourself."

"Great, thanks. He's going in the trunk."

"Awesome, so when I get pulled over, I won't just go to jail for assault but also kidnapping because no one is going to believe me when I tell them the blind man did it."

Lane feels around in the back seat until I hear a crinkling of a bag. He holds it out to me, so I look inside at the duct tape and cable ties.

"Where'd you get this stuff?" I ask.

"García grabbed it for me."

"And when he asked why you needed it, what did you tell him?"

"That you were into S and M."

"Great. Great," I say as I grab the bag and drop it into my lap.

"Put the cable ties around his wrists. Make sure they're tight," he says.

I pick up a thick cable tie before reaching over and pulling his hands together. I wrap it around both wrists and tighten it, but I'm kind of scared it's going to cut the circulation off.

"Now wrap duct tape around them just to make sure," he says. "Duct tape all the way down to his fingertips so he doesn't start playing with shit in the trunk."

"Okay," I say as I start it at his wrists, and then wrap the duct tape around his hands until none of his fingers are showing. "Now what?"

"Put tape over his mouth, but make sure it's not obstructing his nose in any way," Lane says as he hovers over the seat.

"Okay..." I rip off a big piece of the tape and press it against Ryan's mouth. I press it down firmly as I hold him up against the seat.

"Pop the trunk. I'll carry him to it while you make sure no one is looking, alright?"

"Yeah," I say as I look around until I find the button. I push it and hear the trunk pop. Ryan moans, so I quickly get out and look around. The street is dark this far out, and most life seems to be asleep, but there are cars driving by every few moments. "Lane...there are cars..."

He gets out of the car with the duct tape and holds it out to me. I take it from him, unsure of what I am doing with it. "Inside the trunk is an emergency pull. It'll look like...a glow in the dark oval. I want you to tape that up against the trunk lid. He shouldn't be able to reach it anyway, but just in case, we need to keep him from seeing it right away. Then, while you're looking around, there should be a knob to pull that will release the back seats. Pull that."

I scavenge around until I see the glow in the dark pull that Lane is talking about. I rip off some tape and press it firmly against the trunk lid. Finding the seat release takes me a bit longer because it is hidden where I can't see it in the shadows of the trunk. I pull it and hear the seats give as light from the interior of the car peeks in.

"Close the trunk," Lane says as I hear him doing something in the cab of the car.

I slam the trunk closed, and then I rush back to the car where Lane is trying to roll Ryan into the back seat. He has the back seats down, so we can push him into the trunk from the inside. I open the back door and start helping him tug as Ryan moans again.

Ryan's boot gets stuck on the front console, so I yank at his leg and the boot pops free, letting him fall into the back seat like a rag doll. Then we shove his head and chest into the trunk. He's tall and barely fits.

"Before his legs are in, tape them."

I nod and quickly set to work winding the tape around his ankles.

"Now you're going to tape his hands to his ankles."

"More tape? Lane, this guy isn't going anywhere!"

"You'd be surprised what a person can do when they think death is near," Lane says.

"Fine, hold him for me," I say as I force the man into the fetal position. I tape his ankles to his wrists and then push him the rest of the way into the trunk. "Good?"

"Hopefully. Since I can't actually see your work, I'll deem it as mediocre."

"Thanks, doll," I say, and he smiles.

He pushes the back seats up and gets out of the car, and into the passenger seat. I get into the driver's seat and look over at him.

"Alright, now that we have our victim, where exactly are we going with him?"

"Reed's house," Lane says.

"Didn't Mick just try to kill us?" I ask.

"Yes, which is why he won't be at his house. There will be someone watching his house, but when I asked García who was on night watch, he told me it was Yates. And one thing I know about Yates is that he's a shitty-ass worker. He'll either be asleep or playing on his phone."

"He's not going to notice us dragging a human being into the house?" I ask.

"Not at all," he says.

"Okay…" I say suspiciously.

I glance over at the screen on the dashboard of the car and click for the GPS before typing in the address as Lane tells it to me. The back of the car is starting to bounce a bit as I put the car in drive and start down the road.

"This is a bad idea," I say.

"No, we're doing good," Lane says.

"Are we? Because I'm convinced this is a bad idea."

"Don't be."

Sure. Sure.

Lane holds his hand out, so I reach for it. As soon as my fingers brush against his, he squeezes them tightly. I try to pull comfort from his touch.

"Hey, are you doing alright? If you want to back out of this, I don't blame you," he says.

I slow the car as I near a red light. "No…I don't want to back out. I want to help you."

"If you back out of this, you do understand that doesn't mean I'll leave you?"

My stomach tightens as I listen to his words. It's like I hear them, and I understand them, but I'm just not sure I believe them. Everyone leaves me behind eventually. Why wouldn't he? So, despite his assurances, I know that I can't leave. I have to prove to him I'm worth something, that I'm worth keeping around.

"Felix. I'm serious. You could stay with James's wife for a few days and García can help me. I won't leave you," he says.

"I'm fine," I say as the light turns green. "I want to help."

He sighs, and I hear a loud *thump* coming from the trunk. "Felix…"

Something dawns on me at that moment, and I quickly look over at Lane. "Where is my *dog?*"

"Ah…shit," he says.

"*What?* What does that mean, *Lane?*"

"It means we forgot him," he says.

"Where's he at?"

"I put him in the alley, so he didn't draw Gibson's attention to the back seat. He's fine," he says.

"If someone stole my dog, you're going in the trunk with Ryan," I say as I do a U-turn right in the middle of the road, which probably isn't the brightest idea since if I got pulled over, they'd hear Ryan making a ruckus in the trunk. I'm not sure any amount of flashing García's badge would get me out of that one.

"First off, he's not your dog. You stole him. Second, he's a trained dog, he's not going to wander off from his command unless he knows the person asking."

I park in the same spot I'd just left, although the car is now facing the wrong way. "Where is he?"

"Just call him," Lane says, as he rolls the window down. "Copper, come!"

The dog rushes out of the dark alley, and without missing a beat, leaps through the open window onto Lane's lap. He wiggles his tail when he sees me.

"My baby!" I coo.

"You're scrunching my nuts, dog," Lane says as he tries to push him off.

"My poor Copper. Did you think Daddy was going to leave you? No! I wouldn't," I say as I kiss his forehead. He wiggles a little harder as his tail bashes Lane in the face.

"Alright, make out with the dog later," Lane says as he shoves Copper into the back seat.

Copper lands in the back seat and tilts his head as he listens to the ruckus in the trunk.

"I can't believe you," I hiss at Lane.

"The thing is, I can tell you're trying to push all the blame onto me because you feel guilty that you never thought about the dog as you drove away," Lane says.

"No, I'm not," I lie.

He laughs. "Sure."

CHAPTER SIXTEEN

When we open the trunk, Ryan looks *pissed*. His bun is messy, the loose strands are stuck to his sweaty forehead, and his eyes are wide but in an "I'm going to murder you" sort of way. Not the terrified way I would be looking at someone who just shoved me in a trunk and drove me around for forty minutes.

And when he sees me, his look turns even more sour, like if *anyone* else abducted him, it wouldn't be as bad, but I automatically made it ten times worse.

"Ready?" Lane asks. "Reed showed you the pin for the door lock, right?"

I nod and watch as Lane picks Ryan up. Since he pulls him straight up instead of back, Ryan's head smashes into the trunk lid rather hard. Ryan slumps down like a dead weight in Lane's hands which makes Lane stop moving.

"Is he alright?" Lane asks.

"I think you just knocked him out," I say like it is completely fine. Hopefully, it is. "Come on, we're going to get caught."

"Just carrying a drunk friend home," Lane says as he carries the bound and gagged man.

"Remind me to never go drinking with you," I say and Lane laughs.

We'd parked right next to the house since García had told Lane that the front door would be watched.

"What does García think we're doing?" I ask as I rush for the back door.

"I told him that I forgot something inside and needed it," Lane says as he hoists Ryan up a bit higher in his arms.

"Is he really dumb or does he kind of just not give a shit?" I ask.

"I think he just hates Walsh and thinks it's ridiculous he won't let me help," Lane says as we head to the back door. It's quite dark back here, and I'm scared to turn any lights on to see by. Thankfully, I can see the pin pad well enough that I am able to punch in the correct code to unlock the door.

"What if Mick is already in here and ready to kill us?" I ask.

"He's not that dumb," Lane says as he turns sideways to get through the door. "We're going to head down into the basement. Can you help me?"

"Yeah, of course," I say as I move through the dark house.

I feel my way through the room using the streetlights to aid me. When I reach the basement door, I pull it open then reach out to Lane. I take his wrist and carefully pull him after me, so he doesn't fall down the stairs.

"Inch forward just a bit," I say as I watch his feet. He does until just his toes are hanging over the step. "Now down."

He slowly steps down, careful to feel the step under his foot before putting his weight down. Thankfully, Ryan is still a little out of it or both of them probably would have plummeted down the stairs, especially if Ryan started struggling.

Once he's on the lowest level, I run back up the stairs and close the door. Then I turn the lights on, illuminating the room we are in.

"Can you find a chair?" he asks as I head down the stairs.

The basement is unfinished, but it looks like it was mostly used for storage. The first room is filled with boxes and old furniture. In the second room, I find a couple of dining room chairs, so I grab one and set it next to a table in the main room. Lane has the tape that attached Ryan's wrists to his ankles pulled off, so I head over to help him put the man in the chair.

"He still unconscious?" Lane asks.

Ryan's head is tipped forward, his mouth open as drool drips out.

"Oh…yeah," I say. "You knocked his head on the trunk pretty damn good."

"Huh…Get some water. A bucket would be fantastic, but if you can't find one, a big head-sized Tupperware or something will work."

"Okay," I say as I turn from him.

I head back upstairs and go into the kitchen. I look under the sink, but I only find cleaning supplies. I don't know where else to look, so I start pulling cupboards open until I find a party-size serving bowl. I quickly stick it in the sink and turn the water on.

I'm nervous I'll get noticed through the window, so I crouch as I move back to the basement. Admittedly, I have never been very skillful at carrying anything filled with liquid, and as I walk, the water starts sloshing around. I slow as I watch it, but by the time I've made it down the stairs, I've lost a quarter of the water. And gained a quarter of the water on my pants.

The first thing I notice is that Ryan has his eyes open. He's back to looking at us with murder in his eyes.

Because I had been focused on Ryan and not my footing, my foot catches on something as I step off the last step, making me stumble forward. Miraculously, I don't fall, but I *do* manage to spill all the water. I look back at what had tripped me and see that it is a bucket that I somehow didn't notice going *up* the stairs.

"You alright?" Lane asks.

"Lane! I found a bucket!" I announce.

"Great. Please try not to break your leg on it."

"You want it full?" I ask.

"Yeah, fill it all the way up."

I carry the bucket and empty bowl upstairs, so I can fill them full. By the time I return, Ryan is alert. He's struggling against the binds and yelling something that is muffled under the tape. Lane walks over to him and reaches for him until he finds his head. He sinks his fingers into Ryan's hair and yanks his head back as his other hand searches for the tape. He pulls it off and Ryan immediately spits at him.

"What the *fuck* is this?" Ryan asks as his eyes shift onto me. He sounds a little hoarse, probably from the rope that had been around his neck.

"Hey, Ryan...do you mind if I call you Ryan?" Lane asks like we are holding a meeting of some kind.

"Fuck you," Ryan says.

"Alright, so Ryan, I'm looking for a friend, and I hope you could give me a bit of information."

Ryan's eyes narrow as he struggles to break his arms free. "Who the fuck do you think you are?"

"You probably know me. At the time I was going by the name of Chris Owen."

Ryan's expression changes, and for a moment, I think I see a look of fear cross his face. He licks his lips as his eyes flicker from me back to Lane. "I also heard about what happened to you," he says as he composes himself. "I ain't afraid of some blind asshole." The way he is acting shows that he is very afraid of the blind asshole.

Lane nods. "That's okay. You don't have to be afraid of me. You just have to answer my questions. A friend of mine is missing."

"Was he an undercover agent too?" Ryan asks curiously.

"No, he's a detective," Lane says. "He went missing five days ago."

"And why do you think I know anything about it?" Ryan growls.

"I know who you are. I know that you have your nose in every goddamn inch of that shithole business Red is running."

He snorts. "The thing is…I don't quite understand why you think I'm going to tell you shit. You're a cop, you can't do anything to me."

"Actually, right now my license is in review, you know, because I can't see. I'm not very concerned about any of it," he admits. The growl of his voice makes it sound that he *really* doesn't care.

"Fuck you," Ryan says as he struggles against the tape.

"Alright, so tell me something," Lane says.

Ryan's eyes narrow as he stares at Lane. "I don't know shit about the missing person. Now fuck off and let me go."

"Great," Lane says. "Let's see if I can jog your memory."

I watch as Lane picks up the bucket of water I'd filled and carries it over to Ryan. Then he reaches out until he has Ryan's neck in his hand and yanks him forward. With one hand, he holds the bucket still as he pushes Ryan's head into the bucket. Ryan fights hard against him as he kicks the chair back, but Lane easily holds his head down into the water. Water splashes up, out of the bucket, as Ryan's legs kick and his body thrashes.

Lane grabs his messy bun and pulls his head out of the water before letting Ryan drop to the ground.

Ryan is heaving and coughing as he looks up at Lane. "Fuck you! Fuck you!" he says between gasps of breath. He tries to roll onto his knees, but he can't get his feet under him.

"Just give me something I can use, and we can stop," Lane says.

Ryan spits at Lane's feet, but Lane just grabs his head and drags him toward the bucket. Ryan starts thrashing and fighting hard before they even reach the bucket.

"Hold the bucket for me," Lane says to me.

I stare at him with wide eyes before slowly walking over to them. I grab onto the wet bucket and hold it tightly as Lane shoves the man's head into it. Water splashes up around the sides while he kicks as hard as he can. I'm slightly concerned that Lane is going to drown the man, but he pulls him out and tosses him back to the ground.

Ryan starts throwing up the water he had consumed as he remains hunched on the ground. Slowly, he looks up at Lane, but he doesn't look as confident as he had before.

"This is sad, Ryan. I've seen you torture men before, and they didn't roll around or panic like you," Lane says as calmly as a man can sound.

"Fuck you!" Ryan says as he swings his legs around and kicks the bucket. I'm still holding it, but it makes the water slosh up and out.

"Can you think of anything this time?" Lane asks and when Ryan doesn't immediately answer, he grabs him.

Ryan lunges forward, pushing off with his bound feet as he slams his shoulder into me. The bucket tips over and water spills out all over the floor, drenching my already wet pants.

Lane hauls Ryan toward him and throws him onto his back. "Are you alright?" he asks me.

"I'm fine," I say.

"Well, since we are out of water, I suppose we have to move onto something else, which is fine with me," he says before turning his attention back to me. "Can you find Reed's toolbox?"

I slowly stand up and glance around the basement for a toolbox.

"Go to the garage," Lane says. "Grab me a hammer and some nails. Or a box cutter would work as well. Any of that is fine."

Oh God. What is Lane planning on doing?

I'm a little hesitant as I climb the stairs because I don't know what Lane is planning. I don't know if I should be helping. I don't know anything that's going on anymore. Honestly, I'm a little worried that we are going too far, but I know we have to save James. Even so, I feel like this is wrong. What makes it okay for us to do this, but wrong for the other guys? It's because Ryan is a "bad" guy, right? I know he's a bit obsessed with himself, but he doesn't seem like that bad of a guy.

I take a deep breath because I know that I have to trust Lane and whatever he chooses to do.

I remember seeing a junk drawer in the kitchen when I had been looking for the Tupperware, so I head for it. I pull open the drawer and pick up the hammer that is sitting on top. It feels oddly heavy in my hand as I hold it. Almost like it's too heavy to take. Lane knows what's best, right? I just need to trust him. Using the light coming through the nearby window, I peer back into the drawer. In the corner is a small box of nails. They look like wall nails that someone would use to hang decorations. I grab the box, and as I head back for the basement, I grab a knife from the butcher block.

With my instruments of torture, I head down the stairs. Lane has Ryan back in the chair and must have dragged the chipping table in front of him at some point. The chair is flat against the wall with the table pinning Ryan in place. Ryan looks up at me nervously, like I had betrayed him the moment I left to gather supplies.

"Here," I say as I hold the supplies out to Lane.

"Set them on the table," he says as he pats it gently.

Ryan jumps at the sound of the tools hitting the table.

"Alright, what do we want to start with?" Lane asks as I watch his fingers ghost over the objects on the table. When his hand hits the container of nails, they rattle. "You know what? The time I saw you interrogate a man, you did such a splendid job with nails." He opens the package and pulls one out before setting them back on the table. He holds one of the small nails between his thumb and index finger before putting the head of it between his lips. Then he reaches down and grabs Ryan's hands. Ryan fights hard, flailing and kicking, but Lane is stronger and forces his hand up onto the table.

Ryan starts cussing and fighting as Lane places the tip of the nail against the back of Ryan's hand. With his other hand, he picks the hammer up as Ryan and I watch him nervously.

"You were pretty good at this, though you definitely had bigger nails. First…you hammered the man's hands to the table," Lane says as he presses the nail against the duct-taped hand. He sets the head of the hammer against the nail as Ryan yanks back hard. Lane hits the hammer down just as he moves, and the man screams as he jerks his hands free.

"Fuck! Fuck you!" Ryan draws his hands to his chest as he rocks back and forth in his chair.

"Then…you drove a nail under his fingernails. Do you remember that? Of course you do," Lane says. "But man, that guy never said a word. Definitely wasn't acting like you are now. And all of this because he didn't pay back a loan or something, right? Or you suspected him of doing something with the money? Huh…I just can't remember. I do remember how much you enjoyed this though."

Ryan is desperately looking at me, but now that I've heard a bit of what he's done to others, I don't feel quite as bad. Just thinking about a nail being driven under one of my fingernails makes me cringe. I subconsciously clench my fists at the thought.

"Oh, but now I remember what it was. You suspected one of your guys of stealing the money they were supposed to be bringing in. You got him to tell you where it was after you threatened to cut off his testicles. Silly me. I had forgotten. Let's try that one out."

Lane kicks the table out of the way before grabbing Ryan and throwing him onto the ground. Ryan starts letting out a shrill whining noise as he tries to crawl away, but with his ankles bound, he isn't getting far fast. Lane picks the knife up off the table before walking over to Ryan. He flips him onto his back and sits down on his legs as Ryan starts hitting Lane with his bound hands.

"Touch me again and I'll gut you," Lane growls as his other hand unbuttons Ryan's pants. "You can live without your testicles. You'll be fine."

"I'll tell you what I know!" Ryan yells as he looks up at Lane with wide eyes filled with fear. "I honestly don't know about the detective…but there was a disturbance at one of Red's factories a few days ago…probably about four or five days ago. I don't know what the disturbance was. I deal with the loans, I don't deal with that side of his shit."

"Where's the factory?" Lane asks.

"I don't know. I think it's about an hour or more from here. It's a laundromat called Leenson and Sons. I don't know the address. I swear that's all I know…now what are you going to do to me?"

"I'll make a deal with you. You don't tell them about this, and I won't tell them anything about you. I'll drop you off at the station, and they'll hold you for a night or two as they try to figure out if you are related to the case. When they can't get any solid information on you, they'll let you go. Alright?"

"Yes."

"That also means that if the information you gave me is bullshit, I'll know right where you're at," Lane says.

Ryan nods quickly. "I promise that I don't know anything else."

"Alright," Lane says.

He pulls out the cellphone García had given us and makes a call. As he talks over by the stairs, I watch Ryan as he lies on the floor. He's not looking at me now, instead, he's curled up with his pants around his thighs.

Lane walks over to me as he slips the phone back into his pocket. "García is headed here."

"Okay," I say.

"We'll let him deal with it," he explains.

We don't talk as we wait. Instead, Lane leans against the wall while facing Ryan. When García arrives, Lane talks to him, and then reaches out for me. I look down at his outstretched hand. A few of his knuckles are scuffed and red, probably from holding Ryan's head down into the bucket.

I take his hand and interlock our fingers as I head to the stairs. I look back once at Ryan and García, before leading Lane up the stairs. The upstairs lights are on, and it makes it easy to find my way to the back door. Together, we head out to the car where Copper is eagerly waiting. I leave Lane at the passenger door before heading around to the driver's door.

"Are you alright?" Lane asks as soon as I'm inside.

"Yes...you?" I ask as I put the key into the ignition.

He leans against the door of the car as he closes his eyes. "What does it mean to be alright? I mean...even if someone is not 'alright' they say they are."

"We'll find James," I promise. "We're doing...everything we can."

"It's not just that," he says. "When you live a life where you lie all the time and you're forced to become someone you are not, the line between who you are and who you have to pretend to be gets blurred. You have to do shit you don't want to do. Act how you don't want to act. And then, when you get put in situations like that one, you question when it became so easy to take on that role. So easy to just hurt someone and not even care."

"You didn't really hurt him," I say. "And it sounds like he spent his fair share of time hurting people."

"Yeah," he says as he nods, but I can tell he doesn't truly believe me.

"Lane?"

"Hmm?"

"You didn't do anything wrong," I say as I reach out to him. I set my hand on his wrist and slowly pull it away from where it'd been tucked against his stomach.

"Let's go," he says.

"Yeah," I say. "Can I see your phone?"

He hands it to me, so I can research this cleaning service place. It takes me a moment, but I finally seem to find the right company. "Okay...so it looks like this company deals with uniforms and the rags that factories use. Looks like they pick up and clean them for companies each week."

"Anything else on them?"

"No...I mean, I doubt it'll have a tab that says, 'bad guy section,'" I say.

"Don't be a smartass, no one likes a smartass," he says, but it pulls a small smile out of him. "I meant like, different locations...do they have different buildings in the area?"

"Um...looks like just the one location in this area. Apart from that, there isn't really anything else of interest on here about the company."

"Okay, let's go," he says.

I type the address into the car's GPS and watch as it calculates. "Hour and forty minutes."

"Alright, are you tired? Are you okay to drive?"

"Yeah, I'm good," I say as I put the car in drive. "Just as long as you talk to me, I probably won't get too sleepy."

"What do you want me to talk about?"

"What your job is," I decide.

"I have told you all that I can tell you," he says stubbornly.

"You're no fun. Alright...where'd you grow up?"

"Small town in California."

"What about your family?"

"They're still there."

"Why didn't you go to them after the accident?"

"I didn't want to put them in danger," he says.

"Oh, so you'd rather put *me* in danger. Thanks a lot," I say sarcastically.

"I didn't know you. And if you recall, I never wanted a babysitter," he says.

"Tell me about your family," I say as I merge out onto the highway that heads out of town.

"My dad has been a homicide detective for most of his life and was pretty much married to his work…but somehow it just worked for my parents. They're still together if you can believe that," he says.

"I didn't think families stayed together anymore," I joke.

"Yeah, I think my father is paying her. There'd be no other reason for her to stay otherwise," he jokes.

"How did they handle your accident?" I ask.

"They don't know," he admits.

I look away from the road to stare at him in surprise. "*What?* You never told them?" I ask.

"No, because I know that if I did, they would lose their minds and insist I be with them. I want them safe," he says.

"Of course you do, but I'm sure they'd like to know," I say. "Are you not close to them?"

"Yeah, I try to call them once a week," he says.

"And when your mom is like 'oh, how are you today?' you are like 'fantastic!'"

"Pretty much," he says.

"You're ridiculous," I realize. "If I had a parent that would have cared, I would have told them everything," I say.

"When you're in a job like mine, secrets are what you learn to do best," he says.

"I suppose," I say even though I don't really believe any of it. "You have siblings?"

"A sister. She's married and just gave birth to her first child…a girl," he says. "When she told me, all I could think about was how I'll never be able to see the kid."

"Does it matter?" I ask. "You still like me, and you can't see me."

"The only reason I like you is that I can't see you," he jokes, and I laugh.

"Hey, I wooed a man today, quite successfully if I might add," I say. "To the point where he jumped into a trunk for me."

"Just to break his heart," he says.

"Yeah, he did look pretty betrayed when I opened that trunk," I say. "Was it hard leaving your family for this job?"

"Yeah, it was…it definitely wasn't the path I had planned to take, but I kind of fell into it and things just escalated from there. I would like to dream that all this shit just…goes away and I can go back home and not have to worry about endangering anyone I love. It used to be that all I could think about was my job. What I was doing, how I could look into the minds of these people and slowly tear them down as I built up their trust. It was like a high when I found out the truth that would help bring them down."

"I'm sure," I say. "I'm not sure if this past week has exactly been a 'high' for me, but it's definitely made me feel terror, excitement, and the on-coming of death."

He laughs. "I'm not going to let you die," he says.

"Uh huh…okay…*sure*…"

CHAPTER SEVENTEEN

"Now what?" I ask as we sit in the car just outside of the factory.

We're in some small town in the middle of nowhere. The only thing of any size is the factory that is bordering the edge of the town limit. Even at this time of night, the place is in full swing, but there's nothing marking it as suspicious in any way.

If this was a movie, there'd be a fence and guards wandering around with vicious dogs at their heels. Nope. There is just a mundane building sitting in a mundane town. The only area that has a fence is where the semi-trucks and trailers are parked in the back, probably just to keep people out of them as they sat and waited for the next shipment.

"Anything interesting or unusual?" Lane asks.

"No…all of the man-doors are open," I note.

"It's probably hot in there," Lane says. "A lot of people working?"

"I don't know, maybe if we get out and walk the sidewalk along it, I can see inside better. There are…maybe three or four people outside on break. You think they're making drugs here?"

"Could be. It'd be an ideal spot for it. Places like this already deal with chemicals to clean, so hauling things in for drugs could be simple to do. It's right in the middle of town, so people aren't going to suspect that anything unusual is going on."

"That's true…do…we walk by it?"

"Is there a sidewalk along it?"

"Yeah," I say.

"Alright, let's go," he says as he opens the car door. "Bring Copper, we'll look less suspicious."

"Okay," I say as I get out of the car.

I pull open the back door and Copper wags his tail as I snap his leash on. He hops out and we walk around to the other side of the car where Lane is waiting. I reach out and slide my hand into his before giving him a tug. He follows me as I cross the desolate street and head toward the factory.

"What if I went and asked someone to use a bathroom or something? Snooped a bit?" I ask.

"The issue is that they're not going to make it easy to find. If this is an actual drug operation, there isn't going to be a door with a sign on it saying, 'drugs made down here.'"

"There might be," I joke.

"Yeah, trust me, we're not that lucky," he says.

"Then…what are we even doing?" I ask. "I feel like part of it is that you don't want to get me involved, but what are we going to do? Walk a circle around the place? Hope they get so tired of seeing us walk around that they feel bad and just tell us what's going on?"

Lane is silent for a moment as we wait for a street light to change so we can cross. Since there isn't anyone in the area anyway, we probably could have crossed whenever, but I didn't think it was wise to talk about drugs as we circled the building. Or maybe we would draw their attention and they'd feel bad for us and give us the information.

"Just be my eyes, alright? As you walk around, look for anything out of place. I don't care what it is. Someone that doesn't look like they fit. I don't care. Just look," he says.

"Okay," I say as I head across the road. We slowly walk, with me on the right side, so I can gawk easier. "It looks like they're having a swingers' party inside."

"Does it?" Lane asks in mock surprise.

"Everyone's naked."

"Everyone?" he asks.

I laugh. "No...but there's a man and woman outside the door."

The woman is smoking, and the man is on his phone as we walk toward them. She glances up and watches us, making me wonder if I should let go of Lane's hand. There's probably not too much of that kind of thing in this area.

"Your dog is adorable," she says, and I notice she has a thick accent.

I smile at her. "Thank you," I say. "Do you want to pet him?"

She nods and puts her cigarette out on the walkway she is sitting on before tossing it.

I move down the walk toward her as I notice the man looking up from his phone. He seems disinterested as he puts his phone away and heads back into the building.

"Aw, he's adorable," she says as she kneels.

Copper walks up to her as she reaches a hand out. I notice her fingers are a little unsteady as she reaches for him before sinking them into his fur.

"What's his name?"

"Copper," Lane says. "Do you have any dogs?"

She shakes her head slowly. "No...I used to...I miss them," she says.

"You should get yourself one," Lane says with a charming smile. "Everyone needs one of these buds to keep them company."

She smiles as she looks up at him. "I wish. We have such long hours here though."

"I hate that. I just got off work myself. Thought I'd take the dog for a walk before going down for the night. I always prefer walking at night…there's something calming about it."

She nods. "Yeah, I could see that," she says as she flattens Copper's ear with a stroke of her hand.

"I heard some crazy ruckus going on a few days ago when walking by here. I was worried something happened," Lane says.

Her eyes snap up to his before returning to the dog. "Was there? Must have been in the loading department. When you're inside that place with all those machines running, it's hard to hear what's going on. I wonder what happened though."

"Me too, but I guess it's not a big deal as long as no one was hurt, right?" Lane says.

She smiles, but the look is unnatural now. "Well…I need to get back from break. I'm already a minute late. Thanks for letting me pet him."

"Of course," Lane says. "Maybe we'll come this way again sometime, so you can see him."

"That would be nice," she says as she stands up. "Have a good night."

She hurries back into the building, so we head back for the sidewalk.

"What was her expression? I could tell there was a difference in her demeanor after I mentioned it," Lane says.

"She looked kind of startled," I say.

"Anything unusual about her?"

I think about it for a moment. "Not really…"

"What was her race?"

"Maybe Hispanic? I don't know," I say. "She definitely had a Spanish accent, but I don't know what dialect."

He nods. "Alright, let's keep walking."

I continue around the building with Lane beside me and Copper leading the way. His tail never stops wagging as he sniffs the ground.

"We're passing the trucks. They're fenced in, but it doesn't look like anything unusual."

"Did the website state which areas it served?"

"I think just surrounding counties," I say.

"Is the gate open?"

"No, it's closed," I say as we near it. It looks like there is a chain around it, but as we grow closer, I realize the chain doesn't seem to be locked. "It's not locked though."

"Let's go in there. Any windows or doors where we can be seen easily?"

"A few windows that look like they lead to an office area, but they're dark. There's a door that's open though…I can see people wandering around, but no one near it."

"Alright, quiet as you can, unchain the gate and head in."

I go over to the gate and find that "quiet as you can" and "chain" don't fit together very well. As soon as I pick up the chain, it clangs against the metal gate, and Lane turns to me in alarm.

"Quiet," he says.

"Sorry, I forgot what that means," I say sarcastically as I gather the chain into one hand before feeding it through the gate as quietly as I can.

Once it's free, I set the chain in the grass and slowly pull the gate open before leading Lane through it. "What are we doing?"

"Pick a truck that can't be seen very well from the open door."

"Okay…" I say as I head over to the furthest one. Who knows what Lane has planned.

"On the sleeper compartments of some cabs, there will be a little side door. Quite often, they get left unlocked. See them?"

I pass the passenger door and reach a little side door just beyond it. "Yeah?"

"Okay, what I want you to do is climb in through that door—"

I stare at the tiny door on the side of the cab before looking back at him. "I can't fit through there!" I say, but he gives me an apologetic expression.

"I'm sorry, Felix…but with your little dwarf limbs you can," he says. "I'll help you through it. Once inside, you are going to be under the bed. Head toward the front of the truck, there's usually a little flap there that you need to push through, and then you'll be in the cab. I want you to look around for a little book. It's called a driver's log and it's something a semi driver has to fill out, stating things like when they're resting, where they're going, and when they left. Rip the last page out of it and write down every city and state they have headed to that is not within thirty miles of here."

"Yeah…I really don't even know what 'here' is so sure, this will be easy."

"Here's my phone. Don't turn the flashlight on until you are in the bed of the cab, then pull the curtain shut, so no light comes through."

"Were you a truck driver in a past life?" I ask, wondering where he received all this knowledge about trucks from. "Sexy truck driver. We could roleplay that if you want? Oh…trucker, no! Don't bend me over—"

"What? Just go!"

Lane interlocks his hands together as I open the small compartment door. Stepping onto his hands, he boosts me up, so I can crawl through the open door. Sadly, I'm able to pull myself inside without even a struggle. I thought I would have to wiggle around a bit to get through the opening, but nope, I slip right inside.

My first impression is that it's dirty and smells like feet. I find the source of the smell as I knock a pair of disgusting shoes out of the way as I reach out and feel the flap. I weasel my way through it and into the cab. The nearby streetlight is bright enough that I can look around and see well enough to make out shapes.

There are about ten cans of Coke on the ground that I try to avoid as I reach for the glove compartment. I turn the knob, and the compartment opens, revealing a thick booklet on top. I grab it and crawl into the bed area where I pull the curtain shut. I turn on the phone's flashlight as I flip the booklet to the last page. I rip the page out and then begin writing down every location the truck has traveled to since the log started. When I'm finished, I put it back, grab the paper, and shimmy my way back under the bed to where Lane is waiting for me.

"I got it, sexy trucker man," I say.

"Good job," he says, completely dismissing my remark as he holds his arms out. He feels for me as I stick my feet out first. Once he has my ankles, he pulls me through the opening and lets me drop to the ground. "How many more trucks are there?"

"Two more."

"Let's head to the next one."

We creep over to the next one that is clearly a newer vehicle, but it proves to be locked from all sides. That just leaves the truck closest to the open door. We stay on the far side as Lane helps me inside. As I work to write down the locations, the phone in my pocket begins to vibrate. Startled, I jump before flipping it over and looking at who is calling. Since there aren't any names in the contacts, I don't recognize the number. I stick the phone back into my pocket and return to working on the log. Most of the locations are similar, and instead of writing new ones, I start putting a tally next to them.

"Felix, there's someone coming," Lane whispers. "Hurry!"

My stomach tightens as I quickly push the curtain back. I drop the log back in the glove compartment and push it shut as I rush for the area under the bed. The glove compartment drops back open, reminding me that if I don't turn the knob, it doesn't lock, but I don't have time now. I crawl under the bed and reach for the little door as I hear the front door open. I assume it is Lane, trying to find a quicker way to get me out, until I feel the cab dip a little as someone climbs in.

Now I don't know if I should try to open the compartment door and get out or wait for him to leave. Maybe he just forgot something and will just grab it and go.

I hear the jingle of keys as he sticks them in the ignition.

Now I really don't know what to do. What if he's planning on leaving? What if I'm stuck in here for fuck knows how long?

Oh lord…

This definitely isn't the sexy role-playing I had been wanting.

The semi-truck roars to life as the floor begins to vibrate. I reach for the door, finding that Lane hadn't pushed it closed, and start to press against it when the truck begins to move. I lie still, praying he is just moving the truck into the loading dock, and then I can flee after he has left.

I lie as still as I can, breathing quietly as the truck moves around a bit before I hear the air of the brakes.

"We good?" the driver shouts, telling me that someone else must be outside, but I don't know what side they're on. If the driver's shouting to them, it's likely they're on the driver's side, so should I shimmy my way around to escape through a different compartment? The roar of the semi is loud enough that he probably wouldn't hear me even if I make a racket. I begin to push the door open just a bit, hoping to see out of it when the man turns the truck off. I take a deep breath and just wait for him to leave. Once he's gone, I'll make my escape. I'll get out, and I'll run.

Suddenly the phone in my pocket begins to vibrate. Pressed against the hard floor, it begins to rattle as I quickly reach for it, hitting buttons as I feel them. It stops vibrating and I hold my breath.

"What the…?" the man asks as he pushes the flap up and shines his phone's flashlight in. I stare at him as his eyes grow wide. "What…the hell? What are you doing?"

With my foot, I kick the door open. I start pushing myself back toward the door as panic settles in my stomach. I hear the truck door open as I push my feet through the open gap.

"Hey! Someone broke into the truck!" he yells, probably to the other guy that had been helping him.

Suddenly the man from the cab is there. He grabs my ankle and yanks me toward him. I bring my free foot up and kick him right in the face. He reels back, but he doesn't let go of me.

"You fucking asshole," he yells as he yanks harder.

I reach for anything to grab onto and catch something in the dark. I hold on tightly and start struggling as the man yanks at my leg as hard as he can. I lose my grip on whatever I am holding onto as he yanks me from the cab. For a moment, I'm falling, but the drop isn't far before my toes touch the ground. I struggle to get my feet under me, but I lose my footing and fall back onto the ground as the man moves toward me.

Suddenly, there's a streak of darkness as Copper collides with the man. He latches onto his arm and starts dragging him down. The man screams as he's yanked off balance by Copper's weight. I jump up as the second man grabs me. I bring my elbow back, but there was no reason for me to because Lane is already there. He grabs onto the man, grasping the man's shirt in his hand before yanking him forward and driving his fist into the man's face.

"Let's go," Lane says as he pushes the man away.

He moves toward me, so I grab his wrist as Copper continues to drag the man. Lane yells for Copper and the dog releases before running after us.

I lead Lane through the gate and start running for the car.

"Keys…keys…where are the keys?" I hiss as I dig at my pocket for my keys and manage to pull them free. I yank open the driver's door and thrust Lane toward it. "Get in!"

"I'm trying," Lane says as he crawls over my seat and into the passengers.

I send Copper in before jumping in and ramming the key in the ignition. I start the car, throw it in drive, and slam my foot down.

"Well?" Lane asks.

"Well, what?"

"You wanted to role-play. Was it fun?"

"Oh, not funny," I say.

Lane laughs. "Alright, no more joking. Are you alright?" Lane asks.

"Yeah…you?"

"I'm fine. Why is it…why have I gotten into more shit since I met you than I ever did alone? This is definitely a first for me to get caught so often."

"Well…at least I stole one of your firsts," I say as I glance in the rearview mirror to make sure we aren't being followed. I'm not even sure the two guys saw what car we got into.

"That's not true," Lane says. "You've taken at least a couple of my firsts. Like…the first time I was tortured by food."

I look over at him in shock. "I'm going to take away your first time of being murdered if you mention my food one more time. I *never* said I was a good cook."

"Fine, I won't mention it again. So, how'd you get caught?"

"This stupid phone kept ringing," I say as I yank it out.

I see that there are two voicemails as I take a corner going about twenty miles faster than I should have been. The car hits the curb, but thankfully, we don't blow a tire.

"What are you doing?" Lane yells as he tries to find something to grab onto.

"I don't know! Looking at this stupid phone. There are two voicemails," I say as I hit the first one and put it on speaker.

"We have found James, give me a call when you get this."

"What? That's it? No 'he's okay' or anything?" I ask.

"What's the second voicemail?"

"Was that García?" I ask as I slow just enough to make sure we won't get hit before flooring past a stop sign.

"Yeah."

I flip to the next voicemail and press play.

"Okay, so I have a little more information. He's okay at the moment. I believe they have him stable. Give me a call back."

"Call him," Lane says as soon as the voicemail ends.

I press the "call back" button and put it on speaker. The phone starts ringing as Lane reaches over until he connects with my wrist. He slides his hand up until he hits the phone and takes it from me.

"This is García."

"Hey García, you found James?" Lane asks.

"Actually, St. Michael's hospital called us. He had been with them as a John Doe for three days. I know we sent out alerts to nearby hospitals and his name was on the list of missing, but there hadn't been a connection until about two hours ago. They called us up, we identified him, and I ran over since I was the closest to make sure it was him."

"Is he alright?"

"He's in a coma. Suffered trauma to the back of his head. He had been stripped of all ID. A woman found him when she was out walking her dog. Thought he was dead and called the police. As of right now, we don't know anything else."

"Alright, I'll be there. I'm not sure how far away St. Michael's is, but we're headed there now. Has Janice been notified?"

"Yes, I notified her as soon as I identified him. She should be here any minute," he says.

"Okay, great. Thanks, García."

"I'll see you in a few," he says, and I end the call.

"I mean, if he's made it this long, he'll probably live, right?" I ask.

"I guess…but head trauma…especially trauma that has left someone in a coma for days, can be a tricky thing," he says as I slow for a stoplight and plug the address into the GPS. It tells me that it's a four-hour drive, which makes me internally groan.

"So…if a hospital *four* hours from here is currently holding him, then he wasn't involved with the disturbance here," I say.

"Probably not," he says. "It must have just been a coincidence. We basically got nowhere as we ran around threatening people and breaking into places."

"Pretty much," I say. "But at least James is alive."

CHAPTER EIGHTEEN

When we arrive at the hospital it is nearly dawn, and I'm dragging. I had been having trouble keeping my eyes open while I drove, but thankfully we are here now.

We head inside to where García is waiting for us at the entrance. He smiles when he sees us and steps back, so we can pass through the door.

"You two get into any more scuffles?" García asks as soon as we are inside.

"No, we're good," Lane says.

"Did Felix just roll around in the dirt a bit before coming here?" he asks before taking a left as he follows signs for the elevator.

I look down at Janice's nice clothes and realize that they did look quite dirty. "Maybe I like it dirty?" I suggest with a wink, and García laughs.

"That's good," García says as he leads us down the winding halls to the elevator. We get inside and ride up to the third floor. "It sounds like they found James's car about a mile from where he was found. It was parked at a grocery store and had been noted by the manager to have been sitting there for a few days. There wasn't anything unusual in it."

When the door opens, he heads down the hallway.

"Hmm…did they find anything interesting where James was found?" Lane asks.

Copper wags his tail every time we pass someone in hopes they will become his new friend. He doesn't seem to be grieving too much about the disappearance of his owner. I think that's just because he's realized how much better of an owner I am.

"Not yet. The waiting room is right here. Only two are allowed back with him at a time," García says.

"Okay, I'll wait here if you want to take Lane back," I say.

"Alright. Lane, you want to hold hands? I don't mind," García says with a grin.

"I'll take the dog," Lane says as he takes Copper's leash from me and heads after García.

"That's cold, Lane. What's wrong with my hand?" García says, sounding very hurt.

"I don't know, nor want to know, where it's been," Lane says, and García laughs.

I watch them pass through a door before I head to the waiting room. There are two women huddled together in seats at the far end, so I take a seat near the door. I still have Lane's phone, so I pull it out as well as the paper I'd written all the cities on. The majority of the trips had been to a city called Bloomington, so I type the city into the phone. There really isn't much of interest, and I'm not even sure what I should be looking for.

All I do know is that I'm starting to get a headache and the bright lights in this room are not helping. I skim over the cities and states that range from Illinois to Indiana to Nevada to New York. Discouraged, I tuck the paper away and close my eyes, hoping that would help get rid of the headache.

I hear footsteps and open my eyes. When I look over at the door, I am surprised to see Janice there. The moment she sees me, she smiles. "Hey...I was just walking down to get a drink. Do you want to walk with me?"

"Sure," I say as I get up and head over to the door. "I'm not sure where to go."

"Me either. I probably should have asked a nurse...but...I just needed to step out for a moment," she says as she rubs at her face. Her eyes are red and she's clenching a tissue in her left hand. "I know I should be happy, no...I should be *ecstatic*...but it's hard to be when he's not waking up."

"I know, I'm sorry," I say. "Is anyone here with you?"

"My parents and sister are headed here," she says.

"That's good," I say.

She nods and walks in silence for a few moments before looking over at me. "You look a little rough...you doing alright?"

I look down at my...well *her* dirty clothes and try to dust them off until I notice the grease smudges on my hand. "I'm good, I have a headache, but I'm good," I say.

"Oh! I have some pills in my SUV. Let's find a vending machine, you can get a drink, and then you can go grab them. They're in the middle console," she says.

"Awesome, thank you so much," I say.

"Of course," she says as she rounds the corner. "There!" She shouts so loudly that a nurse walking by us jumps.

She rushes over to the vending machine and stares at it in disgust. "Why is it only diet? I just want a fucking Pepsi. Can't I have anything I want?" she asks as she bangs her fist against the front of the machine before literally melting to the ground.

A nurse that had been walking by stops to stare at us as I stare at Janice who is now sobbing on the ground. I quickly kneel next to her, hoping it would encourage the nurse to head off. I want to tell her that the floor of a hospital has to be disgusting, but I'm not sure that is her main concern at the moment.

"Hey, it's okay. They found him, and he's alive," I say as I reach out and take her hand.

She nods as she wipes at her eyes with her wrinkled and well-used tissue. "Yeah…Yeah. You're right. It's just like four days of this shit building up and building up."

"I know, I'm sorry," I say as I squeeze her hand. I stand up and put a five-dollar bill in the machine before punching C2 for a Diet Pepsi and A1 for a water. When the Pepsi comes out, I tear the label off it and hand it to her. "Look, they had a regular Pepsi in there."

She wipes at her face as she laughs weakly. "Thanks. I'm glad you found it."

"I am too!" I say as I give her my hand. She takes it, and I pull her up to her feet. "Come on, let's head back. Did you want anything else?"

"No," she says as she takes a sip of the Pepsi. "It tastes like shit."

"It's probably because your snot and tears are mixing with it," I say.

"Ew, that's so gross," she says as she wipes at her face again.

"I agree," I say.

I walk her back up to the wing James is being held on before she remembers that I was going to head out to get something for my headache.

She holds her keys out to me. "It's in the first row, red SUV. Just press the button if you can't find it, but make sure you lock the door when you're done because my laptop is in there."

"Okay, I will. Thanks," I say.

"Of course. Thank you," she says before disappearing through the door. I check the waiting room to make sure Lane isn't in there before heading back down the elevator. I walk through the front doors, hoping I'll be able to find James's wing again when I come back in. It's a little cool out as fall begins to make its move. The fresh air feels nice as I try to stifle a yawn. I feel like I could curl up and just sleep for a bit now that all the excitement is over with.

As I walk into the parking lot, I can't help but wonder what Lane plans to do now. I mean, he could hide. How far or long would Red look for him?

I find the car easily since the parking lot is almost bare this early in the morning. After unlocking the door and climbing into the passenger's seat, I flip open the middle console. Inside, I find a tin full of pills that I flick through until I find a green and white one that I grab. I stick it in my mouth and wash it down with the water before leaning back in the seat. It's a ridiculously comfortable seat at the moment, or maybe I'd find anything comfortable at this point.

But I know that I should head back in so that when Lane comes out, I'm waiting for him. I reach for the door when I see a messenger bag on the ground. I look around to make sure Janice isn't heading out to the car, where she'd learn that my main personality trait is being nosy.

I flip open the messenger bag and see a laptop peeking out. I pull it out and open it up. The laptop is already on and it doesn't have a password, so I just click the Welcome screen that lets me right in. There are a few Excel documents open that probably pertain to her job, as well as a web browser. I click it and the browser fills up the screen. There are three tabs open. The first is Facebook, the second is a recipe for cookies, and the third is an email.

I move the mouse down to the Wi-Fi and click it. There definitely isn't a strong connection out here in the parking lot, but I am a stone's throw from the door, so it will probably be enough.

I ask it to connect and glance at the door again, but no one is interested in what I am doing. I move the cursor over to the history tab and start perusing through the history section. She'd researched a ton on missing persons cases in the past few days and barely anything else. But I keep going deeper until I'm at about five days ago. That's when I find a few interesting sites. One is called The Honey Ranch. I click it and wait an excruciating amount of time for the page to load in.

It doesn't take long to figure out that it is some type of brothel, as are the next four sites that James had to have visited just before his disappearance.

I stare at the four tabs that are up and click between them before taking my paper out of my pocket. I look at the cluster of tallies next to Nevada.

"Hmm..."

I glance at the paper for a moment before leaning over and looking around the SUV until I find a pen on the ground. I pick it up and write down the names of the four brothels that James had looked at as well as their locations. Obviously, he'd stumbled into something that someone hadn't wanted to be noticed and no doubt this is why he is in his current predicament. I sigh as I close all the tabs and put the laptop away.

The real question is what to do with this information. All Lane had wanted was to find James. They found James, so technically we are done. I could talk him into going somewhere away from all of this. Where we'd be safe and neither of us would be threatened because honestly, what the hell can a blind man and a guy that only knows how to steal do? It was really stupid of us to even go this far. Now that it's over with, I wonder where I could talk him into going. We could try to be near his family. I'd love to meet them. Love to have a family to belong to.

I get out of the SUV and head back for the hospital. I take the elevator up and get lost twice before finding my way back to the waiting room where Lane is sitting.

"Hey, Lane," I say.

"Where'd you go?" he asks.

"So, I totally think they're hauling the drugs down to their factory in Nevada and somehow it's connected to a brothel there. James must have thought the same thing, or he was planning a trip to a brothel." Alright, maybe I am not ready to drop this yet. Maybe I am getting too invested in this. Or maybe I need to stop being nosy. Yeah, it's probably that one.

"What?" Lane asks as he straightens in his seat. "What are you talking about?"

So, I fill him in on my trip to Janice's car and what I had found. He listens closely as I tell him my speculations.

"So...let me get this straight. You're like 'man I have a headache' and Janice is like 'please, go get some headache pills from my car' and you're like 'while I'm in here, I might as well invade her privacy'?"

"Correct," I say.

He shakes his head in disbelief. I'm not sure why because, by this point, I would think he'd know me quite well. "Alright...what do you want to do? James is here, so we could drop all of this, pass the information over to García, and go into the safehouse Walsh had in mind for me."

"*Or* we could solve this case and show them that you are better than all of them," I say.

"That's what you want to do?" he asks.

"Yeah. It may be my sleep deprivation talking for me, but I think we should fuck some shit up," I say eagerly.

"You do realize we're not going to go in guns blazing? I mean, you refuse to even pick up a gun. Once we have concrete proof, we will go to the DEA or the police and get this legally solved," he says.

"That definitely doesn't sound as cool," I realize.

"Alright, as soon as the banks open, we'll head to my bank and withdraw some money. Then off to Nevada we go."

***

We didn't manage to get onto a flight to Nevada until noon. It seemed like everything was a hassle and God was trying to tell us to go *anywhere* other than Nevada. The first issue we had was getting money from the bank. That, of course, took a while because Lane didn't remember his account number and had no form of ID on him since we'd originally left our wallets back at the hotel near home when we'd made our untimely escape. So, we had to sort that out first by hunting down our wallets. Once reunited, we then had to go to the bank and get money. By then, I was absolutely dragging and excited to nap for a few hours on the plane. I thought that I could have taken a nap while waiting for the plane, but I guess it's a little harder to just tell everyone your dog is a service dog when you're trying to get it onto a plane.

They stupidly needed to see "proof" that he is a service dog. And something about having to call in advance.

So, with some finagling I had the dog changed from a "service" dog to a police dog. But eventually, Lane talked me into letting García watch Copper, which I had not been pleased about. Lane had assured me that not only was Copper not actually *my* dog but that García would take fantastic care of him.

Even the kisses García gave Copper hadn't convinced me that he was better with García than on the flight with me.

But now that we are finally on the plane, I am ready for my nap.

"Are you still mad?" Lane asks as he bumps his shoulder against mine.

"I should sue them for discrimination against service dogs," I say.

"Again, Copper *isn't* a service dog," Lane says as he leans against the window.

"Wait a minute…why did you get the window seat?"

"I like the view," he says.

"Funny," I say. "I'm going to take a nap, so turn into a pillow for me."

I awkwardly lean against Lane as I close my eyes. He definitely doesn't feel like a pillow, but I suppose he'll have to do.

"Your arms are too hard," I complain.

"I thought you liked my muscles?"

"Not when I'm trying to sleep," I say, and he laughs.

"Sorry, babe."

I look over at him and raise an eyebrow at the uncharacteristically sweet nickname. I'm sure it had been said with heavy amounts of sarcasm included, and I just missed it.

I snort, which has to be a very attractive thing to do after someone calls you "babe," and close my eyes.

I doze on and off for the rest of the flight until Lane nudges me awake. "We're here."

Slowly, I give in to his prompting, and open my eyes. "We are? No! I wanted to join the mile-high club!" I whine as Lane urges me to get up.

"Well, you should have mentioned that earlier," he says, and I laugh as I unbuckle my seatbelt. I stand up and stretch as I get out of the seat and step into the aisle. Lane rams his hip into a seat, so I reach out and grab his hand.

"First thing we need is a car," he says.

"Do you think we need to check out the factory down here?"

"Hmm…let's try the brothel first. I doubt we are going to learn any more than we had in the first place. They may also be on the lookout for us."

"Do we know which brothel?"

"Yeah, that Paradise one."

"Why?"

"Well, as you were talking about them, it seemed that the Paradise one had an increase in ratings and popularity within the last three years. Which could mean a shift in management. That is also around the time that Red's business began to prosper."

"Good thinking," I say as we walk off the ramp and into the airport. There are signs pointing toward the exit as well as car rentals, so I take a right. "What's our plan when we get there? What are we looking for?"

"Well, it could be where they're laundering the money, or it could be where they're selling the drugs. It's probably both though. With prostitution legal in some areas of Nevada, it could pull a lot of people in. They could be using the prostitution as a front and be selling the drugs through the girls. So, we try to get them to sell something to us."

"Okay," I say. "Drugs…I've learned exactly how to get drugs from my momma. It's one thing she did teach me."

"Um…good?" he says with a cringe. "I'm not sure that's the word I want to use but…that skill may help us out here."

I snort and bump my shoulder into his. "My momma would be so proud of me," I say.

"Eh, fuck that bitch. You don't need her approval," he says. "You have mine."

"Yay! I have your approval on my skill for acquiring drugs! I'm so loved," I say as I squeeze his hand tighter.

Lane laughs and squeezes my hand back. "As long as it's better than your cooking skills, I'll be pleased."

"Alright, we're going upstairs here," I say as I pull him to a stop.

"Right here?" Lane asks.

"Yeah," I say even though there are no stairs in sight. To make it look more legit, I start raising my hand up. I watch in amusement as he steps up, finds no stairs, and stumbles forward. "That's what you get, dickhead. You said you wouldn't make fun of my cooking anymore."

The look of surprise on his face is worth it. "Oh! That was mean!" he says as he yanks me toward him. "That was really mean, Felix."

"Was it? Was it mean? Because my cooking skills have their feelings hurt," I say.

"Good, hopefully that means they'll give up on ever trying to cook again."

"I just want approval," I say with a pout.

Lane wraps his arms around me and hugs me, not caring in the slightest that we are blocking traffic. I guess when you can't see the traffic, you automatically don't care. I sink into his strong arms and wrap my own arms around him and squeeze.

"Alright, I'm sorry. I won't ever make fun of your cooking again," he says as he kisses the top of my head. "Can I make fun of your height instead? I mean, I literally have to crouch to kiss the top of your head."

"No, you don't!" I say.

"You're like travel size. A wittle snack pack," he croons in a babyish tone.

I drop my arms, no longer caring to engage in this heinous hug. "Don't you dare say that mean shit to me while trying to sweetly hug me and give me kisses," I say.

He squeezes me harder. "You love it and you know it."

"Do I?" I ask.

"Of course you do!" he says.

"Hm…sure, sure," I say as we continue over to the car rental.

CHAPTER NINETEEN

I'm not sure what I am expecting when I pull up to Paradise Ranch, but I guess something a bit more extravagant. From the outside, it looks normal. Just a regular stone building that could be used as any type of office.

"We're here. There are huge statues of naked women with their tits like ten feet wide," I say.

"Are there? Man, they must be rolling in the dough. Maybe it's a business I should get into."

"It'd probably be a good business for you because you wouldn't be disgusted by all the ugly, gross men. Oh…but you could still smell them, I guess."

"Ew, don't…just stop there," he says, and I laugh.

I shut the car off and look over at him. "May I have some money for my bunny?"

"What?"

"Well…I thought saying that was better than 'prostitute,' but if you want me to say that instead, I can."

He pulls out his wallet and hands it to me. "Get a cheap one."

"Yes, sir," I say as I stare at the money. "How much is…a cheap one?"

"Take six hundred. Hopefully, you don't spend that much."

"Alright," I say as I pull it out and stuff the six hundred-dollar bills into my wallet before handing him his wallet back. "Ready?"

"Let's get this over with."

"Before we go in, you better not have sex with any of them. I don't share," I say as I slide my hand up his thigh and cup his groin. "This is mine."

"Is it?" he taunts as I lean over and bite his earlobe.

"It is."

He grins. "I'm not going to have sex with them," he promises. "Now let's go before someone sees us then questions why two gay guys are trying to get a prostitute."

"I. Don't. Share," I whisper in his ear. I can see his fingers twitch as if they're aching to reach for me.

"Yes, sir."

I get out of the car and wait for him to get out. Instead of taking his hand, I just step up close to him so that my shoulder bumps into him.

"Good, now let's go," I say as I head for the front door. As soon as we walk in a large man eyes us.

"Can I see your license?" he asks because I will forever look like I'm barely legal.

"Of course," I say as I show it to him.

He checks us in and finally lets us pass. We step into the main area that looks like an elaborate bar. Where they'd clearly forgotten to spend money on the outside, they'd spent it all on the inside. There are leather chairs arranged around the room and stools up at the bar. Music is steady in the background but not loud enough to drown everyone out. There are men wandering around and women entertaining them. Some are wearing dresses, others in short skirts that allow a peek of their ass.

"What do we do?" I whisper as I eye a young woman with a top on that barely conceals her nipples.

"Head to the bar."

"Have you been in one of these before?"

"Yes, I have for work," he says.

With my eyes focused on everywhere other than where I am heading, I walk over to the bar as a beautiful woman saunters up to us.

"What can I get you?" she purrs as she leans forward, and my eyes drop to her breasts.

"Uh…"

"Jack and Coke. You want the same?" Lane asks.

"Sure," I say.

"Coming right up," she says with a purr.

I watch her work and see that it's like a dance she does. Every movement she makes has the men at the bar watching.

"Hi boys," a young woman says from behind us, and I turn to look at her. "Are either of you waiting for someone special?"

"I might have just found her," Lane says as he taps the seat next to him. "Can I buy you a drink?"

What the fuck? How's Lane making this look so easy?

The bartender passes us our drinks, so I grab mine and step away from the bar, leaving Lane to work his magic. I don't take two steps away from the bar before a pretty woman around my height steps up to me. She has rich brown hair that falls in ringlets around her face and is wearing a skin-tight dress with large flowers on it.

"Good evening, I haven't seen you around here before," she says with a smile.

"First time," I say.

"How exciting. Would you like to join me?" she asks. She seems to have an accent, but I can't place it.

"Yeah...sure," I say, and she smiles at me.

I follow her over to a velvet couch that faces away from the bar, where she waves for me to sit. I sit down, and she sits next to me so that her bare thigh presses against my leg.

"I'm Jasmine. What's your name?"

"Danny."

"It's nice to meet you, Danny. What made you decide to swing on by?" she asks.

"Um...just...never been to a place like this before. My friend has, and he suggested it," I say as I nod to Lane.

"You from Nevada?"

"No, we flew in from Illinois," I say.

"Ooh, planning an exciting trip in Las Vegas maybe?" she asks.

"I wish. It's for work, but maybe we'll have one day to have some fun," I say.

"Well, today will be all the fun you need," she says as she slides her hand down my arm and squeezes my hand.

"That's true," I say as I sip my drink because I have no idea what else to do.

"Would you like me to show you around since it's your first time?" she asks.

"Yeah...sure," I say, and she smiles at me.

She pulls me up to my feet and leads me back through a door, into a hallway. The walls are white with some signs throughout, advertising the different rooms.

"Well, we have our Jacuzzi room," she says as she nods. "Of course, a massage parlor or if you're feeling a little naughty, this would be the room for you."

I glance at the white door and can't help but wonder what exactly lies behind it. I almost tell her that I want that room, but I chicken out at the last moment.

"And right here is my room," she says. "Can I invite you in?"

I nod, and she pulls me through the doorway before shutting it behind me. The room is large with a king size bed in the middle. There are decorations scattered about to make it look lived in, but it looks fake. She sits on the bed and pulls me down next to her.

"What would you like to do?" she asks as she looks up at me through her long, fake eyelashes.

"Sex?" I ask like I'm not sure and her lips twitch like she's almost going to laugh, but she composes herself.

"I like you, and you're very handsome. It's rare for us to get someone so handsome in here. What if I give you a first timer's discount and we make it five hundred for the hour?"

"Okay," I say before realizing that I was probably supposed to negotiate.

She smiles at me. "Now that we are done with that nonsense, how about we have a little fun," she says as she swings her leg over, so she's straddling my lap.

A position that I am quite unfamiliar with. Usually, I am the one on the lap of someone and that person usually has a dick.

"Can I confess something?" I ask as I set my hands against her chest to stop her from feasting on me like I'm a piece of meat.

"Of course," she says, looking quite concerned.

"I've never had sex before, and I think I'm gay, but I can't be gay because if I'm gay my family will disown me, so I thought I could…I could…come here and prove I'm not gay."

She stares at me for a moment before smiling gently. "Thank you for telling me. Why don't we slow down then?" she suggests.

"Okay," I say.

"How about we start with a nice massage?"

"I like the sound of that," I say.

"Let's get rid of some of these layers then," she says as she unzips my hoodie before sliding it off my shoulders. Her breasts are pushed up, so I can see them peeking out of her shirt as she leans over me. Then she takes the bottom of my shirt and slowly pulls it up as I watch her.

"I'm so glad you picked me to explore with," she says as she unbuttons my pants. "It makes me feel quite special."

She gets off the bed, and with her butt up in the air, she leans over so she can work my pants down my hips to the ground.

"Can we leave my underwear on for right now?" I ask.

"Of course. But let's get rid of these pesky socks," she says as she slides her hands down my left leg before catching my sock and pulling it off, followed by my right. "Lay down on your back," she says, so I lie down as she makes quite the show of taking her clothes off. Her dress frees her huge breasts and reveals a pink lacy thong. Thankfully, she leaves it on even if I am slightly curious. She crawls back onto the bed and straddles me as she runs her hands up my stomach to my shoulders.

"You're so tense," she says as she begins to rub my shoulders, and I quickly realize that this is definitely worth the five hundred bucks, especially because it isn't my own money. She leans over so her lips are near my ear. "Does that feel good?"

"Really good," I admit.

"Good," she says with a grin as she massages my arms and neck as I sink into the bed. "You've been working too hard."

"I have," I agree.

"Let me help with that," she says as her hand slides down my stomach. Her finger circles my penis, so I quickly grab it and pull it up.

"I don't know if I can do this," I say like I'm nervous. Honestly, I am really upset that my massage is currently on hold. "Do…do you have anything to help relax me? I have extra money."

"Like…would you want to play in the Jacuzzi?" she asks, clearly not getting my meaning.

"No…like…something to calm my nerves…something to help me enjoy this. I have money."

"Oh…I don't have anything like that, I'm sorry," she says as she pulls her hands back and rubs at her wrist.

"Really? A friend of mine said that he got some here," I say.

She shakes her head. "Sorry…must have been a private sell or something…if anyone finds out, she'll get into really big trouble."

"Oh…I mean…I'd tip you if you found some for me," I say.

Her eyebrows knit as she gives me an apologetic smile. "Sorry, I probably couldn't even get you marijuana in this place."

"Oh…okay…that's okay. I guess…the massage will help," I say, deciding that I might as well get something out of this. Maybe Lane is having better luck.

Thankfully, she returns to my massage.

"Where are you from?" I ask.

"India," she says.

"Wow, you came a long way. How long have you been in the US?"

She glances toward the door like she doesn't want to talk about it but knows that she should answer her client's questions. "Two years."

"That had to be scary moving here."

"Yeah…but it was definitely worth it," she says.

"Your English is really good," I say.

She smiles. "Thanks. Do you want to touch my breasts?"

I bite my lip to keep from laughing. It is clearly a ploy to distract me, but it kind of works. "I've never touched a woman's boobs before."

She grins at me, clearly back in her area of expertise and comfort as she takes my hands and slides them up her stomach to her chest.

"They're all natural," she says with a grin.

"Are they?" I ask as I cup one in each hand. She could have told me just about anything about them at that moment, and I probably would have believed her. "They're very nice."

"Thank you. Do you want to feel a little more?"

"No, I kind of like my massage. You can rub my back if you want," I say as I let go of her breasts and roll over onto my stomach.

She laughs gently. "I think maybe…you need to just do what makes you happy."

"I don't know…maybe I can just pretend and make everyone happy," I say.

"Your parents won't talk with you about it?"

"God no, they told me if I brought it up again, they'd disown me. They think that I need to be the perfect, normal kid."

"I'm sorry to hear that," she says.

"Thanks. They'll be ecstatic when they hear that I was here," I say.

She laughs. "That's good," she says.

CHAPTER TWENTY

By the end of the hour, Jasmine has completely given up on getting me to do anything other than admire her skills at giving massages.

She leads me from the room and thanks me for the "wonderful time." When I get back to the main room, I see the girl Lane had been with leading Lane over to the bathroom. He goes through the door and she looks the other way, so I slide past her before Lane has time to lock the door.

"Hey—" Lane says, startled as I burst through.

"You got a problem, bud?" I ask in a gruff Southern dialect.

"Yes, it just entered the bathroom," Lane says.

"What are you doing?" I ask. "You trying to wash the evidence off you?"

He snorts. "I feel oily but that's about it. She lathered me in oil and rubbed her tits down my body, so that was fun."

"I touched boobs for the first time!" I exclaim, and Lane starts laughing.

"Um…Congratulations? Why are we having this conversation in the bathroom?" Lane asks.

"Because I can, I guess," I say.

Lane reaches out to me, but instead of pulling me toward him, he pushes me against the sink as he moves up against me, so I'm pinned between him and the sink. "I might as well get some fun out of going to a brothel," Lane says as he unbuttons my pants. My heart seems to quicken in anticipation as I watch him eagerly. His arms snake around my waist as he pulls me up against him and gently kisses my lips. I open my mouth just enough to feel his tongue as I feel his cock pressed against me.

His hand slides down so he can unbutton my pants before pushing them down my hips.

"This I can handle," I say before nipping his lip. "I was traumatized today, I need you to comfort me."

"By a naked woman?" he asks as I feel his breath against my throat.

"Yup," I say as I slide my hand under his shirt and look at him in surprise as my hand skates right off. "Why are you so greasy?"

"I told you that she wiped oil all over me!" he says.

"You're glistening like an oiled pig!" I say as he starts laughing.

"Shush, you're ruining sexy time talking about pigs," he says as I watch him drop down to his knees.

He runs his hands up my thighs until he reaches my cock. He slides a finger under my length as he kisses my inner thigh before sucking the spot his lips had just been. His mouth moves forward until I can feel his lips on my testicles. As his fingers gently run over the base he takes my testicle into his mouth and sucks it gently. I moan as he sucks before sliding his wet lips back to run his tongue under the base of my cock, all the way to the tip. He kisses and licks the tip before taking the head into his mouth where he then proceeds to circle over the tip before pulling off. I want his mouth back the moment it's gone but he doesn't disappoint, taking me deeper into his mouth as his fingers continue to fondle my testicles.

"Touch yourself," I say, as I brush my fingers through his hair. "I want to see."

He pulls his cock out and slides his hand down his length. I moan as his tongue moves over me, massaging my length as the heat of his mouth encompasses me.

Suddenly, I hear the door jingle as someone tries it. Lane pulls back and turns his head toward the door.

"Oops," he says.

"Fuck," I groan. "Why?"

He stands up and kisses my throat as he pushes his cock against mine. "We can have more fun later," he promises as he rubs his hand down my length. The feeling of his cock brushing against mine makes me push up against him.

I cup my hand against his as I lean into the feeling of his fingers brushing over my cock. The door jingles again, but for some reason knowing someone is right outside excites me and I feel myself right at the edge. Another stroke from Lane's hand is all it takes for my release as I try to hide my moans by pressing my face against his chest. Lane's hand moves quickly as he comes, drawing the pleasure out.

"Is there anyone in there?" a woman asks.

"Just a minute," Lane says.

"What a bitch," I say as Lane steps away from me. I move over to the sink to clean up our mess. "My God, you're a grease ball."

"I told you, she slathered me up and was like 'all done, put your clothes on.' I couldn't even open the doorknob, my hands were so slick."

I start laughing as I try to scrub the oil off.

When we're finished making sure we look presentable, I pull the door open and look over at a very confused woman.

"Sorry, he's blind, so it took us a bit to…get things done…" I say.

"Oh…that's okay," she says as I quickly lead Lane toward the door.

"Good save," Lane says.

"Thank you!" I say and grab my chest like I'm super flattered.

We head out to the car which I start and aim for the nearest hotel. "So?" I ask.

"Nothing. She wasn't biting at all, which really isn't that unusual because, with a business like that, you would probably only deal with regulars, but I was hoping to get something. I mean, I offered her a lot of money and she wouldn't budge at all. Claimed that wasn't her area. You?"

"Same. *But*...I think the girl I had was on drugs," I say. "She didn't act like it...at all, nor did she have the usual evidence of drug addiction like bruises or needle marks. She was alert, focused...but when I mentioned the drugs she got this look on her face. And...it wasn't like...a withdrawal but...my mom would get it when people talked about drugs. Like a craving for it, a need for it even though she was already so jacked up she couldn't function. I also think the woman at the laundromat was on it too."

Lane looks over at me in surprise. "What? Why didn't you mention that before?"

"Because it wasn't a super big tell. Her hands were a little shaky. Again, she didn't scream 'druggie' to me though. So, whatever they're taking, if I'm right, has to be something that doesn't affect focus, or response."

"Where was your girl from?" he asks.

"India, why?"

Lane taps his finger against the dashboard. "What if we're wrong...what if they're not selling the drugs to patrons, but instead they're giving them to their employees? Hooking them on it in exchange for labor?"

I look over at Lane. "Fuck…what if you're right? How do we figure it out?"

"I don't know, let me think about it," Lane says.

"Say we're right. If we got one of the girls to confess, would that be enough?" I ask.

"Oh, if they're trafficking humans into the US and forcing them into sex slavery or forced labor, we will have no trouble bringing them down."

"So…I go back and try to talk one of the girls into letting me help them," I say.

"It won't work like that. They're holding them there somehow. Whether it's through the promise of drugs or maybe through a threat, I don't know. But if any of those girls had a desire to escape, they would have tried."

"But what if they're too scared to try?" I say. "You know if this shit is going on, the girls in there aren't ones that have support. They don't have family or anyone that cares about them. They're coming from shit lives or from other countries and they think this is it for them. That this is all they can do because there isn't another option. What if I try to give her one?" I say.

"I don't know, Felix…why would she trust you?"

"Because when you're in a situation like that, sometimes you will trust anyone just to have someone to trust," I say.

"I know…" he says as he realizes that I'm a bit too familiar with this. "You're good at getting into things. If you can find a sample of the drug, we can at least move from there. You need to get the same girl as last time and build up your relationship with her, but don't press her yet. We will only press her if we aren't getting anywhere, alright?"

"Yeah."

"Okay. Call the place tonight, ask for an appointment with her tomorrow. See if we can get anywhere. If she's keeping quiet, don't push her, alright?"

"Yeah." I pull my phone out and notice that there is a missed call and voicemail. It's from Janice asking us to call her back.

I put the phone on speaker and hold the phone in front of Lane as it starts to ring.

"Hello?" Janice asks.

"Janice, it's Lane and Felix. Everything alright?" he asks.

She lets out a sob and my stomach clenches at what that might mean. "James woke up," she says. "I'm sorry! I'm a wreck! But he woke up. He's really confused right now and doesn't remember anything from the past week, but he's responding some to me."

"That's amazing, Janice," Lane says. "I'm so happy to hear that!"

"I know! I'm so relieved, and I still can't stop crying," she says as her voice cracks. "I'm a mess."

"That's okay. You have a right to be. You tell him that we'll be up to see him as soon as we can."

"I will. He probably won't remember, but I will," she promises. "I need to get back; the doctor is coming in."

"Okay, thank you for calling us," Lane says.

"Thanks for being there for me," she says.

"Of course," he says, and they say their goodbyes.

I turn to Lane and smile. "See? Something good happened," I say as I start the car.

He smiles. "Yes, it did. Are you hungry?"

"Yeah," I say as I turn out onto the road.

"Let's go on a date."

I stare at him in surprise. "A…a…*what?* I thought the only places you know of to take me are ones where my life is put in danger."

"Shut it. Find a steak or seafood place."

"Ruddy's Steakhouse?" I ask as I drive past it.

"More expensive. We're using the money you stole from Walsh," he says.

"Alright…hmm…" I pick up the phone and hold the home button down. "Most expensive restaurant in the area."

The phone thinks for a moment before saying, *"Here is what I found."*

I glance down at the listing that had four money signs. "What about a four in terms of cost?"

"Go for it," Lane says.

"You sure? I mean…I'm just as happy eating at a fast food place."

"No, let's burn through that money," he says.

"Ooh, exciting," I say as I allow the phone to lead me to what it claims is the most expensive restaurant in the area. I park and then lead Lane toward the front door. A woman rushes out and opens it for me as I smile at her.

"Thanks," I say as I'm instantly sucked inside and up to a hostess.

"Reservation name?" she asks.

"Uh…no…"

She stares at me like I'm a fool for not having a reservation. "Hmm…how many?"

"Two."

"It'll be two hours," she says.

"What?" I ask as I look at her like she's nuts. "This food can't be that good that people are waiting for two hours."

She looks shocked that I would say such a heinous thing. "Of course it is."

And that's when I turn off my moral compass and smile sadly at her. "My blind friend here is dying and…this is our last day in Nevada, and I just…really wanted to give him a good time. I heard such great things about this place," I say as I squeeze Lane's hand. "I didn't realize…I needed a reservation."

The woman's eyes instantly turn sympathetic, and I realize that I probably should have told her that I'm the one dying because Lane is probably going to murder me.

"Oh, I'm so sorry to hear that. Let me see what I can do," she says as she hurries off.

Lane yanks me toward him. "Seriously?" he whispers.

"Shh, don't cry. I promise I'll get you in here if I have to wash dishes for the next ten years," I say as I hug him.

About ten minutes later a man comes up to us and smiles at me gently. "We found a table for you," he says.

"Lane? Did you hear that? They found a table for us!"

"I'm so happy," Lane says as I pull him after the man.

He takes us over to a small table in the corner where I help Lane a little more than I needed to.

"Is that alright for you?" I ask Lane. "Are you comfortable?"

"Yes, thank you. This is so amazing I just…wish I could see it. Will you describe everything to me, Felix?"

"Of course," I say, and the man looks heartbroken.

"Your waitress will be with you momentarily," he says as he leaves us.

I turn my eyes back to Lane who is leaning back in his chair. "What happened to being all judgy?" I ask.

"Yeah, fuck that. I'm hungry."

I laugh. "It's not like we were *lying*. You are blind and at some point in your life, you *will* die. Technically we are all dying."

He points at me and nods. "That's true. I knew you were more than a pretty face."

The waitress walks up and smiles at us. "I'm so glad you guys have come here tonight. My name is Kelly, and I'll be your waitress. What brings you to town?"

"We're heading to Las Vegas to get married," Lane says as he reaches his hand out to me. I set my hand into his and he squeezes it gently. "Our state doesn't allow gay marriage, so…this is something we've always wanted to do."

"Aw, that's so sweet. How long have you two been together?"

"Ten years," Lane says.

"Oh my goodness, you two are so amazing."

Lane smiles. "Thank you."

"What can I get you started off with?"

"How about two glasses of a nice Chardonnay?" he asks.

"Of course. Here are your menus. Our specials are on top."

"Thank you," he says, and she smiles.

"Of course," she says before leaving.

"Okay, so who is getting into this now?" I ask like I'm judging him.

"It's actually my job to lie to people," he says. "I've spent a quarter of my life pretending I'm someone I'm not."

"There's one issue though. Ten years? I would have been fifteen and you'd have been twenty-five," I say.

"Twenty-seven actually."

"What? You told me you were thirty-five!"

"I also told you that my name is Lane," he says with a grin.

I stare at him in shock. "WHAT? What's your name?"

He grins. "I'm joking. It is Lane. And I told you that I am thirty-seven, I don't know where you got thirty-five from."

"Huh…I don't know. Maybe I was trying to make it feel like I wasn't with an old fuck or something."

"Thanks, make me feel good about myself."

"You're welcome!" I say. "Shush! The waitress is coming, we have to act like we love each other."

He grins as he holds his hand out, and I quickly take it as I lean toward him just as the waitress nears.

"The decorations are just so beautiful. There are these cute little candles on each table…oh, I'm sorry, I was trying to describe to him what the room looks like…it helps him feel like he can see again," I say to the waitress.

"Aw, that's amazing," she says as she sets our glasses down. "I just brought the whole bottle for you two instead." She pours the rich liquid into the glass as I watch it.

"Thanks," I say with a smile.

"So, are you wishing to go with the small plates? Those are fun to share and what most people order."

"Sounds good," I say. "Uh…Lane, what do you want?"

"Anything you want, I'll enjoy sharing," he says.

"Perfect," I say as I pick multiple small plates for us to share.

"They'll be out shortly," the waitress says.

"You'd be good at my job," Lane says after she's gone. "You're fairly good at conning people."

"Thanks! It's an art form I acquired young. Shush! She's heading back."

Lane doesn't skip a beat. "You don't mind taking my name, right? Mr. Felix Price. I just love the sound of it," Lane says as she sets some bread down in front of us.

"I love it," I say to him and she smiles at us before leaving.

When the food comes Lane and I eat until we both feel like we're going to explode. It is so good that even after I feel close to dying from gluttony, I continue on. Just stuffing the bottomless pit that is my face. And not even a smidge of guilt is able to surface before I am stuffed full.

"Aw, that was so good," I say as I lean back and admire the empty plates.

"It was," Lane agrees as he pats his stomach.

"I wish you were rich, so we could eat here every night."

"I wish you could cook, so we could eat something semi-edible."

"I wish you would stick to your promise of never bringing that up again!" I say as our waitress returns with an older gentleman.

"Good evening, sirs. Was everything good?"

"Absolutely delicious. Best meal I've ever had," I say.

"I completely agree," Lane says.

"I'm so glad to hear that. I'm glad tonight was a special night for both of you and would like to tell you that we waived the bill. So please, just go and enjoy your night," he says.

I'm sure the shock is showing on my face. I think it makes them smile more like they are proud of themselves for doing such a selfless act for two deserving people. "Uh…No! Really! We have plenty of money to pay for it," I say as I pull out my wallet.

"No, it's on the house. Have a good evening, gentlemen," he says before walking away with the waitress.

"*Lane*," I hiss. "Now I feel freaking guilty!"

"I think…we may have taken it too far," Lane says with a grimace.

"You *think?* Oh my God. We're going to hell for this. If I wasn't going to hell for running over that police officer, we're going to hell now."

"Running over an *officer?*"

Oops. "It was an accident. When I stole his car, I didn't know he was in front of it. I didn't break anything, I just kind of…pushed him out of the way. That was like ten years ago. We have more pressing matters such as how we are lying assholes." God, please help me turn that moral compass back on pronto.

"Just leave a ridiculous tip," Lane says. "And then we'll flee and forget this night ever happened."

"Yes, please," I say as I toss the money on the table before grabbing Lane's hand.

We then proceed to make our walk of shame out of the restaurant.

"Lane, I feel so bad," I whine.

"Shush, we're never going to mention it again, understand? We're going to erase it from our memory."

"Imagine if they knew that you dedicated your life to fighting the bad guys," I say. "And then came in and became one of the bad guys!"

"What did I just say?" Lane asks. "We're never going to mention it again!"

CHAPTER TWENTY-ONE

Talking Lane into staying at the hotel while I went to the brothel to see Jasmine was like talking an automatic door into never opening. I assured him that sitting in the passenger seat of the car in the parking lot of a brothel would look a bit suspicious. He eventually agreed and allowed me to drive solo the three miles to the brothel where I park the car.

I head inside but don't even make it to the bar before Jasmine finds me. She greets me with a genuine smile.

"I'm surprised you asked for me again," she says.

"Yeah…I just…thought I'd give it another try, you know? Like if I slowly work my way up to it in maybe a couple of visits…I can go through with it, you know?"

"Of course. We'll just go at your pace," she says as she leads me back to her room.

"Thank you for being so understanding," I say.

"Of course," she says as she shuts the door behind me.

I watch as she undresses me before telling me to lie down on the bed. I do and pretend I'm interested as she strips. Then she gets up on the bed and begins massaging my hand.

"I'm so sick of having to do what my family wants me to do," I say as her hands travel up my arm. "I feel like I just can't be myself. I can't be who I want to be or do what I want to do. I have to go to school for business because that's what my dad wants me to do. I have to take over his business, but I don't want to. I want to be a journalist. What did you want to be growing up?"

"A photographer," she says without hesitation. Then she blushes as she looks away like she said something she shouldn't have.

"A photographer? That's amazing! Hey, maybe you and I should work together. We can create our own magazine. I'll write the articles and you take the photos."

She smiles. "That would be fun."

"Did you take the photographs for the website?" I ask.

"I did…I asked them if I could."

"Really? They are amazing. I thought for sure it was a professional photographer," I say even though I don't really remember even looking at the photos. I might have glanced at a few just out of curiosity, but I couldn't remember if it was this place's website or a different one.

"I really loved doing it," she says.

"So…why don't you go to school for photography while working here?" I ask. "You have to make some good money through this place."

She bites her lip and looks away from me. "Um…no, I'm just…happy with this right now."

"Are you?" I ask, voice calm and quiet. I don't want her to think I'm pressuring her for an answer or I think I'll scare her off.

"Of course," she says.

"When you came over here from India, is this what you expected you would be doing?" I ask.

She looks like she's close to tears, and I know I'm getting somewhere. "Can we please stop talking about this?"

"Are you okay?" I ask as I sit up. I wrap my arms around her because I know that if a human is close to tears the quickest way to get them to cry is to hug them. "Don't be upset, what's wrong?" I squeeze my arms around her as soothingly as I can as she lets out a sob.

"This isn't what I wanted," she says as she clings onto me desperately.

"What did you want?" I ask gently as I smooth her hair away from her face.

"I wanted…to be free…to have the American dream. To be a photographer. I didn't want to do this," she says as she buries her head against my bare chest.

"I can help you," I say. "I can get you out of here. There's a life outside of this place. I can show it to you."

"I want to go," she whispers like if she says it too loud, someone will hear.

"Then come with me," I say.

She pulls back and looks at me. Her thick eyeliner is smeared around her eyes. She shakes her head. "I can't," she says.

"Why?"

"I can't…I'm going to go…to the bathroom. I'll be right back," she says as she quickly pulls her dress back on.

"Okay," I say as I watch her go. As soon as she's gone, I get up and head over to the cabinet in the corner. I pull it open and look in at the small tin box inside. It must be where she stores her private belongings so that others can't get into it. There's a lock on it, so I pull open a few more drawers. I can't imagine where she has her keys for it because she clearly doesn't have them on her.

Instead of finding the keys, I grab two bobby pins. I pull the plastic ends off them with my teeth and spit them out onto the ground. I stick one pin into the lock in order to bend the bobby pin up. After pulling it out, I bend just the tip of the other.

I stick the bent one into the lock and turn it like I would a key, which puts tension on the pins inside the lock. Inside the lock are six pins that need to be pushed up to release the tension of the lock. I slip the other bobby pin into the lock and feel the first of the lock's pins. It slides up and down easily, so I move on to the next. I move past the ones that easily move up and down, and only stop once I find the one that is stiff. I jimmy the bobby pin up. As soon as the lock's pin is free, the tension of the other bobby pin keeps it from falling back down. I move to the next stuck pin and push it up, causing the lock to give, so I can unlock it.

I pull the pins out and set them down, so I can take the lock off. I glance at the door, but it's still firmly closed, so I peek into the tin box. Inside is a purse that I quickly pull out and open. I begin to quickly dig through the purse, looking for anything that I can use, pulling useless things out and dropping them onto the shelf next to the lock. I look down into the empty purse and silently curse. I open her wallet but there isn't anything resembling drugs in there.

I start putting her stuff back in her purse when my finger catches on a tear in the side of the fabric. I slip my finger into the hole and feel something down at the bottom. I catch it with my fingernail and pull it up. With some jimmying, I drag the plastic out through the hole and look at the little baggie. It's a rose-colored powder, unlike anything I've ever seen before. It wasn't like I had an overwhelming knowledge of drugs, but I'd seen my fair share to know what most of the main ones looked like and this isn't anything I recognize.

Quickly, I start shoving everything else into the purse, hoping it doesn't look like someone raided her. Although, she'll quickly find out as soon as she looks for the drugs. I pick up the lock as I hear the door handle turn. I shove the purse into the safe and snap the lock on before quickly shutting the cabinet door.

Jasmine steps in as I walk over to my clothes that are on a chair by the window. I set my hand on the pants as I slip the small baggy into my pants' pocket.

"I'm so sorry about that," Jasmine says. "I'll, of course, take it out of your payment, or we can go over a little longer?"

"Don't worry about it," I say as I sit back down on the bed.

"Where were we?" she asks as she crawls up next to me. She doesn't strip back down this time, and I don't much care.

I just talk to her for our remaining time, but I don't get too private. Just talk about things that I want her to desire. Want her to long for more than anything. But I know far too well that it's hard to convince someone that they want something more than they want drugs.

"Did you want to stay over?" Jasmine asks when I notice that our hour is up.

"No, I have to get going. Honestly, I'm not mad. Maybe I can request you again this week?" I ask.

She smiles at me. "Of course, just let me know," she says.

"Well…are you free some time tomorrow?"

She nods. "Seven?"

"Yeah, I can do that," I say, and she smiles. "I'll see you tomorrow."

I pull my clothes on and check to make sure the drugs are still in my pocket. With my finger, I can feel the tip of the little plastic baggie inside. I wonder if she'll figure out it was me. Honestly, I hope not because I want her to trust me. I want to help her get out of this place.

I want to show her that even if it doesn't feel like it, there is a better world out there.

"Hang in there," I say.

She smiles at me. "Thanks." She rubs at her face as she opens the door.

"I can walk myself out...your makeup is a bit smeared. People will think I was abusing you," I joke.

She rubs a finger under her eye. "Thanks, yeah, I'll get that cleaned up.

I walk down the hallway toward the front area. As I open the door that separates the two, music floods in, and I see a small group of men near the front door. I stop the moment I realize that I recognize the man. How couldn't I? He'd stood by and watched while I was dragged into an alleyway and beaten. Then threatened my life.

I quickly reach for the door leading back into the hallway as he turns and sees me. Quickly, I yank the door shut, but there's no lock on it and of course, it swings outward. I turn around as I see Jasmine step out of her room. She looks at me in surprise as I run toward her.

I grab her shoulders and yank her toward me. "I can help you. I can really help you, but you have to help me. How do I get out of here?"

"Through the front door," she says cautiously.

"Back doors?"

"There are none," she says.

"Fuck. Do you want to be free of this place?"

"Yes," she whispers. "But I can't."

"Yes, you can. I promise. If I get caught, go to the hotel on Broadway Street. Ask for Lane Price, and give him the drug, he'll help you. I swear he'll help you," I say as I pull the baggie out of my pocket and press it to her palm. "You don't have to do this."

I slide past her as I hear the hallway door open. Quickly, I slip through a closed door into an occupied room. There is a man on the bed and a woman standing behind him wearing stilettos and holding a crop.

They both look at me startled as I rush past and over to the covered window. I yank the blinds hard, tearing them off as I grab for the window. It's locked, so I switch the locks off and try again, but the window won't budge. I can hear them outside of the room, so I know that I don't have enough time to find a different room. I pick up a chair and throw it at the window. The window shatters, making the girl scream. The door is thrown open as I use the chair to knock away any jagged pieces of glass. I pull my hands into my sleeves as I grab onto the window frame and pull myself through. They rush for me as I get my foot up onto the sill, so I can jump down.

"Get him. Don't kill him," Red says as I drop down on the other side.

A piece of glass breaks under my foot, so I grab it and hold it carefully as I slip it into my back pocket. A ten-foot-high fence surrounds the place to keep people from being nosy, but it also threatens to keep me in. The only way past it is through the front gate or over it. I jump up, catching onto the chain links as someone tries to fit through the window and for the first time in my life, I realize I'm pleased about being small.

I fumble up the side of the fence, forcing the toes of my shoes between the links. It's hard to do and when my foot slips, I almost fall, but I just manage to catch the top and heave myself over before dropping down on the other side. I lose my balance and fall forward, into the stones. Before I can quite get my bearings, I am already starting to run toward the front where my car is waiting while trying to yank my phone out of my pocket.

I redial the last number that I called, which was García's, and pray to God he answers. As I near the parking lot, I see the men filing out through the front door. They're too close to my car, telling me that they would get there before I would, so I turn toward the road instead. Maybe if I can get to the road, I can get someone to stop for me.

"This is García," he answers.

"García, I'm at Paradise Ranch in Nevada and I found the drugs. I think they're giving the drugs to the workers and forcing them to work for them, but they caught me, and now they're chasing me, and Lane is back at the hotel, and I'm going to die," I say as quickly as I can. My heart is pounding too loudly, and my stomach feels tight with anxiety.

"What?" he asks. "Slow down. You're being chased?"

I glance behind me as two men barrel down on me. "Yes. What do I do?"

"If he catches you, you do anything he tells you to do, alright? No hesitation. Just tell him anything you need to tell him or do anything he asks you to do. What hotel is Lane at?" he asks.

"I don't remember! The one off Broadway Street!" I say.

"Okay. Can you hide anywhere?"

"I'm in the fucking desert! There isn't even a tree!" I yell as I hear one of the men nearing me. His breathing is heavy as his feet fall like bricks with each step. He lunges forward and tackles me to the ground. I slam down onto the hard earth, causing the phone to slip from my fingers and clatter along the ground.

I reach back into my pocket and pull the chunk of glass out before stabbing the man right in the leg. He howls out as he rolls off me, allowing me to scramble to my feet, but the second man grabs me in a hug from behind.

"Let me go!" I yell as I bring my arm down fast. I can feel the glass biting into my hand as I drive it at the man's side. Before I can reach him, he quickly grabs my wrist and yanks it up as he pries at the glass. In doing so, he lets go of my body, so I swing around and kick him in the balls hard enough I had to have burst one. He sounds like a wounded animal as he jerks away from me. I turn to run when I notice Red casually walking up to me.

"You're like a little Tasmanian devil," he says as he continues his leisurely stroll up to where I stand next to my victims. I hold the glass tightly as my blood and the blood of my enemies drips off the tip. The glass is biting sharply into my hand, but I don't loosen my grip.

"Leave me the fuck alone," I say as I stand my ground. "I'll fucking gut you if you get closer to me."

"I see why Lane likes you. You have a bit of a spirit to you. I like that," he says. "Too bad you're so fucking nosy."

His foot hits something, and we both look down at my cellphone. He reaches down and picks it up before setting it against his ear. "Is this Lane?" he asks. "Oh…that's fine. But I think we're going to make a few negotiations…no…*I* will make the negotiations…Oh, you don't have anything that can bring me down. I'm running a perfectly legal business. There's nothing you can pin on me. I've actually done nothing. Currently, this kid has come into my establishment, broken my window, *stabbed* a man, and hurt another. We haven't even touched him. Tell Lane to give me a call so we can talk." He hangs the phone up and tosses it back onto the ground. "Alright, kiddo, let's go," he says.

"I want to see you try," I growl as I hold my piece of glass steadily.

The man I'd stabbed in the leg is now getting up even though his pants are stained in blood. The other man is acting like I kicked his testicles into his stomach.

I might have.

And I will do the same to Red.

He walks up to me, and I rush him. He steps to the side, grabs my wrist as his other hand rolls up my arm, and suddenly I'm face first in the dirt with no recollection of how I got there. He kneels next to me, holding me down with a knee on my arm as he leans over and looks at me.

"You had your fun. Time's up," he says as he pulls the glass out of my hand and tosses it. "Let's go. What the fuck am I paying you two for if you can't control a ninety-pound boy?"

The man I'd stabbed is the first to respond. He grabs my arms and yanks them behind my back before pulling me to my feet. I thrash and kick, but I can't make contact with him. He seems to have a bit of experience with dragging people around.

He hauls me over to the parking lot and up to a car. The other buff guy opens the door, and as he tries to push me in, I set my foot against the door and push back. The man, having none of my shit, roughly shoves me inside as he comes in after me.

"Get me something to tie this damn kid's hands and legs down," the stabbed bodyguard says.

The one I'd made a eunuch returns with such material, so they hold me down against the seat as he loops what looks like a shoestring around my wrist, pulling it tight until it's biting into my wrists before tying it. Then he does the same to my feet as I kick and thrash about, that is until the eunuch leans on my legs, so I can't move them, and ties them tightly.

Red climbs in next to me after I'm tied up.

I glare at him as he smiles at me.

"I'm so glad you could join us today," Red says.

"Thanks, me too," I say sarcastically. Instead, I'm trying not to panic or cry or show any of the emotions raging inside of me. My stomach hurts at the prospect of being whisked off by supervillains, so maybe I'll get sick and throw up on him and he'll toss me out the door.

Instead, Red reaches down to the ground and picks up a shirt, which he wraps around my eyes, blocking my vision. The car begins to move, as my brain runs as fast as it can. I should listen to García. I should do exactly what they say. García and Lane will find me, right?

For the rest of the drive, I'm left in darkness, listening only to the sound of Red playing on his phone.

My mind is racing as I question what will happen to me. Lane was right, I shouldn't be here, pretending like I know what I'm doing. What if they kill me? I mean, they don't care about killing people, right? They've made it this far by expertly covering their crimes up. I'll just be another that is swept under the rug.

Fuck.

My stomach aches as I sit in the seat, hands on my lap as I lean against the cold door. It feels like a ball of anxiety is eating away at my stomach as I question where exactly I went wrong. Maybe all of it?

Fuck.

When the car stops and the engine shuts off, I'm not sure if I'm more anxious or slightly relieved. I want something to happen as much as I want nothing to happen. But I know that right now, in this car, I can't do anything but wait for my fate. I need out. I need to see. I need to do something.

The car door opens, and my ankles are untied. The moment they're free, I'm yanked out. My foot hits hard as I'm dragged forward, blind to the world around me. This is how Lane lives every minute of his life. Unable to tell what is before him. What is coming or what is behind him.

I take a deep breath and try to calm my nerves. I need a clear mind to think all this through. Lane would have helped me calm my nerves, but I don't have him here. So, I have to fight like he is with me.

"I think I need stitches," stabbed guy says.

"You? I think my fucking nuts exploded," the other guy says.

"Well, you're ugly as sin anyway so it's probably a good precaution. You should be thanking the kid," Red says.

"You're welcome," I say, and Red laughs.

"Any other day and I think I would like you, kid," Red says. "But today, you're a fucking nuisance."

I'm dragged through a doorway and suddenly I'm inside. The sound of my feet on the ground changes as my shoes sound on the floor. I'm pulled to the right and given a shove.

I stumble and rub the blindfold off on my shoulder. It slides up enough that I can see Red standing in the doorway.

"Let's talk. Felix, right?" he asks.

"Maybe," I say.

"Alright, have a seat," he says as he waves behind me.

I look behind me to where a small table is set up with four chairs. It definitely looks too civilized to be a torture chamber. I walk over to the far chair that is facing the door and sit down.

Red pulls the opposite chair out and takes a seat. He straightens his suit jacket before folding his hands on top of the table.

"What are you doing in Nevada?" he asks.

"Gambling," I say. "I like to count cards."

"Do you? That's an interesting hobby."

"My mom was poor, and I would sneak into the nearby casino and count cards for money," I lie. I really hope he doesn't ask which card game is the one you count because I don't have a clue. Only card game I know how to play is Uno.

"So, what were you doing at my ranch then?" he asks.

"Prostitutes in Las Vegas are illegal, so I headed to a different place," I say.

"They are. So why my ranch? Why not any of the multiple ranches between mine and Las Vegas?" he asks.

"Ratings," I say.

"Oh, okay. What about my laundromat? What were you doing there?" he asks.

"Now, I don't know what you're talking about," I say.

"Okay," he says as he pulls up a computer and sets it on the table. He opens it up and clicks the play button, so I can watch myself break into the truck lot.

"That's not me," I say.

He looks at the video then at me in mock shock. "It *isn't*? Huh...that's crazy."

"I know, right?" I ask as I watch Lane pushing me into the cab.

"What tipped you off? How'd you find the laundromat?" he asks.

"I watched *Breaking Bad*. In that, they were doing drugs in a laundromat, so I just...automatically assumed you'd do the same," I say.

He laughs as he leans back in his chair. "Tell me."

"I told you!"

His phone begins to ring, the noise sharp in the quiet room. He sighs when he glances down at it. "Perfect timing. Let me take this call and then we can decide what I'm going to do to you. You have a very, very nice face. I bet I could get some men to pay a nice sum for you to spread your legs."

"Thanks, I think I'm alright, but that means a lot," I say.

He ignores me and heads out the door, leaving me alone with the eunuch. He is glaring at me, so I glare back as I mess with my binds under the table. They're really freaking tight, but unlike when Lane and I abducted Ryan, my fingers are free. And Lane is right about how big of a mistake that is.

CHAPTER TWENTY-TWO

My bloody hand stings as I bend my wrists as far as they'll go while trying to pick at the shoestring binding me. It's tight, but I dig at it with a fingernail until it begins to give. Then I shove my finger between the strings and work at them. Slowly, it begins to loosen but by the time the door opens again, I'm still not free.

"Alright, let's continue our chat," Red says. "Who told you?"

"Told me what?" I ask as I work the string down until I get it past my thumb before pushing it down to where it can fall free. Before it does, I gather the string up into one hand and hold it tightly.

Red slams his hand down on the table, making me jump as I stare at him with wide eyes. I really wish Lane was here. Which is a stupid wish, but he seems to give me a boost of confidence that I feel like I can't find on my own. And right now, I could use a big heaping dose of confidence.

"Answer the fucking question. I'm only going to give you five more seconds to answer, or I will *make* you answer," he says as he makes a show of slowly getting up.

I watch with wide eyes as he walks around the table and sinks his fingers into my hair before yanking my head back, so I'm looking up at him.

"Did Lane tell you what I did to him?" he asks quietly as my stomach clenches in fear. "No? You want me to show you? You want to hear about how I had my men drag him down into the basement, strap him down…just think about it, Felix. Think about how strong Lane is and what I did to break him."

I'm shaking as I stare up into his cold eyes, absolutely terrified of what he is going to do to me. The thing is…do I even have anything worth saying that will sate him?

"Oh, Felix, you should have heard the way Lane *screamed* when the acid was poured into his eyes. The way he shook as we broke that man down—"

"Please, I don't know anything," I whisper.

He snorts as he lets go of his grip on my hair and walks back over to his chair. "Oh, trust me, you know something. How about I give you a moment to think about it? Want me to continue my story while we wait?"

I jump up and flee for the door. The big bodyguard takes one step to the right, causing me to slam into him.

"No! Please, I don't want to die, please!" I cry.

I paw at the man as my left hand slips under his jacket and grabs his gun. I pop the strap off the holster and slide it out before either can notice. I turn my body and drop down into a ball, so I can cover the gun up. I slide it down into my pants as the man grabs my upper arm and drags me back over to the table. He shoves me hard onto the ground.

"Sit the fuck down before I have your fucking legs broken!" Red yells. "I told Price that if negotiation goes well, I'll give you to him. But I never fucking said what shape you'd be in. The thing is, I was being kind to you guys. I warned you to stay out of my shit. Instead, I think it made you guys more fucking adamant. And I told you what would happen if you didn't get them to back off. The thing is, I can cover all of this up so fucking easily. And really, it doesn't matter how many of my men I have to use in order to do it. There are more that will replace them. You guys cannot take me down. And if I don't fall, none of this falls."

Sobbing is much easier than it should be as I crawl up into the chair and face the man. The bodyguard goes back to the door so now my two enemies are in a perfect line. If it was like in a video game or movie, I could down them both with one shot. Too bad I'm not a macho video game hero.

Under the table, I slide the safety off the gun and wait for the right moment. Red leans forward, but I wait until he puts his hands on the table. He easily could have a gun even if he is never involved in any of the action.

"Tell me."

I nod like I am finally giving in. "O…Okay. So…it was Lane's idea, not mine," I say. "I thought it was a bad idea. I *really* thought it was a bad idea. I told him I didn't want to do it."

He sighs and folds his hands on top of the table. "Get on with it."

"Okay," I say as I pull the gun up and aim it at his face. "I'll blow your motherfucking head off if either of you move."

Red looks surprised and then furious. "Owen, where's your fucking gun?"

"What? He…" he reaches for it, and I wave the gun triumphantly.

"I said don't move," I growl as I slowly stand up. I'd seen enough movies to know that he could push the table at me and it would make me dramatically drop the gun and it would be game over for me.

I back away so he can't reach me or hit me with anything. Then I toss the shoestring over to Red. "Tie your bodyguard up and grab the car keys from him."

The string slides across the table, and for a moment, Red just stares at it.

He seems to think about the situation before giving in with a nod. "Fine," he says grudgingly. He stands up and grabs the string before walking over to the bodyguard and wrapping the shoestring around his wrist. He ties it tightly as I watch him very carefully.

"Drop the keys and slide them over to me," I say.

He drops the keys on the ground and they clatter so loudly, it's almost deafening. He kicks them with his shoe, and I quickly stoop down and pick them up.

"Alright..." Now what? If he has a gun, he'll shoot me. But I can't get close to him because he clearly knows some type of martial arts.

"Put your gun on the ground," I say.

"I don't have a gun," he says nonchalantly.

"Slowly open up your suit jacket," I say. "If you move too quickly, I'll shoot you."

He unbuttons his jacket so slowly that I regret saying it. When it's unbuttoned, he opens it up and carefully turns around as I look for any bulge that could be a weapon. His suit pants and his button-up are tight enough that I think I would be able to see something, but he appears to be clean.

"Alright, let's go," I say. "Out the door. If anyone makes a move, I'll shoot you."

He just stares at me. He clearly wants me to get closer, but I don't want to get any closer to him than I already am.

"I said move!" I yell.

"The thing is, I really don't think you have it in you to shoot someone," he says.

I turn the gun on the bodyguard and fire it. He cries out as he falls forward, bullet hole right through his lower leg. I don't want to kill the guy, so I'll just assume that will be semi-safe. Who the fuck knows. Oh God! What if I just killed the man?

Red snorts. "Alright," he says as he steps through the doorway and out into the hallway.

"Take me outside," I say.

"Got it," he says as he starts walking, but the moment he turns right, I know it doesn't feel correct. I had been terrified and blindfolded when they brought me in, but I swear we'd turned right into the room.

"You're going the wrong way," I say.

"You think I don't know my way out of my own building?" he asks. "That way we'll go past guards. This way we won't."

"I don't believe you. Go the other way," I say, realizing he'd now have to pass me in the hallway.

"Fine, your funeral," he says as he turns around and starts to pass me. I back up, into the doorway, so I won't be pinned against the wall if he decides to attack me. He watches me closely as he walks by me without incident.

We start walking toward the front door when a man comes around the corner.

"Don't move or I'll kill him," I snap.

The man quickly looks over at Red for his next order but Red doesn't say anything, just keeps walking. He reaches the door and pushes against it, but now I have to watch the other man as well as Red.

"He'll shoot you in the back," Red tells me as we move through the door.

I want to look back at the other man. I want to see if he has his gun drawn, but I know that's what Red wants. "Then I'll shoot you in the head. If he wants you to live, he won't touch me," I say.

He snorts as the door swings shut behind me without incident. He starts walking over to a white car with heavily tinted windows.

"Get in the car. Driver's seat."

He opens the car door as I see the door to the building open and four men come out. I glance back at Red as he dashes around the open car door and runs to the front of the car. With a duck of his head, he's out of my line of sight, and I'm suddenly very defenseless.

I hear a gunshot hit the side of the car as I dive into it and slam the door shut. I stick the key into the ignition, but it won't slide in, instantly telling me it is the wrong fucking car.

I duck down, thanking God the windows are so damn tinted they can't see shit. I lock the doors and scramble into the back seat. I grab the seat release and tug on it. The back seat drops forward, allowing me to crawl into the trunk before pulling the seat back up. It's completely dark in the trunk except for the glowing release. The front of the car is facing the building, which means that the trunk is facing away.

I hear the window shatter, and I jump, startled. There's noise surrounding the car as I carefully pull the release while holding the trunk, so it doesn't pop up high. I push it up, letting light flood in as I hear another shot hit the car. I slide out of the trunk and hit the ground as I dive under a truck parked behind it. I crawl under the truck as I try to think. What did the car look like that brought me here?

I can't even remember the color and there are at least twenty cars in this damn parking lot. I pull the key out and look at the Chevy emblem etched into it.

Okay, so it's a Chevy…and it was a car. I remember that much.

I can see people rushing the car I'd just left as I crawl along the gravel toward the rear of the truck. Carefully, I peek out before moving out from under it to the next vehicle. I lean against the trunk as I look both ways. From here alone, I can see two Chevy cars.

Can I hot wire one fast enough if I'm wrong?

I guess there's only one way to find out.

Quietly, I move from vehicle to vehicle until I reach the closest Chevy. I peek under the car and see that the feet are no longer surrounding the original car but are spread out. When I slide the key into the door of the Chevy, it slides in with ease but refuses to turn.

I pull the key back and move around to the trunk as I look for the next car. There is only one more Chevy in this row, and if it's wrong, I'll have to move onto a different row. Or, I'll have to try to hotwire it if it's unlocked.

I crawl up to the door of the car and slide the key in. I nearly cry when the key turns, unlocking the door. Gently, I pull the door handle and the sound of it giving in is deafening. I drag myself into it, making sure my head isn't showing as I put the key in the ignition and turn it. The car rumbles to life as I shove it in reverse and press hard on the gas. The car leaps backward, and as soon as I'm out of the parking spot, I ram it into drive. The engine screams as I hear a bullet strike the car.

Pain brushes my leg as I look at the tear in my jeans, but thankfully the bullet had barely touched me. Stones spit out the back as the wheels squeal and the car lunges forward. I turn it quickly as I cut through the grass and put the building between me and the gunmen.

By the time I reach the road, the car is up to ninety. I don't know where the road leads or where I'm headed, but I know I'm getting the fuck out of here. I don't have a phone, I don't have any way to contact Lane.

I grab my seatbelt and buckle it as I near a car leisurely heading down the road. I anxiously look behind me before swerving around the car that's going the speed limit and rushing past them.

When I pass the police officer out on duty, I'm going a hundred and ten. I have never been so excited to see a police officer before. But I don't slow until he manages to catch up to me. His sirens are blaring as he zeros in on me. Only then do I pull the car over and turn it off. I shove the gun under the seat as I anxiously wait for him to come to me. I'm scared he'll think I'm attacking if I jump out, but he seems to be taking a leisurely time coming out to see what I'm up to.

In the rearview mirror, I see the officer get out of his car as another car barrels down the road. Unsure of what to do, I turn the car back on and throw it in drive just as the other vehicle swerves past the police car. Realizing that there is no way I would be able to outrun them at this point, I unhook my seat belt and lunge for the passenger seat as the sound of gunfire fills the air. I push hard against the door and leap out into the ditch.

I roll down to the bottom of it, slamming into the murky water as I hear the police officer fire his gun. When I manage to right myself and look out of the ditch, I see that the officer has hit the tire of the fleeing car. The car squeals as it jolts to the side before dipping off the road and slamming into the ditch. The front of the car hits so hard that I swear I can feel it from here. It flips over once before coming to rest on the hood.

"Stay down!" the officer yells at me. I gladly listen as he shouts something over his radio about backup.

"Can I crawl behind my car? I don't want to be shot," I say.

"Slowly, keep your hands where I can see them," he says as he stays behind his car door for cover.

I keep my hands up and use my elbows and knees to crawl over to my car.

"Get on the ground!" the officer yells, telling me that someone got out of the vehicle.

Once safely behind my car, I peek around the edge of the bumper as Red stands up.

"Get on the ground!" the officer yells again.

Red lifts his gun up and shoots. The officer falls back, slamming into the side of his cruiser.

"Felix, come out here," Red says. "You've done such a fucking splendid job destroying my life."

"That's what my mom liked to tell me too," I say as I see the police officer reach out for his gun. He picks it up before slumping back down. He's breathing hard as he holds the gun against his chest.

"I can clearly see why," he growls as he stays clear of the front of the police car.

It tells me that he plans to avoid the camera, killing me and the officer before leaving our deaths for his men to be responsible for. He steps around so he can see me and lifts the gun up as the police officer fires.

Red stumbles back as the officer shoots him three more times. Red is watching me with a look of shock on his face as his eyes widen. His legs drop, and he hits the ground on his back as I stare at him.

"How many others were with him?" the officer asks. Each word sounds pained, and he's breathing hard.

"I-I don't know," I say. "I'm sure at least a few."

"Grab my radio, tell them I need a paramedic," he says.

I nod and rush for the open car door. I step over him and grab the radio. I hit the button. "We need a paramedic. Please, quickly." I drop the radio and rush over to the officer. The bullet hit his shoulder and blood is blooming out around the wound. "Are you okay?"

He nods, but I'm not sure if he's being truthful or not. "Fine. Why were they after you?"

"Because I know something I shouldn't," I say as I set my hand against the wound and hold pressure on it to stop the bleeding. "Can I use your phone?"

He doesn't answer, just continues to stare at the smoking car in the distance, so I pull the phone out and search for a number to contact Chicago's homicide department. By the time I finally get through to someone, I hear sirens.

"I need to talk to García," I say.

"Who is this?"

"I'm with Lane Price," I say, knowing that she won't know me, but might respond to Lane's name.

"García isn't here at the moment."

"Then Walsh! Let me talk to him!"

"Just a moment…"

She must put me straight through because he answers quickly. "Hello?"

"This is Felix, I was with Lane and—"

"Where are you?" he says.

"I don't know. The side of the road. I'm with a police officer, but he's down, and I think Red's dead but there's a bunch of them."

"Alright, stay on the line as I try to figure out your location," he says, as sirens begin to drown him out. The noise is piercing, and I can't hear anything Walsh is saying.

The police cars swarm us as they park, and the men and women exit their vehicles with guns at the ready.

"Hands up!" they shout at me.

"I'm putting pressure on his gunshot wound," I say as I put the hand with the phone in it up in the air.

Two officers descend upon me as the rest move forward. I watch as one checks Red, but he must be dead because the man waves them on. They move over to the flipped car as a woman relieves me of my medical duty and begins working on first aid.

The ambulance is the next to arrive, but by then they've pulled a man out of the car and have him restrained. I can't tell how many more are in the car or whether they are deceased or not.

The paramedics are instantly on the officer as I back off and slump down next to the back tire of the police car. Now that the others are disarmed, they move onto me. A woman kneels next to me.

"Are you alright?" she asks.

"Fine," I say. "What should I do?"

"We'll have the paramedics look you over, but I believe someone from your department is coming to pick you up."

I didn't know I had a department.

An unmarked vehicle pulls up, and I look up. I don't recognize the driver, but I jump up and rush toward the car when I see Lane in the passenger's seat. As he pushes the car door open, I dive in and grab onto him.

"Felix," Lane says as he grabs me. "Oh fuck...are you alright?"

I bury my face against his neck as I squeeze him as hard as I can. "I thought I was going to die," I admit. It's muffled, but I know he's heard me because he squeezes me tighter.

"I'm so sorry, I shouldn't have let you go alone. I shouldn't have involved you in any of this. Please tell me you're okay."

"I'm fine. I'm fine, I promise."

"Hey, is he lying? I can smell blood."

The driver, who had been getting out of the car, ducks his head back in. "I don't know, he's got blood on him, but he's still breathing, so I deem him fine." He heads off to join the others, leaving Lane and me alone.

"I was so scared, but I was so badass, Lane. I like...stabbed someone with glass, stole a gun, held Red at gunpoint, and stole a car. Oh, and I kicked a man in the balls so hard he was crying."

Lane squeezes me harder. "You did good, but you also didn't do anything García told you to do. He told you to just do what Red said and we'd come to find you. I doubt Red told you to do any of that."

"Yeah...García did say that, didn't he?" I say, not really caring at all. The only thing I care about is never moving from this spot again. "Did Jasmine get to you?"

"She did, she gave me the drugs. García has someone talking to her who is getting as much information out of her as we can. Red may be dead, but we have to destroy what he's built and with this, we can. We have witnesses, we have locations, and it sure didn't help that Red shot a cop."

"He was really pissed. I think he thought he could just...kill us both and leave the bodies of his men behind to get blamed."

"I was so scared when I heard that someone was hurt. I was so scared it was you," he says as he kisses my cheek.

I cling to him desperately, scared that this is all a dream, and I am still stuck in that room with Red. "I'm fine. I cut my hand, but I'm fine."

"How bad is it?"

"It's not horrible, but it hurts," I say, not wanting to get off his lap.

"Okay, we'll have someone look at it," he says.

I sink into his warm, strong arms. I don't want to go anywhere else. There is too much safety in these arms. "Lane, I love you, you know that, right?"

"Of course. I love you too," he says as he kisses me on the cheek. And that's all I need. All my anxiousness, my terror, my adrenaline is just washed away, and I'm left feeling oddly raw and vulnerable. But tucked against Lane's chest, I feel safe and loved.

EPILOGUE

With all the proof against Red, his empire came crashing down. They found proof of drug trafficking that he'd gotten away with for so long through transporting it carefully. But what was more interesting, was the unique drug I had taken from Jasmine. They had figured out that the drug he was making didn't provide anything a normal drug gave a person. It didn't make them high or help them feel calm. But the withdrawal was vicious. The only use the drug had was to keep people from ever getting off it. So, he would find young women who had run away from home or had come here from another country and get them hooked. Once they were hooked, he took everything from them. Forced them to sell themselves or work for him. If they left, they would think they were dying from the withdrawal. Thankfully, the drug hadn't spread far by the time we found proof of it. Along with taking down the business, they arrested quite a few people that were involved, including Mick (which meant that Copper is now technically my dog. I don't know if that's how it works, but that's what I told everyone).

By the time we made it to visit James, he was doing quite a bit better. He would still get confused but was able to talk and hold conversations for small periods of time. The doctors told us that they thought his outcome looked very positive, and with some therapy, he would be back to normal before long.

I also visited Jasmine a few times while she was in rehab. The first time was horrible. She wasn't coherent and looked so ill I hardly recognized her, but when I had visited her yesterday, she was doing well. She was happy and had told me about the programs she had joined that would help her start a real life here.

I felt bad leaving her, but she assured me she was fine. That she had friends and a support system now.

***

"Are you ready?" Lane asks as he stands up.

The plane has nearly cleared out by the time I stand up.

"Yeah," I say even though I am more than a little nervous.

Lane had decided to move back home to be closer to his family. He thought we'd done enough detective work for a while, and I couldn't help but agree.

"You alright?" Lane asks since I haven't moved. He seems to have noticed that I'm quite anxious about this.

"Do they even know you're gay?" I ask.

"Wait…I'm gay? I thought you were a woman this whole time," he says as he squeezes my hand.

I smile and shake my head. "Funny," I say, but it at least makes me feel a little better. I lead Copper after us as we exit the ramp. I'm trying to force myself to think about something other than meeting them because I'm terrified of what they'll think of me. What if they don't like me? I couldn't connect with my own parents, what makes me think I can connect with them? "They're going to hate me."

"Why?" he asks.

"I don't know," I say.

"I feel like you've been more worried about meeting my parents than you were when taking down a drug lord."

I think about it for a moment. "Yeah, maybe," I say, and he laughs.

We walk into the airport and I stall by using the bathroom, but eventually, I have to come out. Lane is waiting just outside for me, so I take his hand and lead him down the escalator, onto the first floor.

"Lane!" a woman yells.

The noise startles me but makes Lane smile.

He'd told her about him losing his sight and had made her promise that the family would never look at him with pity or he'd leave again. She rushes up and grabs him, squeezing him tightly as an older man that share's Lane's features, rushes up with a lady around Lane's age. They maul him as he smiles and hugs them back.

"I missed you guys," Lane says. "This is my boyfriend Felix."

His mom grabs me by the shoulders and looks me over as I look up at her, a bit worried. I don't have a lot of knowledge of dealing with moms.

"It's so wonderful to finally meet you! I've heard all about you," she says as she hugs me tightly.

They each introduce themselves to me and hug me as I try to take it all in.

"Come on, let's go. I made your favorite for supper," Lane's mom says as she heads off while Lane's father and sister retrieve our bags.

Lane grabs my hand and pulls me toward him. "They're not so bad, are they?"

"I like them," I say since they're out of earshot.

"I told you that you would," he says.

"They remind me of you."

"Now, I know for a fact they're nicer than me. For example, they'd never make fun of your small stature *or* your cooking."

"You know what? I think I'm going to tell them you jumped on a different flight, and I'll just keep them as my family," I say.

Lane laughs. "I'm sorry, I mean, if we lived through that mess, we'll survive your cooking, so it'll all be fine."

"You're going to make me cry," I say.

"Good, I bet you're cute when you cry," he says as he squeezes me. "Come on, let's go."

I slide my fingers between his and think about how I will get back at him for everything mean he has said to me.

Honestly, I don't care because I have a place to belong. I have a place where someone cares if I am hurt. Someone cares if I come home. I know it might take me a while to open up every part of my mind and heart to Lane after having kept it locked away for so long, but I know that if I can give everything to one person, it will be him.

Acknowledgments

I want to thank everyone who helped me work on this book. A huge thank you to my mom, who has always supported me and helped me reach my dream of becoming a writer. I also want to thank Courtney, who has always been supportive and helpful. I don't think this series would be where it is today without your help! I can't forget to thank Caroline for her assistance with this book!

And of course, I need to thank my readers for supporting me! I couldn't have done it without you!

AUTHOR'S NOTE

Want a free Felix and Lane short story? Subscribe to my newsletter. https://www.alicewintersauthor.com/

One free short story not enough? Join my reader group, Alice Winters' Wonderland, on Facebook! On the group, I have giveaways, teasers, and freebies!

Please don't forget to leave a review!

Printed in Poland
by Amazon Fulfillment
Poland Sp. z o.o., Wrocław